WATER
MUSIC

MARGIE
ORFORD

HEAD
of ZEUS

First published in South Africa in 2013 by Jonathan Ball Publishers (Pty) Ltd
First published in the UK in 2014 by Head of Zeus Ltd.

9 7 5 3 1 2 4 6 8

A CIP catalogue record for this book is available from the British Library.

ISBN (TPBO) 9781781857847
ISBN (E) 9781781857830

Typesetting by Ed Pickford

Printed in Germany.

Head of Zeus Ltd
Clerkenwell House
45-47 Clerkenwell Green
London EC1R 0HT

www.headofzeus.com

For my sister

'All torture is, in the end, directed at the spirit.'
Rogue Male – Geoffrey Household

Friday
June 15

one

The bridle path was rarely used in summer. Never in the dead of winter. Almost never. The low cloud lifted and broke, the dawn sky pale, as a horse stepped out of the trees.

Cassie turned her collar up against the wind knifing up the valley. She patted the glossy bay's arched neck and the horse, reassured, picked his way through drifts of leaves. The reeds closed behind them.

The bay stopped, nostrils flaring, where some leafless poplars stood sentinel. Cassie urged the horse on. The night before, she had jumped the fallen oak on her way home, and she now gathered up the slack reins and coaxed her horse into a canter. As she did so, the wind tore a sheet of plastic from under a tree. The horse reared. The girl fell hard, hitting her head, pain exploding.

Her quick breath, a knife in her chest. Ribs cracked.

The wind moaning in the trees the only sound.

Cassie rolled onto her side in the hard cold mud, drawing up her knees, opening her eyes.

A tiny foot, waxen and white, protruded from under the fallen tree.

A doll, it had to be. One of those kewpie dolls that had haunted her childish dreams.

Cassie closed her eyes, but when she opened them it was still there: a small foot – a child's foot. Cassie yanked at the sheet of black plastic. The hungry wind snatched it from her hands, exposing a swaddled child. Matted black hair, pale bruised skin.

A girl. Maybe three years old. So thin, her knees drawn up to her chest, stick-like arms wrapped round them. The child was blue with cold.

Cassie reached across to pick her up, but her stomach clenched when the girl stuck fast in the mud. She tried again, but the child had been tethered at the waist. Cassie worked the twist of leather loose and pulled her free.

How to warm her? How?

Cassie lifted her top and pressed the cold, limp body against her own warm skin. She tucked her in as best she could, pulling her pink fleece over the little girl.

Her horse, trembling too, stepped closer, touching Cassie's shoulder with his muzzle. She leaned against him, felt his heart rate slowing, felt her own slow in response to the animal's comforting presence. Breathe, she told herself. Breathe, she told the child. Breathe. Please don't be dead.

The horse touched the little girl with his velvet nose, his breath gentle on her face. Cassie felt the child's heartbeat flicker, tentative, erratic. She tightened her arms around the child.

Help.

That's what they needed.

Help.

She found her phone, forced her fingers to work, dialled the emergency number.

The man who answered said: 'Mountain Men.' He said: 'Control.'

'Please, help … the valley bridle path … she's dying, a little girl … my horse, we fell … the valley, yes … she's tied up … alone, yes … she's alone, I'm alone. Please come, please.'

'Keep still, keep warm, keep together,' said Control.

Cassie held the child close, the child kept breathing.

Control was talking. Phoning people, saying, 'Doctor ... police. Help. Hang on.'

Cassie folded her body over the tiny husk of a child. 'Don't die, don't die,' she said.

Her horse, warm against her back, shielded her from the wind.

two

Clare Hart held the narrow strip of plastic in her hand, but no matter how long she stared at it, the test in her hand remained positive. The uncompromising line across the centre confirming what the nausea this morning, yesterday morning, two whole weeks of mornings, had been trying to tell her. Physical evidence that she had ignored. She looked up at herself in the cracked mirror. She hadn't slept last night and it showed.

'Now what?'

Phone Riedwaan, that's what. The thin blue line was his problem too.

In theory.

This was a decision they had to make together.

In theory.

In practice, Clare hadn't seen him for two missed periods. She hadn't spoken to him either. She hadn't been able to. He'd gone undercover – Joburg, maybe further north. He should've been back last night. Clare would not admit it, not even to herself, but she'd waited up for him.

She scrolled through her phone. She knew all his numbers. Home number, office number, cellphone: she'd had them by heart before she'd slept with him. She'd slept with him before she'd known his first name.

She dialled his cellphone.

'Faizal. Gang Unit.' Voicemail. 'Leave a message.'

14

But she didn't. If he was back, he'd see she'd called. He'd phone her back. Maybe by then she'd have decided what to do with this thin blue line bisecting her life just like it bisected the narrow piece of plastic in her hand.

'You OK, Doc?' Major Ina Britz filled the doorway. Black belt, black beanie, grey brush cut: she was never going to win a beauty contest.

'I'm fine.' Clare turned round.

'I thought you were talking to someone.'

'Trying to,' said Clare.

'You look like shit, Clare,' said Ina.

'You were looking for me to tell me that?' Clare dropped the plastic strip into the bin.

'No,' said Ina. 'I'm looking for you to tell you the Mountain Men Control sent through a Section 28 special.'

'What is it?' The band of anxiety round Clare's chest tightened. Past experience told her that a Mountain Men alert meant trouble.

'A horse rider found a little girl on the Orange Kloof bridle path.'

'Anyone report a missing child up there?' asked Clare.

'Not yet.'

'How old is she?'

'About three. Looks like she was there all night.' Ina Britz handed Clare the note.

'She's alive?'

'Only just,' said Ina.

'Christ,' said Clare, scanning the sparse details.

'You'd better get up there before the uniforms arrive and fuck things up.'

'What about the Community Consultation Forum?' asked Clare, watching the black Pajero turning into the muddy parking lot outside their makeshift offices. The new police minister's advisor stepped out of the sleek black vehicle. Jakes Cwele. Leather overcoat. Snakeskin shoes. 'It's scheduled in a couple of hours, and there's Jakes Cwele. What's he doing here so early?'

'He's here to close us down. He told me he wants to wrap up your report on child killings at the meeting this morning, Clare. That's what I was coming to tell you when this came through.'

'Tell him no one's getting the report until I'm done with it. End of June.' Clare pushed her arms inside her damp coat. 'That's when my contract with Section 28 expires.'

'I told him that,' said Ina. 'He wasn't happy.'

'I wasn't employed to make people happy,' said Clare. 'Neither were you.'

'No need to remind me,' said Ina. 'You get up there, get this case going, there'll be no way he can publicly pull this unit if you're in the middle of an investigation. I'll be up there soon as I've told him.'

'What's he got against children?' Clare was checking whether her iPad with its database of missing children was charged. It was.

'Cwele doesn't give a fuck about children,' said Ina Britz. 'It's Captain Faizal and the Gang Unit he doesn't like. So by association that includes you and me and the 28s.'

'You going to cancel the Community Forum?' asked Clare.

'Not for one second,' said Ina. 'This'll turn it against him.'

'We don't know what this is,' said Clare.

'Believe me,' said Ina. 'Whatever it is, this time it's going to blow up in Cwele's face. Now go. Not out the front.'

Clare grabbed her emergency kit and took the fire escape. The wind pounced, pulling at her clothes, her hair, her car door.

three

Clare drove up Orange Kloof until the gravel track ran adrift in the reeds. She parked and walked up the bridle path. This far up the valley, the path was narrow, seldom used. The reeds, fed by the recent rains, reached for each other above her head, enclosing her in their hostile embrace.

It was a relief to reach the clearing. Mandla Njobe, immaculate in his khaki-and-black Mountain Men Security uniform, raised a hand in greeting. He held the reins of a horse, his low voice quieting the nervous bay. Beside him was Gypsy, his wise-eyed Alsatian. Clare held her hand out to greet the dog, and the animal reciprocated with a single dignified thump of her plumed tail. A girl of about fourteen was huddled at his feet, a thermal blanket over her shoulders. Her face was white, her eyes dark smudges. There was a livid gash on her temple.

'This is Cassie,' Njobe said by way of a greeting. He had a wary gentleness that was at odds with his squared shoulders and a past as an ex-soldier.

'I'm Dr Hart.' Clare dropped to her knees beside the girl.

'You don't look like a doctor,' she said. 'Where's the ambulance?'

'On its way,' said Clare, covering her with a thermal blanket.

'Can I see her?'

'You don't look like a policeman either.'

'I work with the police,' said Clare. 'When things happen to children.'

'She knows what she's doing,' said Mandla Njobe. 'Show her.'

The girl lifted her pink fleece, revealing an emaciated child clutched against the bare skin of newly budded breasts.

The child was naked except for a piece of filthy fabric. Her skin, taut over her ribs, her hollow belly, was so pale as to seem translucent. She was three, four at the most. Clare put her fingers against her neck. There was a flutter against her fingers. Breath, as light as a moth's wing, brushed her wrist. Clare cupped one small foot in her hand. The sole so smooth, so unmarked, it seemed never to have been walked on. She lifted the dark hair: a heart-shaped face, a widow's peak.

'Who is she?' asked Cassie. 'Where's her mom?'

'I don't know yet,' said Clare.

She turned to Mandla.

'Any sign of someone else, maybe?' asked Clare. 'A woman?'

She did not need to spell it out. Mandla Njobe would have looked for a woman's body already, a mother's body.

'Nothing yet. No sign of a mother. The patrols saw nothing last night. No vehicles, no lights, definitely not a woman and child,' said Mandla. 'Cops,' he said. 'That's what we need. More cops.'

Clare thought of Riedwaan, her hand on her phone. She had underestimated how little talent she had for waiting, especially for Riedwaan Faizal. But there was no point in calling him. He'd told her he'd get in touch with her when he was able to.

Cassie's voice cut through her thoughts.

'How did she get here, Dr Hart?' Cassie's eyes filled with tears, her own childhood not that remote.

'Tell me how you found her while it's fresh in your mind,' said Clare. 'That'll help us work that out.'

'I was riding down to the beach.'

'Did you see anyone on the way?' asked Clare.

'The sun wasn't up yet. I saw no one, nothing till I got here.'

18

'That's when you saw her?'

'No, no,' said Cassie. 'My horse shied when I tried to do the jump. I fell. I hit my head.'

She put her hand against the oozing gash in her temple.

'When I opened my eyes I saw her little feet. Not a mark, just like a baby's. I pulled away all the plastic and I saw her. With nothing on, just this old red lappie. I didn't know what to do so I untied her – '

'What do you mean, you untied her?' Clare interrupted.

'She was tied to that fallen tree. Here's the belt.'

She handed Clare the twist of leather. Clare coiled it – malignant as a snake – into an evidence bag.

'And then?'

'Then I picked her up, held her against my skin.' Her voice caught in her throat. 'But she's so light, it feels like I'm holding a ghost.'

From a distance, the roar of a helicopter. Cassie started to shake. The cold, the shock, and the realisation that other people, older people were taking charge. Mandla Njobe dug in his pocket and pulled out half a Mars bar.

'Eat this,' he said.

She stripped the wrapper and ate it, a little colour returning to her face. The helicopter was close, the whip-whip of the blades audible.

'Anything else?' asked Clare. 'Did you see anyone?'

'I rode from my house, through the forest and downstream. I saw nobody except the Mountain Men patrol on the other side of the valley,' said Cassie. 'The same as last night. I didn't see anyone then either.'

'What time last night?' Clare's voice was sharp; Cassie recoiled.

'I know it was wrong,' she said. 'Don't tell my mom, please. My dressage lesson was late, so I came this way. It's the quickest.'

'No, no,' said Clare. 'That's not what I meant. You said there was no one here last night. What about the little girl?'

'It must've been five-thirty. It was almost dark.' Cassie concentrated as if she were running a film in her head. 'She wasn't here.'

'How can you be so sure?' asked Clare.

'When I did the jump I dropped my crop,' said Cassie. 'I had to get off to pick it up. There was nothing there.'

Thursday sunset till Friday sunrise. Clare had a time frame. It wasn't much, but it was better than nothing.

four

The red helicopter, its blades slicing the sodden air, landed in the clearing. Clare's anxiety eased a fraction. The paramedics were off and running before it had settled properly, a stretcher between them. A man followed them, unfolding himself from the helicopter. Anwar Jacobs. Child trauma specialist. He and Clare had worked on a dozen or more Section 28 cases in the last six months. He was the fading child's best hope.

'Clare.' He acknowledged his colleague as he got clear of the helicopter.

'Hi, Anwar,' she replied. The paramedics were easing the child out of Cassie's arms and onto the stretcher.

'We should meet in happier circumstances,' said Anwar. 'It's a little girl?'

'Yes,' said Clare, walking with him. 'Girl fell off her horse, found the child. The little girl would otherwise be dead.'

'Was it you who found the little girl?' Jacobs knelt next to Cassie.

She nodded. 'I picked her up,' said Cassie. 'I put her against my skin. My mom does it with puppies if they're born very weak.'

'You did the right thing, Cassie,' He gently touched the contusion on Cassie's head. 'Now you need to let us see to her. And you need to see to her head,' he said to the paramedics.

Then he looked down, all his attention on the child he was laying out on the stretcher.

Anwar Jacobs smoothed the little girl's hair. Her eyes were closed, pain etched on her chalk-white features in a way that did not seem possible in so young a child. It was as if her very dreams were a terror, worse than the nightmare of being abandoned to such a bitter night. His large hands were swift and deft. They dwarfed the spectral child as he tenderly unwrapped her. The tiny girl's shallow breathing seemed as if it might crack her fragile ribs. Her parchment skin, bruised and filthy, was pallid with a greenish undertone.

'I need to stabilise her here,' said Dr Jacobs. 'The heartbeat, it's fading fast.' They erected a tent over the narrow bed. A miniature field hospital.

The oxygen mask was easy, but the hunt for a vein took six attempts. Jacobs found a vein, the single dark drop of the girl's blood swirling into the rehydration fluids the signal of success.

'That list of yours giving you anything there, Clare?'

'Nothing yet,' said Clare, scrolling through the database on her iPad. 'So far, no little girls fit her description. When I can talk to her –'

'She's not going to be conscious any time soon,' he said. 'So she's not going to be able to tell you what happened.'

'She's going to make it, though?'

'That I can't say yet,' he said, opening the girl's tightly curled fists for the obligatory scrape under the fingernails.

'Can you give me anything to work with, Anwar?'

'She's been starved,' said Anwar Jacobs, glancing up at Clare. 'Something I've never seen in a white child in Cape Town. But there's other stuff here I haven't seen before. I need to get her to intensive care now. You coming with us?'

'As soon as things are sorted here,' said Clare. 'We have to search the area, get the forensics done, house-to-house questions.'

'I'll call you as soon as I have something,' he said. 'You call me when you have a name.'

'Her family must be freaking out,' one of the paramedics said, strapping the child onto the stretcher.

'Unless it was them who did it,' said Jacobs. 'Family. Sometimes the most dangerous people a child can meet.'

The medics ducked under the whirling blades of the helicopter. In minutes, it was lifting. Then it hovered a moment, a red dragonfly above the trees. The pilot steadied the chopper in the wind, it tilted away, and the silence rushed back to fill the void.

five

An owl hooted, the sound tipping Clare back to last night's darkness and a little girl too weak even to walk. She had been carried here, that much her unmarked feet had revealed.

Clare knelt beside the fallen oak, reading the tiny marks and disturbances to the soil in a way that another woman might read a book. There wasn't much – just a flattening of the leaves, a frightened animal seeking refuge from the storm, perhaps. Clare looked up at the thick undergrowth that ringed the clearing. The bridle path was a narrow opening in the reeds; beyond, on the other side of the river, a forest where shadows shifted the shapes of the trees.

Clare examined the belt that had held the child fast to the fallen oak. She looked up at the bridle path. The arms carrying her had tired, perhaps, and so the child was tethered to the fallen tree, its branches providing some protection from the sleet.

A movement drew Clare's gaze. A porcupine breaking cover. The creature paused at the edge of the clearing and looked back at Clare, then it turned and ran, dropping a quill as it disappeared into the reeds.

From the other side of the reed bed came the sound of car doors slamming. The voices of the uniformed officers floated above the reeds.

'Jirre, vok. You uniforms could fuck up a crime scene in your sleep. Why your mothers didn't drown you at birth is a mystery.'

24

Ina Britz had arrived, the hapless uniformed police straggling in her wake. 'Secure the place; don't act like a herd of hippos on Viagra, for fuck's sake.'

A constable looped crime-scene tape around the trees in a wide arc. There was a photographer, someone from forensics. The 28s fanning out, searching. A crime scene, not made to order, as on TV, but a good enough approximation.

Ina was stomping over to where Clare stood.

'You managed to get rid of Cwele?' Clare asked.

'How many chances you think snowballs get in hell?' Ina said. 'We'll have a press conference. This is going to be big news. Maybe it'll shut Cwele up long enough for you to finish what you started. What does she look like?'

'Look through those.' Clare handed her camera to Ina.

'I've seen a lot of sick stuff,' said Ina, scrolling through Clare's photographs. 'But what the fuck is this? Who is she? Where does she come from?'

'It's as if we found a ghost.' Clare spread her map out on a nearby rock, but it writhed in her hands, agitated by the wind. Mandla Njobe and Ina held the map steady. From the river, there was a radial fan of bridle paths and dirt tracks. Across from it there was a pine forest. Beyond was the expanse of nature reserve that stretched from Judas Peak across to Hell's Gate, the narrow entrance to the series of dams along the spine of Table Mountain. The waterfall was visible from where they stood. In this weather, with this amount of rain, the area would be almost impassable.

'Did your Mountain Men report anything, Mandla?' asked Clare.

'They had two patrols out on the contour path. The storm was bad last night, even the gangsters stayed inside.'

'The security logs,' said Clare, 'there might be something there.'

'Not many cameras this side of town,' said Mandla Njobe.

'Call them in,' said Clare. 'Everything. CCTV from the whole area. Alarm signals. There are number-plate recognition cameras in quite a few areas now. Get those too – anything that might come up this way. Someone must have seen something. Also a house-to-house search for this whole area.'

'Won't take that long,' said Ina Britz. 'These plots are so big you could fit a whole township on each of them.'

Gypsy cocked her head and whined, looking in the direction of the trees. The roar of the river on the other side.

'Somebody carried her here,' said Mandla Njobe. 'I'll see where Gypsy takes me.'

Ina lit a Lucky Strike as she and Clare watched Mandla Njobe disappear into the trees, Gypsy at his heels. Man and dog moving as one.

'Kak place to leave a laaitie to die.'

'If that's what the intention was.' Clare held out the length of leather. 'She was tied to the tree. She couldn't have got away, even if she'd wanted to.'

'What the fuck?' said Ina.

'That's what I want to know,' said Clare. 'Like you'd tie up a puppy so it won't wander. To keep it safe, maybe.'

'Or a lamb if you're going to slaughter it.' Ina looked up at the expanse of mountain. 'We've got to search this whole fucking area now, and it's just trees and shit.'

'It's nature, Ina,' said Clare. 'It's beautiful.'

'I grew up on the mines on the East Rand,' said Ina, turning her back on the mountain. 'I fucking hate nature.'

A mud-splattered truck appeared, bumping down the track. A man driving, next to him a woman bundled up in a blanket. The driver pulled over and got out. A weather-worn face. Ina Britz blocked him at the edge of the clearing, the crime-scene tape snapping between them.

'I'm sorry, sir. No further.'

'I have to get through,' the man said. 'We live up the valley. The Mountain Men come our way sometimes. What happened here? Was there an accident?'

'A horse rider found a little girl here this morning.'

'Dead?' he asked.

'Not yet.' Ina turned to a warrant officer. 'Let them through.'

The bakkie went on towards the scatter of permaculture farms and retreats that had survived the suburban sprawl of Hout Bay. A couple of beehives, a child's red scooter on the back, the woman's face in the window, turned towards them until they vanished in the trees.

A Land Rover rounded the corner. Inside, a couple. A woman with a tumble of hair, black as Cassie's, opened the door and ran across the clearing. The girl fell into her mother's arms, able to cry at last. The woman helped her child into the vehicle, as the girl's father led the horse away.

A straggle of onlookers: riders, dog walkers, drifters. The tabloid that miraculously materialised at every accident and crime scene, the writer and photographer like some nicotine-stained yin and yang.

'You and you,' Ina was bellowing at the uniformed officers closest to her. 'Get rid of these people. Block the access road. Tell the journalists there's a Community Forum later that'll double as a press conference, but for now they can fuck off.'

Clare's phone vibrated, Mandla Njobe's name flashing on the screen.

'Mandla,' said Clare. 'Found something?'

The uniforms had blocked the gathering crowd and were moving forward, herding them back down the path.

'Looks like someone – maybe a couple of people – were up on the contour path last night.'

'Can you see which way they went?' asked Clare, walking away from the noisy onlookers.

'No tracks, Doc,' said Mandla. 'Not after all that rain.'

'Give me the exact position,' said Clare. 'I'm coming up.'

'What's Njobe found?' asked Ina as Clare tucked her phone into her jacket pocket.

'Looks like someone, maybe a couple of people, were up on the contour path last night,' said Clare. 'Says he saw a place where they seem to have hung around a while. The rest of the tracks were washed away by the rain.'

'Njobe can track anything,' said Ina. 'Says the Bush War taught him.'

'Ja, though he never says which side he fought on.'

'Don't think it matters any more,' said Ina.

Clare walked swiftly between the trees. She took a footpath that vanished up Judas Peak, where Mandla and Gypsy were waiting. An unfurling of crows caught Clare's eye, and she glimpsed turrets protruding from the pine forest. The replica of a Black Forest castle, a rich man's folly that had recently changed hands, according to the *People's Post*.

The surrounding terrain was a nature reserve, with a ravine that led up the back of Table Mountain. Further down, an exclusive estate, each house positioned for privacy as well as security. Razor wire twirled atop perimeter fencing that backed onto the forest and the river. Clare paused to catch her breath. Had the little girl perhaps wandered away from the estate?

She filed the thought for later, pushing on through the trees, soon reaching the firebreak that cut into the face of Judas Peak. Clare checked her orientation and took a short cut towards the contour path, a neglected track where encroaching undergrowth scratched at her. A gate with a gleaming new padlock blocked her path. She ran her hand along the chain, its links icy to the touch. The electric fence spat like an angry cat. The fence was also new, as impenetrable as a game fence. There was live current running through it, the voltage lethal, said the warning signs.

'You looking for something?' The man's eyes were as cold and grudging as the sky. His right hand rested on his holstered gun with the familiarity of a husband's hand on his wife's thigh. The Jeep parked on the other side of the fence was camouflaged, though Clare should have seen it.

'Yes, I am, in fact. A child that was found down the valley this morning.' Clare fished out her ID and handed it to him. 'Clare Hart. This road is public access.'

'I'm sorry.' Joburg accent. 'But Mr Savic has security issues.'

'Did you see anyone last night?'

'No,' said the guard, not too quick, not too slow. 'Just the helicopter this morning. The cars. The dogs – and you, Miss Hope,' he said, handing back her ID.

'Hart,' said Clare.

'Miss Hart,' he said. 'Can I open for you? Drive you through?'

'Thanks. That'll save me time.'

'And effort. The terrain is rough here.' The guard unlocked the gate. There was a spider's web of scars at the back of his neck, the skin puckered and pink in places. He turned his collar up. 'After you.'

The track looped up towards the back of the castle. Two women were walking through the trees. With the forbidding turrets against the heavy sky, they looked medieval. Perhaps it was the long coats, the capes pulled up against the rain.

A gate appeared, opening at the touch of a button. They drove along a road that had been freshly graded, alongside the electric fence.

'There's your colleague,' said the guard.

'Thanks,' said Clare.

Clare scrambled down the hill to where Mandla Njobe and Gypsy were waiting. She could feel the man's eyes on her, between her shoulder blades. It was a relief to hear the Jeep's engine start up.

'There was somebody here.' Njobe squatted down. A chocolate wrapper glinted in a nearby bush. 'You got some gloves?'

Clare handed him a pair, her size, but he got them on. He picked up the cigarette butts and examined them 'Someone who sat here for a while. Two people, maybe. And not too long ago.'

'Could be anyone,' said Clare. 'Hikers, walkers.'

The view down to the bridle path was clear. They could see Ina Britz and the others moving purposefully round the crime scene. Mandla Njobe stood up and flicked mud from his trousers.

'Hikers don't smoke ten Stuyvesants, Doc.'

six

The beggar weaving in front of Clare at the red light was wearing
a cap. He held his handmade sign aloft – *No work. No Fingers.
Plees help* – his stumps pointing to a rough drawing of a fishing
net shearing off all eight fingers.

'Next time,' said Clare, holding up her palms to show that she
had no change. Sharp eyes in a ravaged face. Memorising her
features, her meagre promise. 'I'll be watching for you, lady.'

Her phone beeped. Riedwaan. Her stomach knotted around
her indecision – and unexpected delight at the thought of cells
splitting, folding themselves into life.

She opened the message. *Sorry 4 silence. Delayed. Will explain.
My mother is bad. Back tonight. Will find U. xx R*

What would she say? Once she'd told Riedwaan, the decision
about this baby or not-baby would no longer be hers alone.

The lights turned green. The taxi behind her hooted and she
lurched across the intersection.

She turned into the parking lot outside the 28's offices, three
converted shipping containers. In front of her, three expensive
government cars. The bureaucrats wanting her report profiling
crimes against children, against the women who cared for them.
Wanting her to make her data tell a different story. One of success,
rather than social failure. To her left, a couple of old cars: the few
remaining journalists' jalopies. The Community Consultation
Forum. She should gather her wits, gather the sparse facts she

31

had, and be there already.

Yet Clare didn't move. Instead, she sat in the car and stared un-seeing at the clouds writhing above Chapman's Peak, her phone in her hand.

She had to talk to him. She had to tell him. She had to set the future in motion, but she was unable to do so.

She knew what Riedwaan would want; she'd seen him cradling Yasmin, his only daughter, in his arms. Seen, too, the acrimony between him and his ex-wife. She didn't know if that's what she wanted – to be part of that.

Mother, father, child. It messed with her head; she couldn't think straight. And she had to, she had to. She had to decide. She had to tell him what she'd decided. That was the courtesy a woman owed her lover. It was the least she could do, but fuck it. She couldn't. Not now, not with the job ahead of her, and the child abandoned on the icy mountainside.

She put her phone away and grabbed her bag, got out of the car, and strode across the muddy parking lot to her office.

Ina Britz had a sea of paper in front of her, her glasses slipping down a nose that was dished like that of a prizefighter.

'Those are the missing persons' files?' asked Clare.

'I've pulled up all the missing little girls I can find.'

Ina Britz laid out the photographs of the lost girls, their eyes fixed for ever in the grimace of a pre-school portrait or happily snapped birthday party. Cake, crown, a proud mother's lap.

'It's none of them,' said Clare, flicking through them. She knew each face intimately. They lived in her now, folded into the other faces that populated her dreams. 'What about the international cases?'

'Here's what I've got from FindKidz and Interpol.' The same eyes, the same poses, the same routine of childhood interrupted.

'Where's the mother?' asked Clare. 'That's what I want to know.'

32

'I've got nothing that shows a woman and a child missing together,' said Ina. 'We're looking up some that could match, but so far nothing.'

Clare's gaze moved from one woman's face to the next. Looking for something that might trigger recognition. Pale skin, dark hair, widow's peak. She picked up one or two photographs, but there was nothing. She put them down again.

'I've never dealt with a child that was never reported missing,' Clare said.

'Look at these. The Mountain Men incident reports.' Ina Brtiz handed Clare a list of incidents that the security company had dealt with. Barking dogs, vagrants, break-ins, smashed car windows, a domestic, alarms activated. Lists of phone numbers of the houses that had called in. No sightings of untoward movement in the valley.

'Whoever put the child here knew the mountain well,' said Clare, studying the report. 'There's nothing here.'

Clare closed her office door behind her. She threw the rest of the coffee out of the window, swallowed the wave of nausea and opened her laptop, found the database of missing children. Abandoned babies, wiry kids, teenagers. On the cusp of adulthood, their photographs had the posed stiffness of the school portrait or the graininess of a cheap cellphone shot. Most of them were South African.

With the sparse details she had, she sent out the standard alert.

She dialled Dr Anwar Jacobs, closing her eyes against the headache building in the base of her skull. The momentary darkness was a relief but not an escape. When he answered she could hear the electronic beeps, the clink of metal, the muted voices of nurses, other doctors. The comforting orderliness of the Intensive Care Unit.

'How's she doing?' asked Clare.

'The staff have named her Engeltjie. The little angel's alive, she's fighting,' said Anwar. 'But I need the mother to come forward. I need to know what her history is, so that I can work out how to treat her.'

'I've got a press conference right now,' said Clare. 'I need some detail.'

'I have so little,' he said. Clare could hear exhaustion in his voice, he sounded close to defeat.

'Give me what you have,' said Clare. They'd worked on many cases together. Clare admired his thoroughness, his astuteness, and his compassion for his helpless little patients.

'She's alive, but she's not going to be conscious any time soon. I've induced a coma because her vital signs are so fragile. She has hypothermia and long-term malnutrition.'

'How old is she?' asked Clare.

'By weight, two or three, but if I look at her teeth, bad as they are, then I think she's five, even six. Her growth is stunted in a way I've never seen before. And the pallor, it's as if she's never been in the sun.'

'Sexual assault?' asked Clare.

'Nothing visible.'

The rain running down the windows blurred the world outside.

'Have you got any idea yet who she might be?' the doctor asked.

'Nothing,' said Clare. 'You've got to give me something else, Anwar.'

'But I've never seen anything like this,' he said. 'I'm thinking maybe she's been poisoned. I've sent off for every test you can imagine.'

'I need those results as soon as you get them,' said Clare.

'I should have them this afternoon,' said Anwar Jacobs.

The door opened. Ina Britz was standing there. She had taken her beanie off in deference to the formality of the occasion.

'You ready, Clare?' she asked. 'To be thrown like a Christian to the lions?'

'You shouldn't speak of my former colleagues like that.'

Clare closed her laptop, put on red lipstick, brushed her hair, and changed into a dress and a pair of heels.

'Standing on tiptoes helps you concentrate?' asked Ina.

'Can't think otherwise,' said Clare.

'The press pack is sniffing the bones of a story that could run for weeks,' said Ina Britz. 'Everything's upside down – missing child, no reports, half-dead kid, no weeping mother or suspect stepfather. They think we're hiding something.'

'I wish we were,' said Clare. 'There's so little to go on and I don't like the feel of what there is.' A wave of nausea washed over her again, nausea and a fatigue so deep, so in her bone marrow, that she wanted to lie down and sleep right where she was.

'You go on, Ina,' she said, heading for the bathroom. 'I'll be there in a minute.'

Ina Britz raised an eyebrow, and left. Clare ducked into the bathroom and retched, but there was nothing. She had to eat, but the very thought of it made her want to be sick again. She drank some more water instead. When she looked out of the window a battered blue bakkie was turning in. A man at the wheel – a dog beside him – gesticulating to the security guard at the gate.

seven

Jakes Cwele was out of his 4x4. He blocked her path, a life's worth of anger in his tensed shoulders.

Clare had to stop herself from stepping backwards. He was too close, right inside her space.

'What can I do for you?'

'I'm here to help you.' He smiled. 'It's a big thing, this press conference.'

'We don't need your help,' said Clare.

'Cape Town is my command now.' A blaze of anger in Cwele's eyes. 'But it would be much better if you would cooperate with me while we get this province to focus on the things that matter if you want law and order. It's tough for you. You're a civilian. You're a woman. You're out of your depth. You just tell me when you need advice. About being a cop. I hear that Faizal gives you advice about how to be a woman.'

'Rumour mill, the police,' said Clare. 'Some of us prefer facts and evidence, now get out of my way. I have a job to do.'

'Dr Hart,' Cwele put his hand lightly on her arm. 'By Monday your captain's going to be gone. Then there's no one watching out for you. This is not a place for a lady, and you're not a cop.'

'I'm not a lady either,' said Clare. 'So that balances things out.'

A taxi boomed kwaito music. It throbbed, then turned a corner, leaving silence in its wake. Clare stepped past Cwele, and then she was in the cramped conference room, corralled behind the podium, no water in the jug. Microphones and flashbulbs and cameras and people saying her name – Dr Hart, Clare, Dr Hart. She scanned the crowd. In front of her were bemused Neighbourhood Watch members and others who had tried to stitch connections between the economic gulfs that divided Hout Bay. In front, a group of mothers who campaigned for the right-of-way for horse riders, and at the back three women whose children had vanished in the dunes above Hangberg.

She knew the journalists; some she'd seen that morning. Jakes Cwele came in too, flanked by a trio in sharply tailored suits. There were a couple of other cops too. Allies. Colonel Edgar Phiri, Riedwaan's Gang Unit boss, raised a hand in greeting. Clare was glad to see him there.

At the back of the room sat an old man in a black suit. Holding a hat on his knees, he did not take his eyes off Clare, not for a second. His unblinking gaze unsettled her, the still point in the heaving tide of journalists around her. In the front row was a woman who had tackled Clare on a previous occasion.

'Dr Hart,' she stood up before anyone could stop her. 'The 28s? Why are you called after a prison gang?'

'Section 28. It's a clause in the Constitution that guarantees children their rights.'

'What does it promise them, pray tell?'

'A name, a nationality, safety, security. Love, too,' said Clare.

'All the things that the United Nations likes,' she sneered. 'Ironic, don't you think, that the 28s is also the name of a prison gang? This fact seems to have bypassed the minister completely.' Her voice was rising, she was just getting started. 'Let me tell you what these children get. They get a bullet in the back. But what can you expect from a government like this?'

Ina Britz moved over to the woman.

'We've been over this before, Mrs Sheridan,' said Clare. 'We know how you feel, but we need to move on.'

The woman sat down, but Ina remained close, one black, beady eye on her.

Clare gathered her notes. No lynch mob ever wanted facts, but she was going to give them some. She listed the few that she had and then the questions machine-gunned.

'Is it true it's a white child? Is that why there was a helicopter?'

'Is this to do with drugs?'

'Is it true that the mother was an addict?'

'Is this about drugs?'

'Gangs?'

'Paedophiles?'

'Was the child sodomised?'

'Bewitched?'

'Is our community safe?'

'Who's next?'

'You've got no clue, have you?' A reporter writing down his own question.

Clare could picture tomorrow's tabloid headlines that would whip readers into a profitable frenzy. Nothing sells a paper better than a missing child. The old man slipped out, his black-suited back a column. There was a concentration to him that caught Clare's attention. She watched him go across the parking lot towards her office.

'Any arrests yet?'

The question – repeated – brought her attention back to the room. No, no arrests yet. No suspects yet. Priority being the child's welfare.

'Dr Hart, is it true that Section 28 is being dissolved?'

'Perhaps the minister's advisor would like to take that question,' said Clare.

Everyone turned to look at Jakes Cwele, taking in the leather coat, the fedora.

'Expertise in this area is being redeployed,' said Cwele. 'The new minister is taking the president's instructions to heart. Economic stability is everything. We know that crime is a result of poverty, therefore this must be addressed first.'

A tabloid journalist turned to Clare. 'Your views, Dr Hart?'

'Section 28 was set up by the previous minister after a Community Consultation Forum like this one. You know this,' said Clare. 'The minister laboured under the illusion that voters are owed explanations as to why so many children and their mothers die. She was removed during the last cabinet shuffle, but the 28s are still here, unwanted and unwelcome.'

'For how long, though?'

'I am contracted till the end of June,' said Clare. 'Major Britz is permanent. The Gang Unit – Colonel Phiri is here too – are our partners. We're not going anywhere. And now we have an investigation to complete.'

It was over, and the journalists were shepherded out.

The old man who had caught Clare's eye during the press conference was waiting for her when she and Ina Britz went outside.

'Dr Hart?'

'That's me,' she said.

'I know of your work, Dr Hart, Section 28. It's in the papers, on the TV. You find them, the stolen ones. You'll bring her back to me.' The old man's eyes were hollow. Clare knew that look. 'She's gone. My little girl is gone.'

'Do you know something about the little girl we found this morning?'

He shook his head. 'I'm so sorry for her, but she's not the one I came for, Dr Hart. I came for you. She phoned me.' He was fumbling with a cellphone, the instrument apparently unfamiliar in his work-worn hands. 'Listen.'

Rosa, Oupa, it's Rosa.

There was a flaying purity in the terror of the girl's voice.

Oupa. There's trees outside. Get me help, Oupa, Oupa, come. Please.

A scream, high-pitched as a cat's.

Oupa. Find me, Oupa. Find me please. He's —

The phone fell from the man's hands.

Clare picked it up and checked the log.

'The call came at five this morning,' said Clare. 'It's eleven now. That's six hours ago. Since then there's been nothing?'

'Nothing.'

'There's no number,' said Clare, handing the phone to Ina. 'Can you get a trace on this, Ina?'

'No problem,' she said. 'What's her name?'

'Rosa Wagner. I'm Alfred Wagner.' His voice was rough with pain. 'I'm meant to protect her and I didn't hear her calling. I was asleep.'

'Does Rosa have a daughter?' asked Ina Britz.

'Rosa's hardly more than a child herself.' A tear in the clouds; sunlight slanting through, the golden light mocking the man's anguish.

eight

Alfred Wagner stopped in front of the map with the forest of pins that Clare had placed there over the past six months. She looked at her map through Wagner's eyes: a chart of horror that covered one whole wall of her office. On the adjacent wall she'd pinned up photographs of the little girl on the bridle path. Alongside it were pictures of the fallen tree, the leather restraint, the black plastic, the dark rag she'd been wrapped in. It was pitifully little: the only source of real information was the little girl's mute, injured body.

'What do the red pins mean?' he asked.

'Places where injured children have been found.'

'And the black pins?'

'The ones that didn't make it.' Clare closed the door behind her, shutting out the hubbub of the rest of the Section 28 office. Uniforms coming in and out, phones ringing, dog handlers wanting coffee for themselves, water for the dogs.

'You're going to put in a red pin for Rosa,' he said, a catch in his voice. 'Not a black one.'

Clare guided Wagner to the table in her office. He followed, obedient as a child, the weight of his desperation too heavy for him to stand any longer.

'I went to the police.' Helpless fury in his voice. 'An officer said nothing could be done unless she's been missing twenty-four hours. I asked him to listen. He did, said she sounded like

41

she was on drugs.'

'As soon as we get the number traced,' said Clare, 'we'll have somewhere concrete to start. How old is Rosa, Mr Wagner?'

'Nineteen,' he said.

'This unit is for children.'

'The law might say she is no longer a child, Dr Hart,' he said. 'But I'm her grandfather. My son died, her mother followed soon after. I am her family,' he said. 'There's Rosa, there's me. That's it. Look at her.'

Mr Wagner placed a photograph on Clare's desk.

Rosa Wagner. She lay there between them, an accusation. An ethereal girl in a red velvet dress. Tawny skin, her hair a black cascade around a delicate face. Her knees were parted, a cello cradled between them. She clasped the instrument's slender neck in her arms, rapture in her upturned face. Clare looked at the old man – his face was lined with anxiety and loss, his hands knotted with arthritis and a life of labour. It was hard to imagine how this girl was connected to him.

'She's a musician?' asked Clare.

'A student at the Cape College of Classical Music. Here in Hout Bay,' he said. 'I phoned them. The secretary told me that she had withdrawn.'

'You didn't know?'

'I had no idea.'

Clare pulled her notebook out of her bag, found a pen. 'You'd better tell me what you do know about her.'

'She's a gifted cellist and she won a music scholarship. She left me and she came to Cape Town.'

'When last did you see her?'

'She came home for the weekend. It was a Friday. The twenty-fifth of May was the date.' Mr Wagner picked up the photograph of his granddaughter.

'Today's the fifteenth,' said Clare. 'So that's three weeks ago. How was she?'

'Quiet, but that's how she is.'

'And you haven't spoken to her since?'

He shook his head.

'How often do you usually speak to her on the phone?' asked Clare.

'When it's essential,' he said, touching the hearing aid tucked behind his left ear. 'It's not easy for me, the phone.'

'Did anything happen between you?' Clare was making notes.

'Nothing,' he said. 'We didn't argue. We never argue. She said she'd be back for the holidays.'

'Did she have a boyfriend? Was she unhappy – that she told you about?'

'She never said.'

'Where did Rosa grow up?'

'With me,' he said. 'In Churchhaven, an hour or so up the West Coast.'

'I know it,' said Clare. 'It's like heaven.'

'For some,' said Mr Wagner. 'For a long time it was. Then Rosa wanted more. There isn't even a shop there. No electricity. No running water. It's how young people are.'

'Where are her parents?' asked Clare.

'Her father, my only son, died when Rosa was four. His wife –' his mouth twisted as he spoke the word – 'she brought Rosa here some time later. My son's wife said she'd come back for Rosa, but she never did. The damage was already done by then.'

'What damage?'

'The child never spoke of it.' Mr Wagner looked directly at Clare. 'But there are things that can be done to a child's soul that cannot be measured in bruises or blows. This you would know.'

'Where's her mother now?' asked Clare.

'She died when Rosa was eight. Rosa said nothing at the time. She didn't even cry. There was only the silence her death left in its wake. A silence that Rosa filled with music. That's how we lived together; just me and her and our music.'

Mr Wagner handed Clare an envelope. In it were a few photographs. Rosa in the sun on a wind-scoured beach, black rocks, her eyes slits against the wind. An only child sitting between her parents, her father the image of the man in front of Clare; the woman small, her face obscured by luxurious black hair – but where Rosa's skin was nearly as dark as her father's, her mother's was pale. The rest of the photographs were of Rosa alone on the beach, a three-legged dog beside her. A few more of her playing her cello. One of her standing outside a Victorian building: the Cape College of Classical Music.

'Has Rosa ever disappeared before?' asked Clare.

'No.'

'Never went looking for her mother's family?'

'Not that I know of,' he said. 'But I think it unlikely.'

'There are few children who don't want to find their mothers,' said Clare.

'Even if their mothers have traded their bodies for drugs?' the old man asked.

'Even then,' said Clare. 'Sometimes especially then. We have to consider everything.'

'There is no one that I know of,' he said. 'She came from Joburg. Apart from my son, she seemed to have no one.'

'No school photos?' said Clare. 'Always helpful, old school-friends.'

'I taught her at home,' said Mr Wagner. 'I taught her what I knew. Nothing that would help her, really. About birds and fish. Some Latin and Greek. And music. Rosa, my vulnerable grand-daughter, was my consolation.'

'In what way was Rosa vulnerable?'

'She's a lonely girl,' he said. 'That makes you vulnerable.'

Clare looked at the old man a moment.

'I need a list of everyone she knows, where she goes,' she said. 'Friends, boyfriends, coffee shops, clubs. Phone numbers. Everything you have.'

He took the pen she handed to him and began to write. 'I phoned the music school this morning,' he said, looking up at Clare. 'When they said she'd withdrawn, I didn't understand. She never abandoned anything in her life. There's only love in her hands. That's why she plays like an angel.'

He handed the list to Clare. It filled half a page, his number at the bottom.

'Do you have somewhere to go?' asked Clare.

'I must go home.' He stood up, unsteady on his feet. 'If she's running, that's where she'll be headed. I'm too old and too sick to do anything else but be there when she gets there. That's the only thing I've ever been able to do for her. I'll be waiting for her to come, or for you to phone.'

He turned around, and walked back into the rain.

Clare watched as he picked his way past the row of BMWs. He climbed into a rusted old Cortina and sat with his hands on the wheel. A dog hopped up and placed its grizzled head on his shoulder. Then Alfred Wagner started his car and drove away.

nine

Ina Britz opened Clare's door. She had a packet of biscuits in her hand.

'Eat some of these,' she said.

'I'm not hungry,' said Clare.

'I don't care,' said Ina. 'Do what I tell you. Ginger biscuits – the ginger will help with the nausea, the sugar will help with fatigue.'

Clare stared at Ina.

'Your secret's safe until you give it away,' said Ina.

'How did you guess?'

'I didn't,' said Ina, opening the packet and handing Clare two of the hard, sugary biscuits. 'And I haven't got ESP or feminine intuition. We share the same bathroom here and you're not that good at tidying up after yourself.'

'I put the test through the shredder,' said Ina. 'I guess you'll say something when the time is right.' She assessed the expression on Clare's face. 'Or not. Your choice, girl. I'm behind you either way.'

Clare ate a biscuit. The ginger was working, so was the sugar.

'Rosa Wagner called from here in Hout Bay,' she said. 'You got a trace?'

'I did,' said Ina. 'There's no one there. Just an answering machine. Dutch couple. Summer swallows.'

'You checked?'

'Called the number in Holland,' said Ina. 'He's an IT consultant.

46

Been gone since early May. Won't be back till October.'

'Anyone staying at the house?'

'No one,' said Ina. 'Maid comes in once a week. Security at the estate keep an eye on things. They don't know any cellists called Rosa.'

Ina put the details in front of Clare.

'Sylvan Estate,' said Clare. 'That's the estate near where the child was found this morning.'

'So get there already,' said Ina.

'Rosa Wagner's not a child,' said Clare. 'If I take this on, it just gives Cwele more ammunition against the 28s – and me.'

'Since when did you give a fuck about Cwele or anybody else?' Ina folded her arms. 'Get your arse into gear. Go find that old man's granddaughter.'

Razor wire, electric fences, Alsatians, armed guards in Kevlar. Sylvan Estate residents spent a lot keeping themselves in, and the poor out – unless, of course, they were cleaning, or tending the manicured grounds.

The guards at the gate had their hands wrapped around tin mugs of coffee. It was raining. They waved Clare inside; pretty white women in new cars didn't fit the profile for a stop-and-search. Not in this weather.

The houses were blank-eyed, curtains closed against the winter, their stone-clad facades forbidding. Sunbird Close was a cul-de-sac, number thirty-nine the last house. Green-roofed and white-shuttered. The original farmhouse before the land had been developed. The house was screened by trees, and the land behind it dipped down towards the river.

Clare switched off the ignition. There were no cars outside. No movement. A *Beware of the Dog* sign, but no animal. Clare rang the doorbell and there was a pretty chime inside. Other than that, silence. The windows were closed and the curtains were drawn.

Silence pressed in around her.

She worked her way around to the back.

On the back steps of a small stoep, a saucer with a splash of milk.

The back door was closed. She tried it; the door swung inwards.

She stood inside an old-fashioned scullery. Wellingtons lined up near the door, drying racks on the counter, a washer and dryer, bits of broken glass across the floor.

Clare's heart banged when, behind her, the wind blew the back door shut.

'Rosa?' she called.

Silence. There were two doors, both shut. Clare opened the first one: a neat pantry. A packet of Dutch stroopwafels was open, cinnamon and sugar dusting the shelf.

She opened the next door. It led her into the kitchen. Red-and-white gingham curtains. A scrubbed wooden table, and a cooking island. All the knives in place.

The entire wall opposite was filled with photographs of two apple-cheeked blonde children. A list of emergency numbers written in clear letters, a box of chalk on a ledge by a small blackboard.

A wall-mounted phone next to it, the receiver dangling alongside brownish streaks on the wall that bloomed into a stain on the ground. Clare strode across the kitchen, bent down. She could smell it. Blood.

She stood up, the familiar crawl in her marrow. She had learned to pay it attention.

A solid oak door led from the kitchen into the house. She tried it, but it was locked.

'Rosa,' Clare shouted. There was no reply.

Clare dug her phone out of her pocket and dialled Ina Britz.

'I'm at the house,' Clare said. 'Seems to be the last point of contact with Rosa Wagner. No sign of her, but there's a broken window and blood by the phone. I want forensics here now.'

'I'm on it,' said Ina. 'Are you alone? Stay where you can be seen till we get there. Clare? Clare, answer me.'

But Clare's phone was back in her pocket and she'd already stepped outside, looking for a way into the house. All the windows were closed, all of them intact. She tried each one as she worked her way around the house. Sash windows in the sitting room. Nothing out of place.

She found a stone and cracked a pane. She waited, holding her breath. No alarm. She unhooked the catch and opened the window. She climbed in. She ran through the living room, the immaculate dining room, a playroom where two teddies sat wide-eyed, expectant, amid a pile of toys.

The oak door into the kitchen was locked, the key on the inside of the door.

Clare ran outside again. Nothing but the view onto the wintry garden. Woody rose bushes, lavender, the lawn. Behind her, the roar of security vehicles as they raced towards the house. At the end of the garden the trees swayed in the wind, a branch skimming the electrified wire fence that encircled Sylvan Estate.

She ran down the slope.

The grass here was long, with straggly runners flattened under the fence. A steep bank, invisible from the house, had washed away – the ground eroded by the rain. There were marks in the earth where tiny claws had burrowed under the fence. Nearby, a porcupine quill lay in the mud. Clare picked it up, testing its pointed end against her skin. Neat black-and-white quills, little javelins, afforded the creature protection that Clare envied right then.

The winter-hungry animal had squeezed under the fence to forage in the estate. The tracks used by other creatures surviving on the edge of the suburb were visible among the trees. And it would have been the trees that drew the girl into the forest, closing up behind her. In the woods, Rosa would have been in another world, dark, forested, a refuge. But Sylvan Estate was not a benign place, as the skull and crossbones – small yellow-and-black signs – strung along the fence at eye level, warned. Clare tossed a small branch, and the fence hissed and spat, lethal as a cobra. Voltage like this would have knocked Rosa out – unless the current was off.

Clare slipped the quill into her pocket. There was the semblance of a path next to the fence. It led towards a stand of oak trees fifty metres away. She followed it and her pulse quickened when, among the solid old trunks, she saw a dry-packed wall.

The cottage on the other side was constructed from dressed stone that was a mottled orange-grey from the lichen. Raspberry canes had grown rampant in this corner of the garden, almost swamping the roof and recessed windows. Clare tried the door, but the wood had swollen in the rain and it was stuck. She put her shoulder to it and shoved. It gave way suddenly and she stumbled inside.

Light filtered in through a cobwebbed window. Clare probed the gloom with her flashlight. A pile of blankets and old scraps of carpet in the corner. A snug nest against the cold. An empty vodka bottle on the floor, a half-eaten packet of stroopwafels, the same as those she'd seen in the pantry.

Clare held her breath and went over to the bed. Lying on a grubby blanket was a light bulb, the crystal meth residue streaked across the inside. Tik, the smell of new money. Tik, the smell of fleeting power, the stench of a slow death. A new copy of *Glamour* magazine was jammed between the bed and the wall, a torn scrap marking the fashion spread. Clare slid it out and turned it over, noticing part of a graph and handwritten notes that she couldn't quite decipher. There were a few more scraps underneath the magazine. Clare placed them on one side, all five pieces, evidence to be bagged with the other detritus. One fell to the floor, and as she bent to pick it up she saw the corner of a photograph protruding from under the mattress. She took it out – it was part of a pile of photos, images that erased all other thoughts from her head. She looked at one. Small-breasted, the pubis shaven, childlike. The body bound and helpless. The fear and pain in the girl's eyes as naked as her body. Grainy prints from a mobile phone.

It wasn't Rosa.

ten

Clare went back to the guardhouse at the entrance of the estate. The guard – Kevlar, cuffs, taser on his belt – came out to greet her this time. He did not look happy when he saw her ID.

'Your people have been here,' he said. 'Asking questions this morning about the bridle path and the little boy –'

'A girl,' Clare corrected him.

'The girl they found on the bridle path,' said the guard. 'We gave them the logs.'

'It's not that,' said Clare. 'Someone phoned from number thirty-nine, sometime between three and four this morning.'

'That can't be,' said the guard. 'The owners aren't there. They left for Amsterdam last month. They'll be back in October. There's nobody there now.'

'And the cat?' asked Clare.

'Mavis feeds them Friday afternoon. That's the maid. She's back Monday. Here, look.' He pushed the log over to Clare. 'There she is. They have to sign in every day, the domestics.'

'No one else went to the house?'

'Not according to the log,' he said.

'I didn't sign in when I came,' said Clare.

'Well, lady, you don't look ...'

The silence stretched.

'I went straight past you,' said Clare. 'You have no record of that.'

The man looked away, his job on the line.

'So, who else came in?' asked Clare.

'It's all on the CCTV.'

Clare sat down in front of the monitors that were in the guard-house. There were CCTV cameras everywhere.

'Which cameras are closest to the old farmhouse?' asked Clare.

'These two,' said the security officer. Neither camera showed much more than the facade. 'Both a bit of a distance away. That house has got the most privacy.'

'Or the least security,' said Clare. 'I want your footage of the periphery fence. What do you have?'

'Not much,' he said.

The guard keyed in a code. Cameras dotted the periphery fence that was strung like a noose around the estate – but the screen was blank.

'Where's the footage?' asked Clare.

'We've been checking. It looks like the storm knocked out one of the cameras.'

'And the electric fence? That was on?'

'A branch came down on it near the guardhouse on Sunday night. We had to take it away, so the fence was off then.'

'What time was that?' asked Clare.

'Four,' he said. 'Took us an hour and a half.'

The guard called up the footage. Nothing but rain and branches moving in the ghostly light of the night vision cameras. No other movement at all. Until the time code said four-thirty. A hunched shape moving out of the darkness.

'Stop it there,' said Clare. 'Now go back.'

The dark shape moved out of the trees, hesitant without any cover. It crouched at the edge of the clearing along the fence.

'Go closer,' said Clare. 'What's that?'

The guard zoomed the camera. 'Just a porcupine.'

'Wait,' said Clare. 'Where did it go, can you see?'

The guard had frozen the frame on the animal, silvered by the security light it had triggered. He slowed the footage down, going frame by frame. 'Back into the trees, looks like.'

'No,' said Clare. 'He's not. Look. Go back again, look there.'

'OK,' said the guard, bemused. 'So the porcupine gets into the estate. So what? People pay a lot of money so they can have animals in here.'

'How does it get in?' Clare persisted.

'Ag, lady, they dig,' he said. 'You seen one before?'

'Yes, I've seen them,' said Clare. 'The fence on that side – there's a steep embankment on the other side, isn't there?'

'Yes, it's steep.'

'So they dig in, the porcupines,' said Clare. 'They don't always trigger the electric fence?'

'If they did, the fuckers would fry.'

'If the porcupines can get through, then whoever got in and out could do the same thing.'

'You might be blonde, lady,' said the guard, 'but you're not –'

'I wouldn't say dumb, if I were you.' Ina Britz stepped inside. She flashed her badge at the guard, but spoke to Clare. 'Forensics is here, Doc, at least what I could muster with the cutbacks. Let's get the house searched.'

They drove the short distance back to the house. Clare took her round the back and through the kitchen.

'She slid down the wall and sat here,' said Clare. The phone hung limply on the wall. Next to it was the blood smear, and two faint stains on the floor. 'I think she was naked.'

Ina squatted down and studied the smear of blood. It was in the butterfly-wing shape of a girl's bottom.

'Any other signs of her?' asked Ina.

'This,' said Clare.

She pointed to a clump of hair on a branch, some strands tipped with follicles, on the scullery window. 'It's how she got in, looks like.'

'Man, this is not good,' said Ina.

'There's more,' said Clare.

They walked down towards the stone cottage. Pulling on a pair of rubber gloves, Clare pushed open the door. Again the smell assailed her.

'Cosy little tik den here,' said Ina. 'You think it's kids who live around here?'

'Nothing would surprise me,' said Clare. 'It's *The Truman Show* meets *Desperate Housewives*, this estate. Enough to drive anyone mad.'

The two women worked methodically, bagging and tagging the broken light bulb, the tik straws, the bottles, the magazines, the papers, the leftover food. Sweetie Pies, Nik Naks, children's party food.

'Tik smokers have records usually,' said Ina. 'And teenagers do this shit if they're bored and stoned.'

'Yes,' said Clare. 'But I don't think Rosa chose to be here, and it doesn't look to me like she left the place on her own.'

'Rain last night, so no chance of footprints,' said Ina. 'No scent trail either.'

'Let's work on what we have here,' said Clare. 'There'll be fingerprints in the house too. That packet of stroopwafels – those cinnamon biscuits – must come from the house. Nobody sells them here.'

'Where's the boyfriend?' asked Ina. 'You questioned him?'

'So far, no evidence she had a boyfriend.'

'Doesn't mean there isn't one out there somewhere.'

'Have you checked out the grandfather?' asked Clare.

'He seemed to be who he said he is. Teacher, studied

classics on some sort of Commonwealth scholarship. Retired to Churchhaven a long time ago. He's Rosa's guardian, has been since she was little.' Ina Britz lit a Lucky Strike. 'The techs tell me her cellphone's not been used for three weeks. Last triangulation was the Hout Bay mast. Then it was switched off, and nothing. Same with her bank. Nothing since the twenty-fifth of May. She doesn't have a laptop, hasn't checked her email in three weeks.'

Some rowdy guinea fowl settled in a tree on the other side of the fence.

'There's nothing connecting her with the little girl we found this morning?' Ina asked. 'The bridle path isn't so far from here, as the crow flies.'

'No, nothing that I can see,' said Clare. 'Rosa is nineteen, never had a child. Seems to be an accident of geography.'

'Not unlikely in South Africa,' said Ina. 'Crime scenes are as crowded in on each other as graves in an old cemetery.'

A mud-splattered forensics van pulled up.

'Here's Fingerprints,' said Ina, as Shorty de Lange uncurled his long body from the car.

'Maybe they'll pull the rabbit out of the hat for a change.'

De Lange walked towards the two women. He was in his version of casual Friday clothes, but looked as much a cop as if he'd been wearing full dress uniform.

'It's been a while, Shorty,' said Clare.

'Morning, Clare,' he gave her one of his rare smiles. 'What a pleasure to see your face and not Faizal's. Morning Britz, you know he's the cop this beautiful woman is usually cursed with,' winking at Ina.

'When I called I said I wanted help, not trouble,' said Clare.

'Captain Faizal,' said Ina. 'He's a man who gets you into trouble.'

'From what I've seen he gets you out of it too, nè Clare?' said De Lange.

56

'Been known to happen,' Clare laughed. 'You want to check things out?'

'What you got?'

'Someone's been smoking tik in there.'

'That means Faizal will find you soon enough. Brings that Gang Unit out like bees to a flower,' said De Lange, ducking into the cottage.

He appraised the familiar scene: the drug detritus of addicts who all too often dragged others into the vortex of their nasty, brutish lives.

'Fuckers,' he said, picking up one of the photographs. 'You want it all tested?'

'Searched and tested,' said Clare. 'Where's your help?'

'Minister's got some ceremony going today,' said De Lange. 'Seems they have to be there to make him look good.'

'And you?' asked Clare.

'I'm a dinosaur,' said De Lange. 'I just do my job. That never made any politician look good.'

Clare left De Lange to get on with his work. Curious neighbours loitered at the front of the house as she walked back to the bottom of the garden. Ina Britz joined her, and the two women looked towards the forest that seemed to absorb the early-afternoon light.

'I want a search of the forest,' said Clare. 'This girl didn't just disappear.'

'But there's no one to do it.' Ina put her hand on Clare's shoulder. 'Cwele's pulled everything. Says the priority is economic stability. Not domestic incidents. Money's a higher priority than people these days.'

'He thinks this is a domestic?' said Clare.

'He told me there's no evidence to justify resources.'

'How does he know about this girl?'

'When I was checking the numbers, he came in.'

'Ina, we'll pretend we're looking for this girl, but you know and I know that what we'll probably find is a body. What on earth must I tell that old man?'

'My hands are tied,' said Ina. 'There's no one who can help.'

'There's Mandla Njobe,' said Clare.

'OK, ask him. He'll do it. Cwele's cut all overtime for the 28s and he wants to authorise each and every expenditure we make,' said Ina. 'He told me this just before I came here.'

'Can he do that?' asked Clare.

'He's found some clause that authorises him,' said Ina. 'I've got our lawyers looking at it. You carry on in the meantime. I'll cover for you. Just get the fuck out of here before he arrives.'

Clare looked at the trees jostling in the wind. 'She's out there. Somewhere. We'll find her.'

eleven

Clare nosed her car into the afternoon traffic. She imagined the CapeTalk anchor, snug in his heated studio as he rattled off plummeting solstice temperatures. There was snow on the mountain ranges that hemmed in Cape Town. The power lines were going down and the passes were being closed, one after another. The station cut back to the weekend's main news story.

'Another of Dr Clare Hart's little girls was found early this morning. She had been abandoned on a Hout Bay bridle path,' the reporter was saying. 'Major Ina Britz of Section 28, established to replace the Child Protection Unit, has appealed to anyone who has information to come forward or to phone the Section 28 hotline 0800 KIDZLIVE. At an explosive press conference this morning it was revealed that the 28s themselves are under threat because of new government policies regarding service delivery riots and the newly established Economic Stability Unit. We have in our studio Jakes Cwele, the man behind this new policy drive. Good afternoon, sir.'

'Good afternoon to you and your listeners.' Cwele's unguent tones were not good for the debilitating nausea that Clare had briefly managed to get under control.

Clare shut him up by switching stations to Fine Music Radio. Bach. The music swelled, its slow beauty bringing into focus the irredeemable ugliness of the day. E minor, the cello rich and full, the plangent music calling to her. Almost missing the sign for the

Cape College of Classical Music, she had to brake sharply before turning into the oak-lined driveway.

There was a faded grandeur to the front entrance; the heavy door was surrounded by mullioned windows. *Cape Town's Juilliard*, said the banner that hung above the stairs. The school's claim to the famous New York School of Music was not that far off the mark. Only the most talented survived the school. They thrived – winged to fame by their voices, or their ability with an instrument. Hard to know what happened to those who fell through the cracks.

At the entrance, a poster: musicians surrounding a lovely blonde with kohled eyes. *Soprano: Lily Lovich*. She already had the look of a diva, thought Clare. At the edge of the group, Rosa in a red sleeveless dress, a tumble of black hair down her back. She had her cello clasped as if to keep herself upright. A list of the other performers, *Rosa Wagner: cellist* struck through with a heavy black line. Today's date, the performance later that evening. Clare pushed the double doors open.

She walked over to the receptionist, a fat woman with crisp grey curls.

'Hello,' said Clare. 'I'm looking for Rosa Wagner and I'm hoping that you'll be able to help.'

'Rosalind,' she said, pausing her fingers over her keyboard. 'She hasn't been here since Easter.'

'I'm trying to trace her,' said Clare. 'Her grandfather is very concerned.'

The receptionist went at her keyboard again.

'I explained to him that Rosalind is an adult,' she said, without looking up at Clare. 'She wrote to us saying she was withdrawing. A waste, I told the director. I knew it, these country girls with nothing but raw talent never last in Cape Town. Out of their depth. Trouble follows them.'

Clare took a breath, made herself be polite.

'I would like to see your director,' said Clare.

'Director Petrova is very busy.'

'So am I.' Clare handed the woman her Section 28 identity card. 'Phone her. Please. Say I am on my way up.'

Clare's card looked too official to ignore. The receptionist hedged her bets and dialled.

'Director? A Dr Hart is here. From Section 28. She's insisting on seeing you,' she said. The receptionist listened to the voice at the other end of the line; the momentary silence was filled with the warm swell of a cello, the sound drifting through the cold air.

'You can go up,' said the receptionist.

'Thank you,' said Clare. 'It will save us all time if you could find Rosa Wagner's file, make me a copy and kindly bring that upstairs.'

The woman's mouth turned down with disapproval, but she got up and went to poke at the filing cabinet as Clare took the stairs. A door opened, emptying a classroom. Students flowed down the stairs – a river of chatter and plans and talk about coffee and drinks and who has a light? And an image flashed unbidden before Clare's mind's eye. Her own arrival in Cape Town at fourteen, a scholarship girl from a farm in Namaqualand. Then she had felt like a fish finally slipping into her element – the anonymity of a city where she could make herself up, far from the eyes of those who knew her. She pushed the disruptive genie of memory back into the bottle of the past.

A door on the second floor opened; an angular woman in an austere suit was silhouetted against the light. On the wall next to her door, a sign in elaborate copperplate: *Irina Petrova. Director.*

'Dr Hart.' Her Russian accent was unchanged by the decade she had spent in Cape Town. 'Please. You come in.'

She held the door open for Clare. Chanel No. 5. A heavy

perfume, for a woman who meant business even when she took her pleasure. The director's office was grand. A Persian rug, two leather sofas, velvet curtains, a fire flickering in the grate.

'You sit, please. How may I be of assistance?'

'I'm looking for Rosa Wagner,' said Clare. 'Can you tell me where she is?'

'I wish I knew,' she said. 'I cannot tell you how much I wish it. As I explained to her grandfather this morning, Rosa Wagner left the college.'

A pair of students hurried past, curious eyes on Clare.

'I suggest we discuss this privately,' Irina Petrova continued, closing the door.

'Rosa Wagner withdrew, you say,' said Clare. 'And you weren't concerned at this?'

'Yes, I am – now that you are here,' said Petrova. 'This morning Mr Wagner said the girl disappeared, but he also said that this morning Rosa phoned him. I took this to mean that all was well. This is not so?'

'Director, I am afraid for Rosa.'

'Then I must help you,' said Petrova. 'Ask me what you need to know.'

'Why did Rosa leave? ' said Clare. 'Did she give any reasons?'

'What little there is, it is in the file.' She picked up the phone, summoning her secretary.

A knock at the door. Handing a slim folder to the director, the secretary said, 'Rosa Wagner's records.'

'Thank you,' said Petrova.

She handed Clare a letter. It was handwritten, in a generously curved script.

Handel House
24th May 2012

Dear Director Petrova,

This is the hardest letter for me to write. I am sorry. But I have to tell you this. I'm not brave enough to tell you in person. I'm withdrawing from the College. I will play the exam piece so I won't let anyone down (except you.) Please believe me, that I am sorry. And believe me when I say how grateful I am that you gave me this chance. It's my fault that I can't live up to things.

You gave me so much. But right now I need to do other things. One day, if you forgive me, I can maybe explain. Thanks for the chances you gave me. I'm so sorry (again!) that I let you down. All my stuff is out my locker and I took my things from Handel House so there won't be trouble there. I didn't have time to clean my room, so please say sorry to Agnes for any trouble.

Yours sincerely,
Rosalind Wagner (Rosa)

Clare looked up to find Petrova watching her.

'I don't understand. What's going on here?' said Clare.

'I called the girl in,' said Petrova. 'But I was very angry, I found it hard to hear what she was saying.'

'And what was she saying?'

'Nothing more than what she writes there,' said Petrova. 'That she was sorry, but she couldn't carry on. I know you think I sound hard, but it is hard for me to find money for European music when there are children up the road with no food. I have been fortunate. We do have one or two generous patrons, but for me if a student drops out, I have failed. I have wasted their money. I suppose I was afraid there would be talk.'

Clare flicked through Rosa Wagner's file. She scanned the application forms, audition dates, concerts, credits, cello and composition information. A list of contact numbers that recorded only two numbers: her grandfather and the college doctor, Melissa Patrick. Two doctor's bills – both of them paid by the college.

'Do you have any idea why she saw the doctor, Director?'

'Flu, a cold? The Cape winter. It makes everyone suffer.'

'She'd been depressed?'

'Not that I know,' said Petrova, folding her hands in her lap.

'Anxiety, maybe,' said Clare. 'She went to the doctor the morning of her last performance. The same day she wrote this letter.'

'I was her teacher, not her mother, so I have no idea,' said Petrova. 'For that you must see if Dr Patrick will breach patient confidentiality.'

'Tell me about the concerts, Director,' said Clare.

'There's nothing much to tell,' said Irina Petrova. 'This is a professional music school. The students get the chance to perform at all sorts of events.'

'And they're paid?'

'A small amount,' said Petrova, 'but they have to play. They need the experience. They need to be seen in public. It is the way to other things, better things.'

'Better-paid things?' said Clare.

'Even artists must eat.'

'Did Rosa play often?'

'All our best students do,' said the Director. 'She is beautiful, she plays well, the cello – it's the closest approximation to the human voice, so an easy way to hear unfamiliar music. She was often invited to play. The list is in the file. It is all our usual benefactors and friends. They give a great deal, this is what we can give in return.'

'So, she would've played at the Winter Gala?'

Petrova looked disconcerted.

'I saw the poster outside, the picture of the beautiful girl.'

'Lily, of course. Our Prima Donna,' said Petrova. 'She's quite a favourite, so she'll sing. I must assure you, Rosa's troubles have nothing to do with the school. There was no reason for me to suspect anything other than what she wrote in that letter. I am so sorry now, of course, but what would you have done in my place?'

'How did she come to be here?' asked Clare.

'I heard her play at a wedding in Churchhaven,' said Petrova. 'The cello. She plays like an angel. I had to have her; I could not leave her to languish in the middle of nowhere – and her grandfather encouraged her to come.'

A log rolled forward in the grate, showering sparks.

'Who were her friends, Director?'

Petrova's brow furrowed as she hesitated.

'You mentioned Lily,' Clare prodded. 'She's singing tomorrow, and Rosa would have been in the orchestra. They must know each other.'

'I never saw them together,' Petrova stood up. 'But you can ask Lily if you like.'

A disharmony of sound floated down the stairwell as the director led Clare to the first floor. Cellos and a violin, flutes and clarinets, pianos, and a soprano practising her scales.

Petrova was about to knock on a door marked *Rehearsals*, when it opened. A group of students surged out, a blonde at their centre – the striking girl in the poster. The other students were swept along in her wake, calling 'Lily, Lily,' and then 'Evening, Director.'

Clare stood in their path as they dammed up behind Lily. 'Rosa Wagner. Anyone know where she is, who she's with?'

'I haven't seen her, oh for ages, no.' Lily turned to her entourage, her voice lilting, smoky. 'You seen Rosa, anyone? Jonny, you seen her?'

'No, man, she keeps to herself,' said the boy in a raffish suit. Dreadlocks, Bob Marley handsome. 'You wouldn't know if she was here or not.'

'She hasn't been around for a while,' said a girl with a sleek black bob. 'All she ever did was walk on the mountain by herself, and practice.'

'She probably had her first kiss,' said Jonny with a smirk.

'You tried and failed, Mr Diamond?' Director Petrova's tone froze the chatter.

'Why you ask?' Lily's green eyes on Clare.

'She's in trouble.'

'I'm so sorry,' said Lily, holding Clare's gaze for a moment. 'Of course we call you if we see Rosa, yes Jonny?'

'Of course we do, darling,' said Jonny Diamond, hooking his arm around Lily's waist.

'Speak to Katarina,' said the girl with the bob. 'They shared a practice room. She might know something.'

'Come, Lily, we'll be late.'

Clare watched as they flowed down the stairs, heard the clang of lockers being opened and shut. The chatter flowed again, plans and talk about a club and getting a taxi. Doors opening, closing. The silence left in their wake was broken only by a dove trapped at the window of the clerestory above, thudding against the glass.

'That's your star?' asked Clare.

'Lily is, yes,' said Petrova, 'she mesmerises on the stage.'

'And her friend Jonny?'

'An effective musician,' said Petrova, 'But cold, I think. He will never be great. Now for Miss Kraft, who will never be more than adequate either,' said Petrova. 'She's here, in the last room.'

Without knocking, the director opened the door. Concert

posters on the wall, a girl seated on a stool. She looked up at them, her bow suspended above the cello. Titian hair, creamy skin, a crop of spots around her small mouth, green dress too tight on her plump body.

'Katarina, this is Dr Hart. She's looking for Rosa Wagner.'

'She's gone,' said Katarina, her eyes wide. 'The Director,' she said, glancing at Petrova, 'she told us that Rosa had withdrawn, forfeited her scholarship.'

'I thought you might know why,' said Clare. 'And where she may have gone.'

Katarina shook her head, dropped it to her chin.

'It might be better if Katarina and I speak alone, Director,' said Clare. 'Would you please excuse us?'

'Of course,' said Petrova, her mouth a straight vermilion line.

The door closed behind her with a sharp click.

twelve

The director's footsteps receded, her heels tapping a staccato rhythm on the polished corridor floor. The silence that came when Petrova turned the corner was a relief. Clare turned to Katarina.

'You're playing at the Gala tonight?' she asked.

'Only because Rosa left,' said Katarina. 'It was made quite clear to me that this is a one-off. At short notice. Because I know the pieces Rosa was going to play.'

The wind blew open a window. Katarina closed it quickly, but not before it had scattered her score across the floor. Clare helped the girl pick it up.

'What is this?' asked Clare, scrutinising the annotations – the curves of the handwritten trebles, the plump clefs.

'I found this piece that Rosa composed.'

'Can you play some of it?' asked Clare.

Katarina picked up her cello. Her nails were bitten to the quick but the music flowed with a haunting lightness, though with an ebb of something darker.

Abruptly, Katarina stopped. 'Rosa said it was what the lagoon sounded like, the one near where she grew up,' said Katarina. 'Beautiful and strange.'

'A bit like Rosa herself?'

'I suppose so,' said Katarina. 'She should have handed it in; all material produced while students are here, is copyright of the school. It is in the contract we sign, but she must have forgotten it.'

'Where did you find it?'

'In her locker.'

Clare looked at the row of lockers, opening the one with no name on it.

'Was this one hers?'

'Yes. I looked in there after she left,' said Katarina. 'It was at the bottom, there was nothing else there. She must have taken everything else.'

'What did you think when she didn't come back, Katarina?'

The question seemed to startle the girl.

'I didn't,' she said. 'It's been exams. She just left. She didn't say goodbye, nothing.' She snapped closed her cello case.

'Are you happy here?' asked Clare.

'It looked like such an opportunity …' she began.

'But it isn't?'

Katarina did not reply.

'Where're you from?' asked Clare.

'Luderitz,' said Katarina, 'Namibia.'

'That's a small place,' said Clare. 'Like Churchhaven. You and Rosa must've had a lot in common.'

Katarina tore a sliver of skin along her nail.

'So when Rosa didn't come back, you understood, didn't you, Katarina?' said Clare. 'But why didn't you look for her?'

'She didn't want to be here any more.'

'Why not?' asked Clare. 'What happened?'

'Nothing,' said Katarina, turning away. 'It was nothing.'

'Tell me. You must, if I'm going to help Rosa.' Clare took the girl by shoulders, made her look at her.

'She hated it here, OK?'

'Why?'

Katarina shrugged off Clare's hands and picked up her instrument. 'She wasn't used to it. The people, the practising, being away from home. She just wanted to escape. Be herself again.'

'So you didn't hear from her after she left?'

'No,' said Katarina. 'It's what she wanted. To get away.'

'That didn't worry you?'

'I've been too busy,' said Katarina. 'There's my own work, and now the concert. I haven't had time to think about anything, not with all the rehearsals.'

'I saw in Rosa's records that she went to see Dr Patrick a couple of times,' said Clare.

'She's the college doctor,' said Katarina.

'Did she say what was wrong?'

'You'll have to ask her,' said Katarina. 'She never mentioned anything to me.'

Clare found the number in her notes but the phone went to voicemail, the doctor instructing her to leave a message. Asking Dr Patrick to call her back urgently, Clare walked over to the poster tacked onto the wall. It was the same one she'd seen at the entrance.

'Tell me about Lily,' said Clare, pointing to the blonde girl at the centre.

'What's to tell?' said Katarina. 'She's perfect, she has a voice that makes people forget things, forget pain, unhappiness. Everybody loves her.'

'Do they love her, or do they want her?' asked Clare.

'Isn't it the same thing?'

'Her friend Jonny Diamond, he's good looking,' said Clare.

'I suppose.'

'You know him?

'A bit,' said Katarina, the colour in her cheeks deepening.

'Is he a student?'

'Not any more,' said Katarina. 'There was trouble.'

'What sort of trouble?'

'The usual.' Katarina evaded Clare's gaze.

'Drugs?' asked Clare. 'Was he dealing?'

'That's not what we were told.'

'But it's what you heard?'

'There are so many rumours in a place like this.'

'I've seen boys like him before.' Clare watched Katarina's face. 'Smooth, beautiful, cruel. Is that what he's like?'

Katarina said nothing.

'Any rumours about Rosa and drugs, Katarina?'

'No,' said Katarina, her voice sure once again. 'She said she liked to feel like herself.'

'And Lily?' asked Clare.

'That's not my world.' Tears welled in Katarina's eyes.

'Katarina, what is it that makes you so unhappy here?' Clare reached into her jacket pocket for a tissue. As she did so, she pricked her finger on the porcupine quill. The tissues were in her other pocket. She gave one to the girl, and dabbed at the blood on her finger with the other.

'Thank you,' said Katarina, blowing her nose. 'Nobody cares about you here. We're just music machines. We have to be perfect, perfect. All the time.'

'Is that what made Rosa so unhappy?'

'It's too much. Rosa escaped.' There was a flash in Katarina's eyes.

'Where did she go?'

'Didn't she go to her grandfather?' asked Katarina. 'She would've done anything for him.'

'She didn't get that far,' said Clare. 'So you really don't know why she went to see Dr Patrick?'

Katarina shook her head. She was packing up her things,

avoiding Clare's gaze again.

'Are you going back to your residence?' asked Clare.

Katarina nodded.

'Then let's take a look at Rosa's room.'

thirteen

Handel House was tucked away in the corner of the grounds, an old stable that had been converted into student accommodation. A gnarled olive tree spread its branches around the house, protecting it from the worst of the wind. On the stoep, stained-glass windows pooled reddish light.

Clare and Katarina stepped inside, where a worn-looking woman in a blue housecoat was flicking through a magazine.

'Hello, Agnes,' said Katarina. 'This is Dr Hart. She's looking for Rosa.'

'That's bad,' said Agnes, sharp eyes on Clare.

'Rosa was Agnes's favourite,' said Katarina.

'Her grandfather hasn't seen her since the weekend before she withdrew,' said Clare.

'No one has seen her,' said Katarina.

'Can we have the key to her room?' asked Clare. 'I'd like to have a look.'

'Are you the police?' asked Agnes.

Clare nodded.

'I knew there was something wrong,' said Agnes, leaning her broom against the wall. 'Come with me.'

Clare followed her down the passage, where she unlocked the last door on the left. The air that escaped smelt like stale breath. Clare switched on the light; it flickered, revealing the cramped room. There were two posters on the wall: Maria Callas, and

Yo-Yo Ma holding his cello. A stripped bed, a side table, an old desk, a chair, sagging curtains over a window that opened onto a rectangle of litter and weeds.

'Was Rosa involved with anyone?' asked Clare, checking the desk drawers. They were empty. Nothing on the bedside table. It was empty too.

'Rosa is a good girl,' said Agnes. She glanced at Katarina. 'No boys. She never brings them here. Not like some of the other girls.'

'Did you know of any boys, Katarina?' asked Clare.

'No one special.' Katarina blushed. 'She wasn't into that stuff really. She got teased, but she kept to herself.'

'Teased, how?' asked Clare.

'Some people called her the nun,' said Katarina. 'Thought she was too good for everyone.'

'It's all rubbish,' said Agnes. 'Rosa knew what was right, what was wrong.'

'Where did Rosa usually go when she went out?' asked Clare. 'Who did she see?'

'She practised nearly all the time,' said Agnes. 'She didn't have friends so much.'

'Not even weekends, or Sundays?'

'She went home for weekends,' Agnes said to Clare, twisting a button on her housecoat. 'To her Oupa, mostly. She liked that. She'd bring me things. Sometimes a fish her Oupa caught, or some konfyt. Things from up the West Coast.'

'What else did she do?' asked Clare. 'Who did she see?'

'They work too hard, these students,' said Agnes. 'The director always tells them where she grew up there was no time for dreaming. Only work. So most weekends they play their instruments. Here, for weddings, for parties. She played on the yacht for the tourists. *The Siren*, the one that belongs to Milan Savić.

He's that guy who owns the castle.'

'Did Rosa know him?'

'Why don't you ask him that?' said Katarina. 'He'll be at the Gala tonight. I'll be doing Rosa's solo.'

Clare turned to Agnes.

'Why do you think she left, Agnes?' she asked. 'You seem to know her quite well.'

'Ja, I did know her. She'd come and sit in the kitchen with me and drink tea,' said the woman. 'I thought maybe the rain got too much for her. She said she missed her Oupa, she wanted to be with him more, but I don't know. She loves the sun, Rosa. It's because of where she grew up. On the West Coast the sun is hot. Very hot. She used to go walking. That's what she'd do a lot. Walk, here on the mountain. I told her mos about the skollies that go up there. How people walk up and never come back. She wouldn't listen, though. She'd just tell me, Agnes, I'll be fine. I know how to look after myself.'

'Did you see her before she left?'

'Ja, I saw her, but I didn't speak to her. I went to clean her room.' Agnes adjusted her headscarf. 'But everything was gone. All she left was a jar of honey for me and her trunk in the storage. I've got the honey still. We can go down and look in her trunk if you want.'

They followed Agnes down the steps into the chilly basement. The single light bulb hesitated before illuminating a jumble of trunks and boxes, and Agnes made her way over to a battered old army trunk.

'That's her stuff,' said Katarina when Clare opened the trunk.

Shoes neatly packed in pairs. Size five. Panties, bras turned in on themselves. An Aran jersey and jeans. Underneath, folded summer dresses, shirts and a red scarf. Some paperbacks right at the bottom.

Clare flicked through a book, and flyers for an organic pro-
duce market fell to the floor.

'We went there once in February when it was really hot,' said
Katarina. 'It's just up the valley. Me and her and a couple of
other girls went up one weekend. Played some folk music there,
jammed with the drumming circle. It was nice. We all ate off one
big platter. Like we were a real community.'

'Did she go there again?'

Katarina shrugged. 'If she did, she didn't ask me to go with
her.'

The light flickered and went out.

'Man, there's a spook down here,' said Agnes. 'You need anything else?'

'Not down here,' said Clare, pocketing the flyer.

Agnes and Katarina followed her up the stairs.

'I've got to practise before supper,' said Katarina.

'I'll see her out, Kat,' said Agnes.

'Phone me,' said Clare, 'if you think of anything.'

Katarina slipped Clare's card into her pocket and took her leave
with a wan smile. Her bedroom door, two down from Rosa's,
closed with a quiet but definite click, then the sound of scales
floated along the corridor.

'They work hard, these students,' said Clare.

'Ja, much too hard,' said Agnes, moving towards the door.
'They are young, they need to live.' She walked Clare to the front
door, and said, 'What's happened to Rosa, where is she?'

'I was hoping you could tell me, help me find out.'

'I can't say anything,' said Agnes. 'It's not easy to get a job, a
woman like me with no education.'

'Is there anything you want to tell me about the college?'

'I can't say,' said Agnes. 'I just do my job, make sure the girls
are all right.'

'But Rosa isn't, is she?'

Agnes shook her head, had nothing more to say.

'There's one thing,' said Clare, turning towards the housekeeper. 'You said Rosa had left you some honey just before she left.'

'She's very generous,' said Agnes. 'She thinks of others.'

'So it's not the first time she gave you honey?' asked Clare.

'No, she was mos generous, like I said.'

'Do you know where the honey came from?'

'Not from the supermarkets,' said Agnes. 'It's thick, tastes like farm honey to me.'

'Can I see it?' asked Clare.

'Come this way.' Agnes led her down a dark corridor. The housekeeper's room was narrow and cold. An iron bedstead, a hotplate, a boxy TV. Agnes opened the cupboard above the stove, pushing boxes and tins out of the way.

'Here.' She held a bottle up, the honey gleaming against the afternoon light. A hand-painted label with a beehive. 'She just brought a bottle sometimes when she went away. She said it makes her life sweeter. Maybe it can make my life sweeter too. She forgot about my diabetes, maybe.'

'She didn't get this up the West Coast,' said Clare, putting her hand in her jacket pocket and pulling out the flyer from Rosa's trunk.

'It's the same, mos,' said Agnes, comparing the two images. 'She must have got it there.'

'So she didn't always go home, then,' said Clare.

'You never know about people, do you?' said Agnes.

'Can I keep the honey?' asked Clare.

'You can take it,' said Agnes, walking Clare back to the front door. 'It'll kill me if I eat it.'

Clare got into her car and Agnes walked back to her chilly room.

Katarina Kraft, standing at the window, watched as Clare disappeared down the darkening driveway. She stood for a moment, felt in her pocket. The Valium was there, small, yellow, comforting. She put the pill in her mouth and swallowed it dry.

fourteen

The Whole Soul Food Market looked bedraggled in the rain; some of the stalls outside were closing, the dim afternoon drifting towards night. In the old barn, a few stalls were still open. Hand-knitted jerseys, bunches of limp herbs, glistening loaves of bread.

Clare parked and went inside. It was warm and smelt of straw and fresh bread and incense.

A man in a tie-dyed shirt was selling hot cider.

'Can I help you, sister?' he asked, doing the lazy-gaze wander: lips, breasts, hips. He didn't seem to disapprove.

'This girl.' Clare put the photograph of Rosa Wagner onto the counter. 'She played music here in the summer. Have you seen her?'

His eyes widened. 'You a cop?'

'No,' said Clare. 'Not really.'

'Look, sister, cops are like virgins: you either are or you aren't,' he grinned. 'So, what are you?'

'I'm almost a cop,' said Clare.

'Ja, fuck, like you're almost a virgin.'

'When last did you see this girl?'

'Actually, I don't know if I've seen her,' he said, his gaze averted.

'If you want to know just how close I am to being a cop, carry on fucking with me,' said Clare. 'So think hard and fast. She bought honey here.' She showed him a photograph of the jar.

'Paradys honey,' he said. 'It's good.'

'So where's their stall?'

The man looked around so slowly that Clare had to put her hands in her pockets to stop herself from knocking the New Age peace and dopiness out of him. 'I didn't see them today.'

'Who's them?' asked Clare.

'Noah Stern,' he said. 'And his wife. She wears these dresses like those Amish chicks did in *Witness*. You've seen that movie? Harrison Ford. It's like the same. They've got a boy. He comes too sometimes. Just sits there all quiet. It's like a closed community they have. Like a retreat. They could live up there for ever if the world ended.'

'When was the last time they were selling?' asked Clare.

'A while ago,' he said. 'It's nearly solstice now, so it was before the equinox, for sure.'

'So where could Rosa have bought this honey in the last couple of weeks?'

'Maybe she went up to their place,' he said.

'Have you been up there?'

'Ja, Paradys,' he said. 'Of course I've been there. It's cool. Organic, off-grid. They grow this organic stuff, like I said. Everyone buys their honey. It's got healing properties and every-thing,' he said. 'But they keep to themselves, they like to live like people did in Bible times. Maybe she hung out with them a bit. I think I remember that. Her talking to the wife. Nancy.'

'Paradys,' said Clare. 'How do I get there?'

'It's hard to get a car up the road,' said the cider man. 'It's in the nature reserve. Go slow. It's easy to miss the gate.'

'I've got a 4x4,' she said.

He walked around his stall and outside with Clare. 'Take that road,' he said. 'Goes straight up the valley. You take the third to the left. The gate at the end of the road. No other way to go.'

80

A gust of wind swirled some winter leaves.

'It's cool. People go up there because they want to, like, step outside the rat race. You should try it. You look like you should chill a bit.'

fifteen

Clare bumped along the rutted track that ran between the river – fed to bursting by the mountain waterfalls – and the road that led up the valley. Trees pressed in close as she drove up the track. The rain had sluiced off the topsoil and the car lurched from pothole to pothole. She'd have missed the turnoff completely if she had not known to look out for the gate. As it was, she drove past it. She let the car slide backwards and then turned in, her wheels spinning in the mud.

It was darker among the trees; the sound of the growing storm shut out, together with the waning light. When Clare stopped to open the gate, the quiet was eerie.

Another track, even rougher; up ahead was the old farmhouse. The windows, too few and too small, gave the facade a pinched look. The homestead had thick walls, a new thatched roof and wide ox-blood steps leading up to the verandah.

Clare went up the stairs and knocked on the front door but there was no answer. She pushed the door open and stepped into the chilly air. There seemed to be no one about. She stopped, waiting for someone to come. For once, she welcomed the loud moan of the wind in the trees. She went into the kitchen: cups and plates – three of each – were draining on the sink. There was a bowl of green apples in the centre of the table and a spray of red sterretjieblomme – star-shaped flowers that bloomed in the dead of winter.

She opened the back door. The yard was run down, the out-buildings dilapidated. She walked past empty stables towards a shed. The building was filled with farming implements, an old tractor. On the floor were vehicle tracks. At the back, a white bakkie was parked.

A movement at the back of the shed drew her attention into the gloom.

'Hello?' she called. Light filtered through a broken window, and Clare made her way past old engine parts. A cat slunk under a pile of dusty metal that toppled over, sending an old number-plate flying. Clare picked it up and leaned it against the mud-spattered bakkie. Like the one she'd seen on the bridle path that morning, bumping up the road where they had found the little girl. It felt like a lifetime ago.

Voices – a woman's and a man's too – low and urgent, drifted in at a broken window. Clare looked around, but there was silence again, broken only by the rhythmic thud of a spade cutting into wet earth.

'Hey, what are you doing here?' A man striding towards her, the light behind him.

'I was looking for someone,' she said, moving out of the shadows. 'I thought I heard something in here.'

The man stopped, studied her face in the dim light.

'It's Dr Hart, isn't it?' he said. 'I saw you this morning at the Community Forum – the child that was found on the bridle path. I was there with my wife, it's too awful.'

Mud-streaked boots, waterproof jacket. A gentle face, deep-set eyes as warm as the hand that gripped hers.

'Noah Stern.' The skin round his eyes crinkled when he smiled. 'You'll forgive my rudeness,' he said. 'We're not that used to visitors up here. The police were here this morning for our statements. They did look around, I'm not sure why.'

'They're searching everywhere nearby,' said Clare. 'Trying to find the girl's mother.'

'I'm sorry we had so little to offer them,' he said. 'I imagine you are here for the same reason?'

'No, I'm looking for someone else, an older girl,' said Clare. 'She bought some of your honey. I had the impression she visited here in the summer, maybe a couple of times.'

Clare held out the photograph. 'Her name's Rosa Wagner. She's missing.'

Stern took the picture, looked up at Clare, his dark eyes filled with concern. 'Rosa, lovely Rosa. She never needed to buy honey. We gave it to her. Always. What's happened to her?'

'She came up here recently,' said Clare.

'Months ago, I think,' said Stern. 'We're not so fixated on time up here, you know. It was summer. She came a couple of times. Always went back to her life, back to face whatever it was that drove her here in the first place.'

'What was she facing?' asked Clare.

'I wish I knew.'

He did not move a muscle, but Clare sensed his concentration.

'But she's troubled by something?' she asked.

'Rosa is very precious to me, to us,' he said. 'We did all we could, but she wasn't ready for this life.'

'She stayed here, did she? Could you find out when exactly that was?'

'I'll check for you. Come inside.' He touched Clare's arm, ushered her into the kitchen. It was warmer there, an Aga burning. Floor-to-ceiling shelving stacked with jams and preserves, a table and a couple of benches, a shelf with books on it, flagstone floors, and windows that leaked in cold forest air. Clare followed him into a sparsely furnished study. His diary lay on the desk. He opened it, paging backwards through the months.

'Here's her first visit,' he said, pushing the book towards Clare. She recognised the curvy handwriting, noted the flamboyant signature, a heart next to it. 'There are a couple of those. She came again later, March or April.' He flipped a few pages. 'She didn't write in the book that time, must've forgotten. In any case, she came alone then. Would you like to see where our guests stay?' he asked. 'Who knows, you might also need a sanctuary one day.'

Right now, thought Clare, that's exactly what I need. Somewhere to hide. Somewhere to wait until all this has passed.

'Please,' is what she said instead.

The communal room was off the verandah. Stern pushed the door open, revealing a large room with a double bed in the corner and some bunk beds. Clare swept her hand along the top bunk. It was stripped of bedding.

'So you haven't seen her since?'

Stern shook his head.

'And your wife?' said Clare.

'Nancy,' said Stern. 'Yes, perhaps you should speak to her. She might've been more of a confidante.'

Clare followed him outside again. The smell of pine trees and freshly turned earth. Late-afternoon rays illuminated a woman in white, bending over rows of turned earth. A boy of about five squatted nearby, playing. He stood up as Clare and Stern approached, pulling his brown beanie low onto his forehead.

'Nancy.' Time and the weather had clearly been unkind to the woman. She glanced at her husband and gave Clare a tentative smile.

'My hands,' she held them out, muddy. Without shaking hands, she looked Clare over, rather in the way one assesses livestock. The boy pulled down his beanie, his dark eyes fixed on Clare's face.

'Dr Hart wants to ask you about Rosa, Nancy.' Stern placed his hand on his wife's shoulder. She did not flinch, but it seemed to Clare that she was relieved when he took it away again.

The boy came to stand by her side; she drew him towards her.

'Rosa was here in the summer,' Nancy said. 'A couple of times she stayed. But then she didn't come back.'

'You expected her to return?'

A gust of wind tugged at the woman's plait, whipping stray strands across her face. She replaited her hair, her fingers nimble.

'She didn't say so, but she needed sanctuary,' said Nancy.

'What do you mean?' asked Clare.

'Rosa didn't seem to fit into the world below.' She gestured towards the valley, Hout Bay hidden by a ridge that hid the homestead. 'Noah offered, but she wasn't ready.'

'Ready for what?'

'For this life we lead,' said Nancy. 'This peace. Has she done something?'

'Rosa is missing, Mrs Stern,' said Clare. 'Her family is very concerned. She hasn't been seen for three weeks.'

'Well, she hasn't been here,' turning to the boy with solemn eyes, 'has she, Isaac?'

He shook his head.

'Nancy, did she mention anything to you? Some place she might have gone?'

'Not to me,' said Nancy. 'She was determined to stay in the world. We offered her sanctuary. But she refused it.'

'You asked a minute ago if Rosa had *done something*,' Clare said to Nancy. 'What were you thinking of?'

'Rosa has been troubled,' Noah Stern chipped in. 'Things have happened to her.'

'Things?'

'When she was a child,' said Nancy. For the first time, she

looked straight at Clare. 'Her mother had problems. There'd been many stepfathers. It came out the first weekend. We did a cleansing ritual. She spoke about it all. It seemed to relieve her to say it.'

'Did she mention any names?' asked Clare. 'Was there anyone she was afraid of? Someone from that time in her life?'

Husband and wife looked at each other, shook their heads in unison. The little boy drifted back towards his toys – wire cars that he'd probably fashioned himself.

'Not that she mentioned,' said Nancy, 'but who's to know? Rosa liked to keep her secrets.'

Clare's phone beeped; a muscle in Stern's jaw jumped.

'Sorry,' said Clare. 'There was no reception earlier, so I didn't put it on silent.'

'Yes, it comes and goes. We forget about it, though, because none of us use these cellphones,' said Noah Stern as Clare opened the message.

It was from Anwar Jacobs.

Your little patient is stable. She's ready 4 you.

Clare felt an irrational surge of hope.

'You've been very helpful,' said Clare to the couple standing in front of her. 'If Rosa contacts you, here are my numbers.'

Stern looked at the card Clare gave him. Nancy picked up her hoe and applied it to the bed she had been working.

'We'll be sure to,' he said walking Clare to her car. He opened the door for her. 'We'll pray for her safety.'

sixteen

The Children's Hospital: a vigilant sentry, it stood between the leafy suburbs and the wind-scoured Cape Flats that fed the hospital with a steady stream of young patients.

Anwar Jacobs had been in Casualty when Clare had called. He was back there now, and it was mayhem. A keening woman, heavily pregnant, was clutching her bleeding son in her lap, the medical officer cutting off his Batman pyjamas. The boy's father – split knuckles, his arms folded around a prison-skinny chest – shouted that he would kill the nurse if his son died, threatening that in the Bible it said it was an eye for an eye.

'Ag, vok of jy,' said the mother. 'Jy't die kind so geslaan, jou mal hond. Jy't my ook geslaan.' She pushed up her sleeve and pointed to a bruise. 'Kyk! Ja, kyk hierso.'

The man lunged at the woman as the guards moved in on him. She ducked and, despite her large belly, deftly avoided the blow. She held her little boy in her lap, protecting him. Her bag flew across the floor, spilling its contents.

Clare bent down and picked up a pack of cigarettes, an empty purse, a lipstick and a pale yellow card. She turned it over in her hand; on the front was the logo of the Ministry of Health. A clinic card. Clare handed it all back to the woman.

'Sedate the mother. Remove the father,' Anwar Jacobs instructed the medical officer who had come to relieve him. 'Get Social Work for the child. This is the third time he's been here in as many months.'

He turned to Clare. 'Welcome to tik hell. And those who make the money drink Johnny Walker Blue while taking in the Cape's beautiful views. I patch up these kids and it's like sending them back out into the killing fields. You saw that woman's antenatal card, she's pregnant again. She and that scum making sure I never run out of patients.'

'It's the devil's merry-go-round,' said Clare. 'Poverty is a gold-mine: abalone, cash, drugs, cash, gangs, cash, then the merry circle starts all over again.'

They took the lift to the second floor. 'I was expecting you earlier,' said Anwar.

'So was I,' said Clare. 'Another case came in this morning.'

'Another child?' asked Anwar.

'Missing teenager,' said Clare. 'A cellist. Rosa Wagner. Vanished three weeks ago.'

'And you're only looking now?'

'Seems like nobody missed her either.'

The doctor pushed open the doors to Intensive Care. The little girl was in a room of her own.

A muted electronic orchestra played along the managed borderline between life and death. Beeps for heart rate, blips for temperature, the accordion wheeze of the oxygen mask. The little girl was curled up on a sheepskin to protect her fragile skin. She was so thin that she seemed hardly human. Though attached to a rehydration drip and oxygen tubes, she seemed less spectral than the previous day.

'Jesus Christ,' said Clare. 'The things people do to children.'

'Don't think about it,' said Anwar. 'Think about what we do instead. Just react. Don't analyse. You'll go mad otherwise.'

'You said you got the test results back.'

'The preliminary ones,' said Anwar. 'Infections and chronic

diseases eliminated.'

The IV beeped. Anwar Jacobs replaced the hydration fluids, got it going again. Clare knelt beside the little girl, her tiny translucent face inches from hers.

'How's she doing, Anwar?' She cradled the child's hand in hers.

The girl's tenuous breath fluttered in her chest, and Clare thought she felt a faint pressure from her fingers.

'She's alive,' said the doctor. 'What a little fighter she is. All the odds against her. She's struggled to breathe and her heartbeat was erratic but that's better now, much better.'

Anwar Jacobs bent over the child. Clare watched his deft hands move gently over the little girl's body, re-counting the injuries on her back.

'She's got more than twenty-six marks on her back. There are some nasty scabs at the back of her neck under her hair. Whatever has happened to her has been going on for a long time.'

'And these?' asked Clare, indicating two ridged scars across her back.

'That's from a sjambok, I'd guess. I've seen this on farm kids a few times. Less so in town. In the meantime we'll keep her sedated. It's who she is and what's happened to her that I need to know. As soon as I have that, I'll know what's wrong with her and what she needs.'

'So far we've had nothing,' said Clare. 'Ina's just done a press conference, though, so maybe that'll result in something. You said no sexual assault?'

'No semen traces, no tears in the vagina or the anus, no burns on the nipples, so none of the usual stuff, if that's what you want.' Anwar's voice was pruned of all emotion. 'Those two scars across her back are from a beating that's long past. We X-rayed her, and it looks like the beating fractured some ribs, but there are a number of other fractures too.'

'Beatings, you say?'

'Maybe,' he said. 'But it could be rickets – vitamin D deficiency that's made the bones brittle. She's like a little old lady – her bones are like meringue.'

'That's the malnourishment you mentioned?' asked Clare.

'Could be,' said Anwar. 'But I think it might be more than that. Her case is so severe, must have been lack of sunlight.'

Clare looked at the child's wan face. 'How do you manage that in South Africa?'

seventeen

Clare left the Children's Hospital. It was only a handful of days shy of the winter solstice, and the darkness came swiftly. She thought of Rosa. Girls vanished without trace, that she knew, but unless the earth opened and swallowed them up there was always someone who knew where they were. And why.

That's what Clare wanted to know. Where. And why.

The black dress she kept for sartorial emergencies was in its dry-cleaning bag under the seat. It was dark in the parking lot, so she slid her seat back, stripped, and eased herself into the dress. She found the heels she had abandoned after the press conference and slipped them on.

Clare flicked down the sun visor and the mirror light came on. Her angular face seemed that of a stranger; the two vertical lines between her brows lingered even after she had finished frowning. She dug a comb out of her handbag and ran it through her hair. She dug deeper, and was rewarded with foundation and a lipstick. The former erased the dark rings under her eyes; the latter restored colour to her lips and cheeks.

That should do, she thought.

She drove over Constantia Nek and down into Hout Bay, transformed into a place where all lights sparkled equally. The democracy of darkness. She turned in at the College of Classical Music. The gravel parking area was filled with cars, some with drivers hunkered down, engines idling to keep the heating on, but Clare managed to find a place that wasn't completely illegal.

The noise of the Gala spilled out of the front door where a pretty usher stood at her post.

'Welcome, ma'am,' she said. 'You have a ticket?'

Clare flashed her official ID and the girl took a step back to let her pass. Four girls wearing expensive shoes and not much else, despite the cold, trotted in after her, but the usher continued to stare after Clare as she strode towards the reception.

A waiter at the door had a tray poised – sparkling wine, Bloody Marys, whiskey. The warm notes of a cello wove through the cocktail party chatter. Caviar and trays of carpaccio – too raw, too red against the silver.

The musicians were grouped on a raised dais. Irina Petrova had a conductor's baton in her hand and her back to Clare. Katarina Kraft was there too, pale, her cello cradled between her knees. Lily smiled briefly as she tossed back her hair.

Laughter erupted on the other side of the room. A tall man at the centre of a knot of people. Mid-forties. A hard good-looking face. A hard good-looking body too. Good suit, good shirt, bad shoes.

'Mr Savić,' Irina Petrova called out to her guest of honour. 'A toast. Welcome. The programme begins in half an hour. For now, enjoy.'

The merest hint of a frown as she noticed Clare in the crowd.

'Dr Hart. This Winter Gala is the highlight of our calendar. I must ask you what you are doing here. Surely this is not a time for an investigation?'

'Irina, darling, this is wonderful, what a crowd.' It was the good-looking man. He smiled at Clare.

'Dr Hart, may I introduce Mr Savić,' said Irina Petrova. 'Mr Savić is one of our sponsors, he is the one who has kept this college alive, is that not so, Milan?'

She laid a hand on his arm. Savić patted it. 'I give money to soccer teams, of course. But who could resist you, Irina? Who could resist all this?' he said, with a sweep of his hand.

Clare felt his dark eyes on her before he said, 'You are a music lover?'

Irina coldly interrupted, 'Dr Hart thinks there may have been an incident with a former student.'

'Which one?' he asked.

'Rosa Wagner,' Clare replied.

'The lovely cellist?' he asked. 'What has happened? She cannot be allowed to drop out. I was so looking forward to hearing her this evening. That beautiful piece she played last time she entertained us. She's one of the highlights, you know.'

'Rosa's grandfather reported her missing this morning,' said Clare. 'She called him before dawn this morning, very distressed, there has been nothing since.'

'You were up at my residence this morning, no?' Savić was looking intently at Clare.

'One of your men let me through,' said Clare.

'Mikey,' said Savić. 'He told me.' He seemed pleased at the surprise on Clare's face. 'We've had security issues. Not everyone in the valley appreciates our conservation efforts. There were some beehives up there that we had to move.'

'Paradys Honey, you mean?' asked Clare.

'Yes, them, Noah Stern and his wife,' said Savić. 'You know them?'

'I was up there today,' said Clare. 'Seems as if Rosa Wagner spent some time there.'

'An eccentric man, Stern,' said Savić. 'We have not been able to see eye to eye. But he's a hippy type. Harmless, I believe.'

Clare ignored the observation and said, 'How well do you know Rosa?'

'She's one of Irina's special girls,' said Savić. 'She's played at events at my residence. I have a yacht, *The Siren* – you may know it?'

Clare nodded, recalling news reports of the luxury vessel.

'In the summer, she played there too. I hope she returns soon. She has a great gift.'

Irina Petrova was clearly impatient with the conversation. 'Rosa is young and impulsive. She will turn up,' she said. 'It would be a pity for the name of the school to be sullied.' She rested her hand on Savić's arm, and said, 'I assure you, this has nothing to do with the school; it has nothing to do with our partners.'

'The thought never crossed my mind, Irina,' said Savić.

'I'm truly sorry about this,' said Petrova. 'But you will still be able to hear the piece. Bach. I know you love it.'

With a tight smile, she said to her companions, 'Come, they're due to start in half an hour. Let's first find my lovely Lily, and then we take our seats.'

Clare watched as the director and the patron walked towards the front row. It was then that she became aware of being watched herself. She turned to look for Katarina. Instead, she saw Jonny Diamond, without the luminous Lily this time, leaning against a wall. Clare worked her way around the room towards him.

'Hello, I'm looking for Katarina,' she said. 'Do you know where she is?'

'The bathroom, I'm sure. Throwing up,' said Diamond.

'Is she sick?'

'Nervous,' said Jonny Diamond. 'An ugly sister trying to fit into Cinderella's shoes.'

'You do have a charming way with women, Jonny,' said Clare, turning on her heel.

She found Katarina in the bathroom splashing her face.

'Hello,' said Clare. The girl looked up, startled.

'I have to go on soon,' she said.

'I need to ask you more about the farm Rosa used to go to. The one up the valley. Paradys.'

'Yes,' said Katarina, drying her hands.

'Rosa went back.'

'That's no big deal. Rosa liked the little boy. He was home-schooled like her, and she taught him a bit. The person she really liked was Nancy, though. I thought she was a bit weird, but Rosa liked that she was so devoted to her husband.' Katarina picked up her bag. 'I suppose she was the opposite of her own mother.'

Clare walked with her towards the door. 'Then why did she stop going there?'

'I didn't know she went again,' said Katarina. 'I don't know anything about that. She didn't talk to me about it.'

'You didn't like it, then?'

'The place was a bit too old-fashioned for me. And I didn't like all the Bible stuff. I told her that, then she didn't talk about it again.'

'What are the other places Rosa went to that you're not telling me about?'

'Look, we studied together, we shared a rehearsal room. Does that make me my sister's keeper?'

'Tell me what you know.'

'I have to go. I'm on now.'

Clare took her arm, and just then Irina Petrova opened the door.

'Is everything alright, Katarina?' she asked. 'Dr Hart, please, this girl must perform now. Why are you upsetting her?'

'I need to know if she is withholding information about Rosa,' said Clare.

'Are you, Katarina?' asked Petrova. 'This would not be wise.'

'I've told you what I know, Dr Hart.'

96

'Good girl,' said Petrova, her hand in the small of Katarina's back, guiding her into the corridor. 'Everyone is waiting to hear you play, Katarina. You will make me very proud.'

The door swung closed behind them. She slipped into the back of the concert room. It was a charming room, pale blue walls and grey velvet curtains draped across the tall, narrow windows. The small orchestra was gathered at the far end, and the light gleamed on the instruments. Katarina looked out over the audience, but when she caught Clare's eye she dropped her gaze. She clasped her instrument, her bow moving rapidly over the strings. Clare listened to her play Rosa's solo. It was technically perfect, but even as the music swelled, filling the room, there was no heart.

eighteen

It was later than she'd have liked when she got into her car. Sea Point was quiet, just the occasional car hissing along the wet roads. Hungry waves leapt over the sea wall, scattering tangled strands of kelp across the Promenade. There were no lights on in her flat, and no sign of Riedwaan's motorbike outside her flat.

Fritz was sitting on the top step, slit-eyed with disapproval, when Clare opened the door.

'Hello, kitty-cat.' Clare picked her up and, with her body warm and purring in her arms, went through to the kitchen. Just as she'd left it that morning: half a cup of coffee on the table, burnt toast in the sink, wet washing in the machine. She tipped some pellets into Fritz's bowl and put the clothes into the tumble dryer.

The kitchen table was littered with old photo albums, the funny haircuts and the too-tight, too-short shorts of her childhood. She and Constance: her twin and her doppelganger. Their birthday tomorrow. Clare packed away her efforts at making a collage of their shared lives – something her sister would love, and something that Constance was incapable of doing. She pushed it all away and opened her laptop, the Marie biscuit she was nibbling settling her stomach. She typed in Rosa's name, Google-trawled it.

Rosalind Wagner was listed as a student at the Cape College of Classical Music – a formal shot of her playing the cello, a brief note about her scholarship, notices of concerts, a shot of her playing on a yacht. Hout Bay harbour in the summer. A few entries for her performances, and a Facebook page.

Clare clicked on it.

Life's about the journey. A stock image of a mountain scene, a waterfall plunging down a cliff face, and some pictures of cats and laughing babies. Stupid, Clare thought. She scrolled through some of her posts on other people's pages. Lacking the glibness essential for easy Internet socialising, very few of them had a response. A few photographs – in all of them, Rosa had merely been tagged. Rosalind with her cello, some group shots with her class. A small number of friends, and none, apparently, that preceded her arrival at the college. The last time she'd posted was the middle of May.

The electronic spiderweb that bound people to a communal life was absent. Where's the busy virtual life of a pretty young woman, Clare wondered.

Clare checked the time – late enough to be sure Ina Britz would be at home.

'Anything more on Rosa Wagner's phone?' asked Clare when Ina picked up.

'It's a pay-as-you-go. Small top-ups. Apart from calling her oupa, she didn't use the phone much. And she didn't use it at all after the twenty-fifth of May. I've put her details up on Facebook and Twitter. We'll see if that triggers anything. The papers are running something tomorrow. But listen, go to sleep now. There's nothing more to be done right now. I'll see you first thing.'

'OK. See you at nine,' said Clare.

'You need to get here before that, sister,' said Ina.

'I'm going to the doctor first thing.'

'*Vroulike kwale?*'

'You could put it like that,' said Clare, hanging up.

She walked to the bathroom, Fritz at her heels. The light was harsh, the mirror unkind. She looked wan, drawn around the eyes. Sleep. She was desperate for it. She closed her eyes against the headache building in the base of her skull. The momentary darkness was a relief, but not an escape.

Escape. The reason why many people disappeared. You just vanished. And then, somewhere else, sometime later, you could just make yourself up again.

The phone call, the blood on the wall. Rosa hadn't wanted to escape; she'd been trying to get home.

Clare opened the bathroom cupboard and rooted through the jumble of medicines and cosmetics. There they were: the sleeping pills.

Do not combine with alcohol, said the package insert. *Not safe during pregnancy.*

She popped one out of its foil blister and placed it on her tongue, but she gagged, her body rebelling. She could not get it down. She spat out the pill.

She was tired enough, in any case. She'd sleep, she'd sleep. She lay down, her limbs leaden with exhaustion, though she willed herself to get up, to shower, to eat something. But it would be morning before she awoke – the warm creature against her back the cat rather than Riedwaan.

Saturday
June 16

nineteen

'Relax your leg against me.' The gynaecologist gave her knee a firm pat. 'Come on, Clare.'

'I hate this,' she said.

'I know. You tell me every time there's a moon blue enough to make you come and see me.'

Clare forced herself not to tense up while the speculum parted her flesh. She lay still while the doctor adjusted the light, looked at whatever it was he needed to look at, probing what he needed to probe.

'All done.'

He pulled the towel over her knees.

'All fine,' he said. 'No infection, healthy cervix. The test says you are about a hundred percent pregnant. You're a bit on the thin side, but you're a strong woman. You'll push out that baby, no problem.'

'I don't want it,' she said.

'Nobody in their right mind *wants* a baby, Clare,' said Dr Evans. 'But sometimes people get lucky.'

'Lucky?' said Clare.

'It's your birthday today,' he said. 'In case you'd forgotten.'

'I hadn't,' said Clare.

'One wouldn't, I suppose, being born on the day that the whole country convulsed. Seventy-six. You and Constance, born as those children were being shot at in the streets.'

'The events are unconnected,' said Clare. 'My mother went into labour early. Tell me why you think I'm lucky to be sitting here like a careless teenager in trouble.'

The doctor leaned back in his chair and regarded her for a moment. 'Clare, you're thirty-six today,' He glanced at his notes. 'In two years' time it'll be much harder to conceive. Four years' time you'll be forty. You've read the articles, you know the numbers. For women, biology isn't fair.'

'It's not for me, motherhood,' said Clare. 'It's inconvenient.'

'Inconvenient.' Dr Evans looked at her over his glasses. 'You are one of the most inconvenient people I've ever known, Clare. Since you were born you've made a career out of it, like your father did when he was alive, like you are now with that unpleasant policeman I heard on the radio this morning.'

'Jakes Cwele,' said Clare. 'I'm quite enjoying inconveniencing him.'

'Are you afraid?' the doctor asked.

'I just think I should terminate,' said Clare.

'Have you discussed this with that unsuitable cop of yours?'

Clare shook her head, looked at Table Mountain framed by the window.

'It's a hard thing to decide alone,' said Dr Evans. 'A hard thing to do alone.'

'Maybe you should do that scan after all,' said Clare. 'Let me look at it. Then I'll decide.'

'It'll make it harder if you do,' said Dr Evans, putting his hand on her shoulder.

'I've never not looked what I plan to do straight in the eye,' said Clare. 'Let me see this.'

The doctor spread a thick film of gel across Clare's concave belly. He ran the scanner's arm over her skin. A pale green snowstorm appeared on the screen. Here was the solid cradle of the pelvis, cupping softer, darker parts of her body. Dr Evans moved the instrument with precision, naming the organs that did their quiet work unnoticed – bladder, liver, kidneys. Then a different spherical shape, the uterus. The doctor zoomed in, pressing the eye of the sonar firmly against Clare's belly, bringing the inside of her into sharp focus on the screen. A window into another world. The bulge of what would be a head, the curve of a bottom, flipper-like arms, tadpole legs curled into a chest. It was of her, but not her. At the epicentre of this ordered, alien accumulation of cells, a steady pixel-pulse. A beating heart.

'Everything's there, everything looks right.' The doctor was concentrating, measuring.

'It's a mistake,' said Clare.

'Nothing wrong with mistakes.' The sonar spat out a print of the scan. He handed it to her. The blur of her belly, the womb where the tiny foetus floated, oblivious of being spied upon in its safe, watery cave.

'This is not a mistake I think I can make,' said Clare.

The doctor wiped the gel from her skin. 'Get dressed, and then come through and talk to me.'

On the broad, blank desk was a paperweight, two paperclips, a family photograph. Her file, lying open. Clare watched him write up his notes, the sound of his pen scratching at the silence in the room.

She felt as if she were floating, or drowning. It was surreal. An unforgivable slip-up that had landed her at the edge of a precipice. She had to decide. Whatever she decided would be absolute and irrevocable. This was the moment between Before and After. Baby. No baby. There was nothing in between. Two halves of herself: her desire to shield the vulnerable; her fear – a terror, really – of losing her independence, her hard-won solitariness. She felt as if she were being drawn back into being half something doubled. A twin – and now a mother. Potentially a mother. She looked at the small black-and-white image in her lap, and her throat closed up.

'Did you hear me, Clare?'

She jerked back to the present, to the room, to the window with the mountain caught in its frame, to her doctor's voice. Her father's friend, and the man who had reassembled Constance's broken body – Constance, her other other. This doctor who had known her since before she was born. His eyes were on her now, gentle, knowing, without judgement.

'You're further along than you think, Clare,' he repeated. 'Ten, eleven weeks.'

Clare felt the shackles of indecision and anxiety tighten.

'How do you know?' she asked.

He opened a drawer and pulled out a card. The Ministry of Health's coat of arms was on the front, the bird at its centre more Zazu-from-*The-Lion-King* than the eagle rampant Clare presumed it was meant to be. Dr Evans opened the card – three elegant diagonal lines plotted on a graph.

'What's that?' asked Clare.

'A state antenatal card,' said Dr Evans. 'This graph gives you a good idea of uterine development, which helps estimate fairly precisely how far along you are. This here shows –'

Clare was on her feet.

'Thanks,' she said.

'Clare, sit down,' said Dr Evans. 'I'm not finished. Your condition is not something you can hide from. You're nearly twelve weeks,' he continued. 'And you're thinking of terminating. If you wait much longer it will be far harder.'

'I know,' said Clare. 'But I can't think about that now. Can I have that card?'

'Are you afraid?' He handed it to her, bemused.

'I'm terrified.' Clare stood up abruptly, knocking the chair over. 'But there's something I have to check.'

'Don't worry with the chair,' he said, righting it. He put his hand on her shoulder. 'It'll be fine. You'll be fine.'

A film of tears covered Clare's eyes. 'I'll come see you again. Tuesday, maybe. You can tell me the rest then.'

With that, she was gone.

Dr Evans walked over to the window. He watched as Clare ran across the rain-slicked parking lot. Her hair flashed against her blue coat. It made him think back to when she and her twin had been schoolgirls. He closed his eyes, remembered the summer's night eighteen years before. Constance, ever the shy twin, climbing out of the window of her boarding school, following Clare – always impatient, always questing – who had a liaison with her first love. Dr Evans opened his eyes, saw still the sinister park where Constance – born second, born smaller, incubated for weeks, unable to bear being apart from her twin – had followed Clare. But instead of finding her sister, Constance had been set upon by five gangsters. Two had knives, one had a hammer. When they'd finished with her, they left her for dead. Clare had found her twin, mutilated, maimed; she had forced Constance to live. Forced her. And ever since, Clare had tried to atone.

twenty

Clare tried to order her thoughts as she drove back to Hout Bay.
The simple solution seemed impossible. And the complicated
solution, not taking action, was also impossible. She had to brake
sharply for the horsebox at the traffic lights, the acrid smell of
rubber bringing her back to her surroundings.

There were few people about, two horse riders on Main Road,
an intrepid group of cyclists overtaking them. Women – domestic
workers, cashiers, packers – trickled out of the tin shacks
that clung to the mountainside. Boys in immaculate soccer kit
streamed down to the muddy poor-boy pitches lower down on
the Disa River. Light gilded the corrugated iron walls, and for a
moment Imizamo Yethu looked like the City of God. Then the
sun was gone and it was a slum again.

As Clare turned into the Section 28 parking lot she could
hear the first cheers of the gathering crowd. The rally was the
prelude to the Saturday morning soccer matches. There were
posters. Free T-shirts were being handed out. The familiar image
of Hector Petersen borne in the arms of a youth whose face is
forever frozen in fury and pain.

Today, in Cape Town, on this muddy stretch along the Disa
River, there were Cokes and Kwaito music. Soon, politicians
would make speeches filled with promises that would dissolve
in the rain.

Clare parked her car, the wind catching her door as she got out.

'Sweetness, let me help you.' It was Jakes Cwele holding her door, blocking her path. He thrust an enormous bunch of white lilies at Clare as she got out.

'I signed for them. Says here: *Clare. Sweetness, see you at dinner, Birthday Girl.*

He smiled. A row of perfect white teeth. Blank eyes.

'Thank you,' said Clare. She had no choice but to take the flowers. Having her hands full made her feel vulnerable. He had boxed her in between her car and the fence. 'I'm surprised to see you here,' she said. 'I thought you'd be at the rally, telling the youth what a wonderful job the police are doing to keep them safe, ensuring that they enjoy all the rights promised in Section 28.'

'Just came by to wish you, to tell you take the day off.'

'And why would I want to do that?' said Clare.

'I'm your commanding officer, remember,' said Cwele. 'I'm here to help, to guide, to advise. You feminists, you think you have to do everything yourselves, but try it. Sometimes a man can help.'

'It's so kind of you to offer,' said Clare, 'But right now, neither Major Britz nor I need your help or your advice,' said Clare.

'Your time is up, Dr Hart.'

'Not quite,' said Clare, pushing past him. 'You check my contract, you check the mandate of Section 28. You're not getting rid of me yet.'

'Clare,' his voice was low. 'Watch yourself. If I find out that you have done something out of order, you will pay.'

Clare turned to face him.

'What are you implying?'

'I've been told that resources are being spent on things other than children's welfare,' said Cwele. 'That's a serious offence.'

'Cwele,' she said, 'you might be my commanding officer, but I will say this to you. You have no interest in justice.'

'You watch yourself, little lady,' he said. 'Captain Faizal and Phiri are not going to be able to watch out for you that much longer.'

'Are you threatening me?' asked Clare.

Cwele held his hands open, palms up. 'I'm your friend,' he said. 'I'm looking out for your welfare.'

'That's something I'd prefer to do myself.'

Clare slammed the door behind her.

Ina let out a low whistle when Clare walked in.

'I watched that,' said Ina Britz. 'Looks like Cwele really got to you.'

'That's one way of putting it,' said Clare, propping the flowers in the sink as she washed her hands. She hadn't realised they were shaking.

'Don't take it personally,' said Ina, dunking a doughnut in her coffee. 'He hates all women, especially the ones who backchat.'

'Ja, I know,' Clare gave a wry smile. 'But he'll be out of the way today. He's scheduled to be the minister's poodle at the Youth Day rally.'

Clare watched Cwele manoeuvre a million rand's worth of official car out of the parking lot.

'It's a farce,' said Clare, turning away from the window. 'We're still getting kids shot in the back. Some days it feels as if we're handcuffed to history.'

'You're philosophical for such a cold morning,' said Ina.

'Not me,' said Clare. 'Salman Rushdie, I was reading *Midnight's Children* again. That phrase, right there on the first page – it jumped out at me. Seems to sum up the Cape.'

'Thinking about dead or nearly dead children on Youth Day would drive anyone to philosophy,' said Ina. 'But last year we had over two hundred cases like this, girlie, so I wouldn't go all New Age and see it as symbolic. Happens pretty much every weekend.'

'Anything from Shorty de Lange yet?'

'Not yet,' he's working on it. 'But the rubbish that they found in the cottage is photographed and up now. The rest is bagged and tagged in the incident room. The photographs from the house in Sylvan Estate are up there too.'

'You're like Wonder Woman, Ina,' said Clare.

Clare went to look through what had been found. The order in the room dispelled both the fury and the fear that Jakes Cwele had managed to trigger in her. She focused on the evidence, working methodically through the detritus that had been sorted and labelled.

'Ina,' said Clare, 'where does this come from?'

She was holding a photograph of five scraps of soiled yellow paper.

'It's part of the rubbish from the cottage,' said Ina.

'Where is it?' asked Clare.

'It's there, with all the other evidence. I'd planned to take it over to De Lange this morning.'

Clare opened the box on the table – marked and labelled and signed for. She broke the seal, signed again, and tipped out its contents. She laid out the plastic sleeves, one by one. Pictures of the girls, each telling its predictable story. Clare pushed them out of the way. Not what she was looking for. The magazine was there, the sweet wrappers. She found what she was looking for in the last bag.

She arranged the five torn scraps of paper, like a jigsaw puzzle. She Sellotaped them together. They were smudged and damp and it was hard to make out the details. A Ministry of Health logo, at least. Graphs and some smudged numbers. Like the one she'd picked up for the pregnant woman yesterday in Casualty. Like the one Dr Evans had shown her an hour ago after he had done her scan.

'Ina,' she said, clutching the card. 'I've got us an ID.'

twenty-one

The Sentinel, the lopsided hill at the harbour entrance, loomed over the fishing village that had clung for centuries to its wind-scoured flanks. Hangberg straggled above the harbour, its humble houses shuttered against the storm.

The Community Clinic was situated in the no-man's-land between an abandoned warehouse and a crescent of rundown council flats. It was ringed by a razor-wire fence and had grenade mesh on its windows.

The sign outside said *No Guns Allowed*. It also said that Saturday was for emergencies only. A Kevlar-jacketed security guard checked Clare's bag for weapons and patted her down.

She pushed the door open. The waiting room was packed. Friday night in Hangberg produced more than its fair share of emergencies. Women looking worse for a night's marital wear and tear, coughing children slumped against their grandmothers, fishermen with bandaged hands, boys in hoodies leaning their bandaged, bloody heads against the wall.

There was a scrum of people at Reception.

'I need to see the head sister,' Clare demanded.

'So does everybody,' said the receptionist, looking up at Clare. She scanned her hair, her clothes, her authority. Then she said, 'Let me call the sister for you.'

'Can I help?' The nurse was immaculate in her white uniform. A plump, pretty face; tired eyes.

'I need to know something: is this one of yours?' Clare said, holding out the patched-together clinic card to the nurse.

'It is,' said the nurse impatiently. 'As you can see, we are short-staffed and busy.'

'Like the police,' said Clare. 'But please, I need to know who it belongs to. The name is smudged.'

A ripple of silence was spreading out from where Clare stood. This was not a community that shared its secrets with outsiders. The nurse's glance shifted to the watching patients, then back to Clare.

'Sorry, I don't have the time now,' she said.

'This won't take long, Sister.' Clare proffered her ID, and the nurse capitulated.

'Come through, then.'

She followed the nurse into an office that doubled as an examining room. A raised bed, steel instruments, a light, lubricant, an empty box of tissues, posters about breastfeeding.

'Right, Dr Hart,' said the nurse. 'What do you need to know?'

'I want to know whose card this is,' said Clare.

'Patient information is confidential, Dr Hart,' said the sister. 'Do you have a warrant?'

'No,' said Clare. 'But a young woman has gone missing. This was found in a cottage on an estate near Judas Peak. Looked like people had been smoking tik there. I'm hoping it was someone who can help us with the enquiry.'

'The gangsters don't come in here much,' said the nurse. 'If they need attention, they go private so there's no record.'

'Please take a look at the card,' said Clare.

The nurse scrutinised it.

'This is an antenatal card.' She held the card up to the light. 'DesRay Daniels. Fifteen years old, weight fifty kilos, third trimester.'

'When last was she here?' asked Clare.

'Her last appointment was Friday. Yesterday.' She rifled through a drawer, pulled out a file. 'She's due in a month,' said the nurse.

'And the father,' said Clare. 'Do you know him?'

'Not personally, no, but I see a version of him every day.' She ran a finger down the notes and said: 'The side effects of pregnancy. Nausea and tiredness: yes; black eyes and split lips: no. Two of DesRay's visits have been because of assault.' She pushed the notes over to Clare.

'Do you know his name?' asked Clare.

'No,' said the sister. 'But I can tell you where DesRay lives. Her chance of surviving will be much higher if he's in jail.'

Clare stepped out of the clinic. The boy sitting on the pavement watched as she walked by. She could feel his eyes on her, two knives in her back. A dog with swollen dugs was scavenging in the gutter next to Clare's car. The boy picked up a stone and aimed it at the bitch's scrawny flank. The animal howled, then disappeared among the crowded houses. The raw sensation in Clare's stomach was way beyond morning sickness. She started the car and drove up the steep cobbled street. Past the crèche, past the barricaded sports centre and the Anglican Church to where Vulcan Close petered out into a footpath that ascended the contour of the mountain. Number twenty-six was the last house, but there were no signs of life when Clare knocked on the door. She could feel eyes watching her from behind shabby lace curtains that hung in all the windows on the desolate crescent. At the Daniels's house, someone had planted a geranium in a tin. It nodded a pretty red flower at Clare as she knocked on the bright yellow door.

The bolt shot back and the door opened a crack.

'Mrs Daniels?' asked Clare. The woman was about Clare's age, though a very different life had been scripted on her once-pretty face. A wiry little boy clung to her legs. A television, tuned into Cartoon Network, rat-a-tatted and squealed.

'Hello, I'm looking for DesRay.'

'What for?'

'Can I come in?' asked Clare, aware of the watchers behind the windows arrayed behind her. Mrs Daniels seemed to have the same concern, as she quickly opened the door and ushered Clare in.

'Why you looking for her?' Belligerence and fear in her voice, Mrs Daniels stood in the middle of the living room with her arms folded. Outside, two black-and-white maid's uniforms were pegged on the washing line. Inside, a flatscreen TV, a puffy leather lounge suite that crowded the small room, a sound system. Costly possessions, on a cleaning woman's wage.

'DesRay,' said Clare. 'Is she in?'

'Ja, she's here.' Arms folded across her chest. 'She's asleep.'

'Could you wake her?' asked Clare. 'I need to speak to her.'

'Why, what's she done?'

'Is she pregnant, your daughter?' asked Clare.

'What's it got to do with you?'

'Her clinic card was found in a house down the valley,' said Clare. 'Something seems to have happened in there. I'd like to talk to her about it.'

'It's hard for her. She hasn't got a father,' said Mrs Daniels. 'My husband, he drowned in a fishing accident. A girl needs her father in a place like this. That's what I say. Otherwise she goes with gangsters. What else can she do? They don't take no for an answer.'

'What's his name?' asked Clare.

The shoulders of the woman's dressing gown sagged.

'Chadley,' said the little boy who was wrapped around her legs. 'Chadley Wewers. He's mos there in the Wendy house at the back.'

116

twenty-two

Clare knocked on the flimsy wooden door.

'Who's it?' A rough voice.

'Child Protection,' said Clare, not quite truthfully. 'Open the door.' She didn't need to knock twice. A man opened the door, his jeans buckled low. Calvins a white stripe against his belly. His chest was inked blue with the gang chappies he'd earned in prison, the tattoos giving a detailed history of his relationship with the law. He looked to be twenty-one, an old man by some standards. He had a gold bridge where he'd had his Flats passion-gap filled – the abalone he'd fished out converted into mouth bling.

Clare flashed her badge. 'I'm looking for DesRay.'

A girl appeared in the doorway, the cold wind moulding her pink nylon nightie against her breasts, the tight curve of her belly, her bare legs. Bambi-eyes, full mouth, her bleached hair windblown.

'You're DesRay?' asked Clare.

'What you want,' she said. 'I did nothing.'

There was a gap between the two young people and the door. Clare stepped inside. It was dim – the windows salted up and grimy from the stiff wind that blew in off the ocean. Another flatscreen television, a sound system that looked like a spaceship. The room smelt of cigarettes and takeaways and sex. DesRay's clothes lay in a heap on the floor. An orange hoodie, black leggings, muddy Nikes.

'You went mountain climbing last night, DesRay?' Clare picked up one of her tackies. Size three.

She looked at Clare and shook her head.

'I was here,' she said.

'He was with you?' asked Clare.

'We were together.' The girl glanced at her boyfriend. He put his arm around her narrow shoulders.

'You been on the mountain too, Chadley?' asked Clare. 'There's mud on your jeans. I've never seen mud in Hangberg – all you get here is sand.'

'Why you fucking with us?'

'Like I said, Child Protection,' said Clare. 'Is that your baby?'

'Of course it's my fucking baby,' said Chadley.

'Do you go to the clinic with DesRay?'

'Of course I go,' said Chadley. 'I got to see what she must eat. What she must do. I check what they write there, it's mos our baby. I take DesRay and the card to the clinic. I know what they think of me, but I'm not a monster. I'm making it right.'

'I found DesRay's clinic card on the other side of the valley,' said Clare.

His hand went instinctively to his empty back pocket.

'You dropped the card?' asked Clare.

'I didn't drop nothing,' he said.

'What were you doing up there, Chadley?' asked Clare.

'I wasn't there,' he said.

'So how did this get into Sylvan Estate?'

'Maybe I lost it.' DesRay's hands went round her belly, a flash in her eyes. 'Maybe somebody picked it up.'

'Like I say, why you fucking with us?' He stepped forwards, but Clare didn't move. His eyes were bloodshot, and on his breath was the smell of decay of an amphetamine user.

'Chadley, d'you know a girl called Rosa Wagner?' said Clare. She didn't step back, didn't drop her gaze. 'There's traces of her

118

blood close to where this card was found. It would help if you told me what you were doing up there.'

'I did fuck-all, so fuck you.' He fumbled in his pockets for a lighter. Leaned over and took a box of cigarettes out of the shopping bag on the table.

'There were a couple of Sweetie Pie wrappers there too,' said Clare. She lifted a shopping bag from the mess on the table. Inside it were Nik Naks, a Sweetie Pie, a bottle of milk, a cash slip.

'The KwikShop on Valley Road,' she said. 'That's far from here.'

'It's pregnant women. You mos know what they're like. Want weird stuff all the time.'

Clare smoothed out the slip. 'So you walked up there at three this morning?' She pocketed the receipt.

'I know my rights,' said DesRay. 'You can't come in here and take my stuff without a warrant.'

'Should I get one?' asked Clare.

DesRay shrugged and the sweater she'd tied around her shoulders slipped, exposing her skinny upper arms. Five fading fingerprints on each.

'I'd like to know what you and your boyfriend were doing up there,' said Clare.

'We's mos family,' said Chadley.

'So that's why she's got those bruises?' asked Clare.

DesRay covered her upper arms with her hands.

'Chadley was with me all the time.' Her face mutinous.

'You were both up there,' said Clare.

'You can't prove fuck-all, lady,' said DesRay. She looked at Chadley, her eyes question marks.

'Not yet,' said Clare. 'But I soon will.'

Clare headed home, past narrow streets, cramped cul-de-sacs and graffitied walls. This is where he was most at home. This was Riedwaan Faizal's territory.

twenty-three

The Gang Unit building had a state-of-the-art security system that had never worked. Riedwaan Faizal went through the motions anyway

He placed his yellowed index finger on the scanner. It flashed red. He did it again. And a third time.

'State-of-the-art se moer, Captain.' The security guard spat, lifting the heavy boom. 'Welcome back. Where've you been, Captain?'

'Joburg,' said Riedwaan.

He had been awake all night. His mother, spry as a city sparrow, had fractured her hip while he was away. Leaving suddenly to see her would have broken his cover and the precarious trust he had built with his twitchy source. So he'd done what had already cost him a marriage: he put work before family. The most he could get from his job was a bullet in the head. But with family came reproach and yearning and the long, slow twisting of the heart.

Still, he had come back, and last night he'd been at her bedside, her bony hand in his, the hollow feeling in his chest growing as he watched her fade. *And* he'd broken his promise to Clare. He was in shit.

The building was only a year old, but the brass plaque commemorating its opening had not been polished in twelve months. The police commissioner who had done the honours was now serving fifteen years for racketeering. Or corruption;

Riedwaan could never remember which, and in the end it didn't really matter.

He took out his phone as he pushed the revolving doors open, and dialled Clare's number. He counted the rings as he walked past empty offices along the Gang Unit corridor. Eight offices, eight rings. The specialised units bleeding, bleeding. What he'd worked for twenty years to create was a husk of the dream he had started out with.

Clare was not picking up.

He kicked open the door to his empty office. His desk was a mess. Coffee cups, ashtrays, no one to nag him about it. He lit a cigarette.

'Don't smoke inside.' Clare walked in, the tip of her nose red from the cold.

'Sorry I didn't make it back last night.' No sleep and too many cigarettes had put gravel in his voice. He put his arms around her. She did not soften.

'At least I slept, and Fritz was happy.'

'That cat hates me,' said Riedwaan.

'Where've you been?'

'My mother broke a hip,' said Riedwaan. 'I couldn't leave her.'

'I missed you.'

'Ja, well. But you knew I was undercover,' said Riedwaan. 'I couldn't call you.'

'Whatever.' Clare felt the tears. She stepped out of his embrace and walked to the window. Gulls squabbled outside. A couple of homeless men were tipping dustbins. Friday night's KFC packs fluttering in the wind.

'My mother's on her way out,' said Riedwaan. He took Clare by the shoulders, turned her round to face him.

'Why didn't you just phone me?' The weight of what she had to tell him pressed against her ribs, but the bleak police building could not contain what she needed to say. 'I ask you for so little. Just this. Let me know you're safe.'

'I'm doing one thing,' said Riedwaan. 'That's where my thoughts are. I don't think till after, and then it's too late.'

'It's called male brain.'

'Don't hide behind that, Clare,' said Riedwaan. 'Don't disappear into yourself.'

She turned away.

'What's wrong?' he asked. 'What are you not telling me?'

'I'm fine,' she said. The lines around his eyes did not disappear when his smile went. Clare wondered when that had happened, why she'd never noticed this before. 'Just tired, and sick of all this.'

'So that's why you phoned me early this morning?'

'No,' Clare looked ahead. 'It's not why I called.'

'You going to tell me?'

'Later,' said Clare. 'At dinner.'

'Oh, fuck,' said Riedwaan. 'It's your birthday.'

'Ja,' said Clare. 'It's my birthday.'

'That's why you're so the moer-in with me?'

'No, Riedwaan. It's not.'

'The little girl,' said Riedwaan. 'Tell me about it.'

'You heard?'

'On the news.'

'She's alive, she's in hospital,' said Clare. 'Anwar Jacobs is looking after her. She'll pull through. That's the most important thing. The rest – who did it, why – that'll come later.'

'So that's not why you're here?'

'Chadley Wewers,' said Clare. 'You know him?'

'Why are you asking?' The name snagging a memory that wouldn't quite rise to the surface.

'A girl went missing. Rosa Wagner, she's a cellist,' said Clare.

122

'Been gone for three weeks. Then she calls her grandfather. We find no trace of her. Except for some blood by the phone. Also a torn-up pregnancy clinic card in a cottage near the house where she phoned from. A whole lot of tik paraphernalia, sweet wrappers, cigarettes, some charming schoolgirl bondage porn. Mandla Njobe and Gypsy found the same tik stuff and rubbish half-way up the mountain. Turns out the clinic card belongs to a fifteen-year-old called DesRay Daniels. Wewers is her boyfriend.'

'You've met him?' asked Riedwaan.

'Yes,' said Clare. 'A gangster.'

'Wewers,' said Riedwaan. 'I've heard the name, can't place it. There's lots of them. You've got your map?'

'This is where they were.' Clare spread out the map of Hout Bay. She'd marked where the child had been found, marked where Chadley Wewers had sat smoking and eating Sweetie Pies while a child was freezing to death in the slush. Marked where Rosa had made her last call, marked where the building was where she'd found the antenatal card and the tik lolly and the pictures of the bound and naked girls.

Riedwaan studied the terrain. Seeing what fitted together, what didn't. Clare stood beside him, her shoulder brushing his. It was easiest this way – the two of them comrades absorbed into the heartbreak of others.

'When I went to DesRay's mother's house this morning, I found a slip from the KwikShop in the Wendy house at the back, where DesRay lives,' said Clare. 'Chadley was at the KwikShop; I saw the CCTV footage. He was also on the mountain and in that cottage at Sylvan Estate. I want to know what he was doing up there.'

'Chadley,' said Riedwaan. 'The girl's probably the only person who calls him that, apart from his mother – if you could find a woman who'd confess to having given birth to him. Gang

123

Records. They'll have him down as that too. Let's see what we can get out of Tracy Darke. She's in. I just saw her car.'

They walked to the opposite end of the corridor, Clare inscrutable beside him.

'You've gone silent on me,' said Riedwaan, as they waited for the lift. 'What are you not saying?'

The doors opened, but there were two officers inside. When they got out on the ground floor she simply said, 'Nothing.'

She was lying, Riedwaan knew that, but he didn't press her. He was afraid of the truth; he was afraid she'd say that this last absence was one too many. That he wasn't worth the wait. *That he couldn't hear* – not now. So he said nothing either, and the doors opened and they were in the basement and Riedwaan was tapping in the code for a reinforced steel door.

twenty-four

Gang Records. It was the Gang Unit's creation, massive and malign. An elaborate family tree of sorts, tracking the connections between members – formal and informal – of the gangs that ruled Cape Town. A vast family, bound by blood. A sinister web of loyalties and traded violence, operating inside the prisons, and also on the outside. Tracy Darke had transformed Riedwaan Faizal's vision of ordered information into a reality, and Riedwaan treasured her for that.

'Tracy,' he said when she opened the door. 'Where've you been?'

'I've been right here,' she grinned at him. 'Come in. Hello, Clare.' Tracy had been pretty once, her father's little princess decades before, and that's how she still dressed. Frills and curls and clips and too much lipstick.

'Captain.' Heart FM was schmaltzing in the background. 'You missing me?'

'Always, Tracy,' he said. 'Always.'

'Ha, you're telling me that because you want something from me.'

'Tracy, don't be like that.'

'Men,' said Tracy, rolling her eyes at Clare, 'Not that hard to figure out, hey? OK, what do you want to know?'

'Chadley Wewers,' said Clare. 'Can you get his record for me? His connections?'

'Hey, you know how many Wewerses there are?'

'But I only want one – Chadley.'

'I'll see what I can get.' She settled her spectacles on her tip-tilted nose. 'Wait over there.'

Tracy Darke's long red nails attacked her keyboard, digging into the database she had so painstakingly built, one depressing case at a time.

'I think you're going to be very happy with me, Captain,' she said, leaning closer to her screen, clicking her way through the links that appeared.

'I'm always happy with you, Tracy,' said Riedwaan. 'Show us.'

'What's in it for me?' She turned to face him; Riedwaan knew the deal.

'Dinner,' said Riedwaan. 'Roxy's in Rosebank. Wednesday. I'll pick you up after work. But now: Chadley Wewers.'

'I have a couple here,' said Tracy. 'One Chadley Wewers from Hanover Park, one from Hangberg, one from –'

'Hangberg,' said Riedwaan. 'That's the one I want.'

'Pollsmoor Prison,' Tracy read off the screen while the information printed. 'That's where he was until a couple of weeks ago. Been a gang member since he was nine. The Sexy Boys. Been in and out of jail since he was fourteen. His uncle was a general in one of the prison gangs. He had his record wiped when he turned eighteen. All the usual,' said Tracy. 'Dealing, rape, attempted murder.'

'The latest charge?'

'Assault,' said Tracy. 'The victim was a drug dealer, by the looks of things. A foreign national.'

'So why's he out?'

'Paroled early,' said Tracy. 'Good behaviour, participation in rehab programmes, anger management classes, an offer of work.'

'Wewers – Colin – of course,' said Riedwaan. 'Rang a bell.'

'He's dead now, Captain,' said Tracy. 'Murdered in prison. But hang on, there's one more thing here.'

Clare waited. More typing, more Heart FM schmaltz.

'Here it is,' she said. 'The new thing in the government's programme is community bridging. Meant to make citizens part of
the crime solution ... hang on a minute, bloody database is slow
today.'

Another love song. Whitney Houston wailing from the other
side of the grave. Clare thought her head might explode.

'The FAF, Captain,' said Tracy. 'That's the name of the Justice
Department approved body. Stands for Fresh Air Fund.'

'People get paid for this?' asked Riedwaan.

'Apparently.' Tracy Darke turned around to face them. 'Kind of
outsourcing. They say here that they're helping the less fortunate,
giving a second chance. All that bullshit. You want the director's
name?'

'Tell me,' said Riedwaan.

'The director of FAF, which has its office in Hout Bay harbour,'
said Tracy Darke, turning around to face them, 'is a Mr Stavros
September.'

'Tracy,' said Riedwaan. 'You're the hottest thing in Records.'

'Anything for you, Captain. Sorry, I have to take this call – it's
my father.' She picked up her phone. 'You'll find your way out?'

Clare and Riedwaan walked along the corridor towards the
entrance.

'D'you know this September guy?' asked Clare.

She pushed the revolving door open. It was cold outside, even
the gulls complaining.

'Been watching him for years.' Riedwaan lit a cigarette.
'Everyone calls him Stavros the Greek – in honour of the man
who may or may not have been his father, who may or may not
have been Greek. Not even Stavros's mother knew for sure.'

'He's from Hangberg?'

'Born and bred,' said Riedwaan. 'Knows the sea and the mountains like the lines on his face.'

'What's his business?'

'The usual. Abalone and tik – the Cape's economy,' said Riedwaan. 'Rents out rubber ducks to the abalone poachers, skippers yachts for men who can afford them but don't know how to sail them.'

'So how's he connected to Wewers?'

'I'll go ask him.'

'Right now?' Clare unlocked her car.

Riedwaan's phone beeped. He checked the message. 'I must talk to Phiri first. He's on his way.'

'There's so little time, Riedwaan,' said Clare, starting her car.

'It'll be OK. Phiri thinks you can do no wrong.'

Riedwaan watched the colonel's white Isuzu turn into the entrance, a brief altercation with the guard. 'There he is now. I'll sort things.'

twenty-five

'Faizal.' Colonel Edgar Phiri got out of his vehicle. He was a tall man, spare, hair graying, eyes that saw much and revealed little. 'Do I look like a nobody, Captain?'

'Not at all, sir,' said Riedwaan. 'Why?'

'That guard,' said Phiri. 'Every time he forgets my face. Every time I come he asks for my ID. It's like I'm a spook.'

'You're not a ghost, sir,' said Riedwaan. 'Not yet.'

Phiri pulled his briefcase out of the Isuzu.

'That was Dr Hart you were talking to,' he said as he straightened up. 'She didn't seem happy.'

'How d'you guess?'

'Body language.'

'I'm in trouble,' said Riedwaan.

'Tell me something new, Faizal.' Phiri pocketed his keys. 'I've had Cwele on my case. Tells me you've been making some high-ups uncomfortable. Ina Britz has had the minister's advisor yapping for Clare's report. If he finds the two of you are working together it's not going to be easy for me.'

'I'm sorry, sir,' said Riedwaan.

'You don't look sorry,' said Phiri. 'Tell me, what's going on?'

'I want to look at some yachts,' said Riedwaan.

'You come into money, Faizal?'

'The opposite,' said Riedwaan. 'My divorce came through. I'm a free man, but I'm flat broke.'

The wind was biting, but Phiri made no move towards the entrance.

'Jakes Cwele was telling me about the search-and-seizure operation in Mpumalanga that didn't go quite according to plan,' he said. His eyes on Riedwaan, sharp as a hawk's.

'Something like that.'

'You find anything?' asked Phiri.

'Not a fucking thing,' said Riedwaan. 'There were some difficulties,' said Riedwaan. He was struggling to light a cigarette. 'Cwele's involved. How, I don't know. Why he is here instead of there, I don't know either. But it's why I had to take some extra time.'

'That's why Clare's angry with you?'

'Women,' said Riedwaan.

'Don't give me that nonsense about women, Faizal,' said Phiri. 'If she's angry, she has a reason. If Cwele's angry, he has a reason too.'

'What did he tell you?'

'Cwele says that's his territory. Says the Gang Unit must run our operations past him. That you didn't have authorisation.'

Riedwaan managed to get his cigarette going.

'You notice his shoes, Colonel?' asked Riedwaan.

'Not on the phone.'

'Gucci,' said Riedwaan. 'That's an expensive pair of shoes for a man paying two lots of maintenance.'

'OK, what do you want, Faizal?' asked Phiri.

'Some latitude,' said Riedwaan. 'Sir.'

'Give me one good reason I should give it to you again.'

'I want to find out who's being paid off. We've lost two more Gang Unit members. Bullets in the head like they were stray dogs. I can't write them off. I've got this feeling, sir –'

'Don't tell me that, Faizal. Your feelings only ever cause trouble.

130

I get Cwele on the line every time you move. He wants you transferred back to uniform. He wants you out of the way. And you give him every excuse. His bosses are my bosses. They prefer Cwele to me. And everybody wants to get rid of you.'

'Except you, sir,' said Riedwaan. His career hung by the slender thread of his boss's loyalty, a thread that was on the verge of snapping. Riedwaan knew it. Some days, though, the prospect of being cut loose seemed a seductive option.

'I'm not so sure of that any more,' said Phiri. 'I need more information from you. I need to know what kind of trouble you are going to get me into.'

'There's a girl that's gone missing now,' said Riedwaan.

'Clare's little girl?'

'One's in hospital,' he said. 'But there's another girl, a music student, who's gone missing. That's why Clare was here. Some gangster was around when she disappeared – near to the spot where the other child was found.'

'And you're telling me there's a connection to the Gang Unit?'

'Cwele wants Clare off it,' said Riedwaan.

'Why?'

'That's what I want to know,' said Riedwaan.

'You've got forty-eight hours, Faizal. You report to me, OK? You don't make a mess – and nobody dies this time.'

'No, sir.'

Phiri watched as some starlings settled on the cables overhead.

'I'd keep an eye on Dr Hart,' he said. 'If I were you.'

'Yes, sir.'

'You should marry her, Faizal,' said Phiri 'I had a woman I loved and I didn't marry her. I've regretted it all my life.'

'She marry someone else, sir?'

'She was killed in Mozambique,' said Phiri. 'Letter bomb. Blew her head off.'

'I'm sorry,' said Riedwaan.

'So am I, Faizal. So am I.'

Phiri walked past the tarnished sign that said *Gang Unit* and disappeared into the recesses of the building.

twenty-six

'You look pleased,' said Ina, as Clare walked into the 28's office. 'Well, maybe not pleased – just less miserable. You get anything more on that little girl this morning?'

'Nothing yet,' said Clare. 'But I did ask the Gang Unit about Chadley Wewers – it was his girlfriend's clinic card that we found at Sylvan Estate.'

'The Gang Unit.' Ina followed Clare into her office. 'Everyone in the Gang Unit's been seconded, except for Colonel Phiri and Captain Faizal.'

'So?' said Clare.

'So you mean you asked Riedwaan Faizal.'

'I needed specialist help.'

'Help. Exactly. You need help, Clare. Not trouble.'

'He knows how to find people,' said Clare.

Ina stared, raising an eyebrow.

'He knows Cape Town like the back of his hand,' Clare said.

'He's got how many disciplinary actions hanging over his head?'

'One,' said Clare. 'Three charges were dropped.'

'Excellent,' said Ina, leaning back in her chair. 'Only one.'

'The deceased was a gangster,' said Clare.

'Now you're talking like a cop,' said Ina, 'which is the one thing you were hired not to be.'

'Riedwaan knows all about girls who go missing,' said Clare. 'It happened to his own daughter, you know. That's how I met him.

He came to me for help.'

'He was the main suspect, for fuck's sake,' said Ina.

'Custody war with his ex-wife.'

'So you slept with him,' said Ina Britz.

'Turned out I was right about him then,' said Clare. 'All he ever did was protect that little girl. What happened to Yasmin was not his fault.'

'Spare me,' said Ina. 'Straight women have no sense in their heads. If Faizal's involved, your best hope is that Jakes Cwele can't decide which of you two he hates most.'

'At least that'll keep his mind occupied,' said Clare. 'I got the tapes from the KwikShop. He was there.'

Clare pulled out the CCTV grabs and spread them on the desk. Ina looked at the photos. Wewers in his hoodie, buying cigarettes, bending over the sweet shelf. On the forecourt, a handful of people, a woman in a nurse's uniform filling her car.

'What's his story?'

'He was at home, DesRay had a craving for chocolate. He went to get some for her.'

'Who's he with?'

'He told me he was alone,' said Clare.

There was a knock on the door.

When Ina came back, she was grinning.

'So the cat got the cream?' said Clare. 'What is it?'

'Fax from Shorty de Lange,' said Ina. 'You hit the fucking Lotto, girl. Wewers's prints are all over the stuff in the cottage.'

twenty-seven

The marina was sheltered, but still the yachts pitched and rolled, the swell muscling in. A sprinkling of luxury cars was moored outside the Yacht Club. Further along, a group of women were gutting fish. As Riedwaan walked by, a woman stared at him, her knife hovering over the fish she was filleting. She plunged the knife into its belly, flicking the entrails towards gulls squabbling over bloody innards.

Stopping at a run-down warehouse, Riedwaan pushed open the door. A woman of indeterminate age, short and squat and ugly as sin, was sitting at the front desk. Her eyes narrowed as he walked into the airless office. She could spot a cop at a hundred paces.

'Name's Faizal, Mrs September,' Riedwaan addressed the woman, holding up his ID. She didn't even glance at it. 'Your son. Is he in?'

'What do you want with him?' she asked.

'Couple of questions, that's all,' said Riedwaan. 'For now.'

'I'll see if he can make the time.'

'No need. We know each other,' said Riedwaan. 'It'll be like old times when I used to work for the Vice Squad. Me, your son and some fourteen-year-old he'd underpaid for services rendered.'

'He's a married man, my son,' said Mrs September. 'A father, a businessman. Why don't you go and look for the proper criminals – these foreigners selling drugs on every corner.'

'I'll speak to him first. For old times' sake,' said Riedwaan, opening the door opposite her desk. The office was a shambles – boat parts, papers, pieces of wood. At the far end was a desk. The man looked up. Small, shrewd eyes set deep in their sockets, his skin pitted by acne and a life lived rough.

'Stavros the Greek,' said Riedwaan.

'Look what the cat brought in,' said Stavros September. 'I still need a deck hand. You come for that job at last?'

'And taking in paroled Sexy Boys gangsters is also part of the business plan?' said Riedwaan. 'How much do you make for that?'

'You heard of human rights?' demanded Stavros.

'I've heard of them,' said Riedwaan. 'Haven't seen them much. Listen, Chadley Wewers got his parole because you said you'd give him a job and keep an eye on him.'

'The laaitie's like my son,' said Stavros. 'And his father, he fished for me when I started out with crayfish. Like family, mos. He drowned when one of my boats went down.' He leaned forward. 'You cops wouldn't get this, but I feel responsible for the boy.'

'You still baiting the traps with the people you don't like?'

'Fuck you, Faizal.' The veins in his neck bulged.

'Where is he?'

Stavros the Greek hesitated.

'You fuck with me,' said Riedwaan. 'I get everything searched, every bit of paperwork checked. You want that?'

'He works that side.' Stavros jerked his thumb to where fishing trawlers were moored. 'But right now you'll find him in bed. He's one of my best divers, he only works nights.'

Riedwaan sauntered towards the door. 'Send my regards to your wife,' he said.

'Fuck you, Faizal,' he said again.

Mrs September was standing in the doorway. Riedwaan stepped aside so that she could enter.

'Sies, Stavros,' said his mother. *'Moenie so vloek 'ie.'*

A vehicle was parked next to Riedwaan's bike. A man leaning against it, texting. He looked up when Riedwaan approached.

'Faizal.'

'Cwele,' said Riedwaan. 'What you doing here?'

'It's a free country,' said Cwele.

'No thanks to you,' said Riedwaan. 'What does it cost to get you to run around for him? Fifty bucks, a hundred?'

Cwele, weight-lifter's shoulders, beer-drinker's gut, moved in on Faizal.

'Sorry, I forgot. You'd do it for a bottle of Johnny Walker Black – make you feel like the politician you want to be.'

'You're on borrowed time, Faizal,' said Cwele. 'You're out of your area. Phiri warned you. I know he did. I told him to. You've got maybe forty-eight hours, and Clare Hart, that skinny little bitch of yours, she's had her nose where it shouldn't be. She's got even less time.'

'You've spoken to her?'

'I advised her of these facts.'

'She loves advice,' said Riedwaan. 'How did she take it? Say "Yes, sir," like a good woman should?'

'Eish, Faizal,' said Cwele. 'You want advice from me? I'd keep an eye on that woman. She spends a lot of time with Ina Britz. Unnatural bitch.'

Riedwaan thought how much Cwele's face would be improved if he broke his nose. Instead he said: 'You learned nothing on your hate crimes orientation course?'

'What the fuck do you mean?'

'Sexual orientation, women's rights. Equality.'

'Bullshit,' said Cwele.

'I suppose,' said Riedwaan. 'To learn anything, you have to

have a brain to start with.'

'You should get a job doing stand-up comedy,' said Cwele, opening the door to his car.

'Already got one,' said Riedwaan. 'Show's called *The Police Force*.'

Riedwaan's phone rang as Cwele sped off. 'Clare –'

She cut his greeting short.

'Shorty de Lange just called me. He got a couple of prints off a vodka bottle they found in the cottage – it's in the garden of the house where Rosa Wagner phoned from.'

'Chadley Wewers,' said Riedwaan.

'The same,' said Clare. 'He ran the other prints too. Doesn't have a match yet, but we've got Wewers; he'll lead us to Rosa.'

twenty-eight

The house on Vulcan Street was locked, but the eyes behind the curtains were as vigilant as the last time. Clare and Riedwaan went around the back to the Wendy house.

The door opened before Riedwaan knocked.

'Hello, you going somewhere, DesRay?' said Clare.

The girl made a move to shut the door.

'Chadley Wewers here?' Riedwaan pushed the door open.

She knew when not to resist, but this didn't make her cooperative. 'Who are you?' she said.

'Dr Hart you've already met,' said Riedwaan. 'I'm Captain Faizal. Gang Unit.'

Her arms still folded, DesRay stepped out of Riedwaan's way.

'Blue, green, purple. Butterfly skin, that's what he gives you with the pizza?' The bed was unmade. The smell of a man in the air, mingled with a stale garlic smell, the smell of tik.

Two takeaway boxes on the table.

'Debonair's.' Riedwaan opened a box. 'My favourite's the Margarita.'

DesRay looked at him. Then she looked at Clare. The eyes of an old woman in her fifteen-year-old face.

'Where did he go, DesRay?' Riedwaan's hand as near as on his gun. She pulled her cardigan close around her bulging belly.

'Tell us,' said Clare. 'It'll be better. For the baby.'

Tears spilled down the girl's cheeks. For her boyfriend,

perhaps. For what might happen to him, for what might happen to her. For what he would do to her – whatever she said, or didn't say. Her eyes fixed on a door at the back. She didn't need to say anything.

Riedwaan kicked it open. Chadley Wewers in his underpants in the musty bathroom. He was wired, the familiar amphetamine twitch in his limbs, eyes shifting to where he'd run.

Riedwaan's gun out; on him.

'Get dressed.'

'You can't arrest me, *jou vokken naai*.'

'Rosa Wagner has disappeared,' said Clare. 'Fingerprints put you right near the place where she last was.'

'I don't know nothing about no Rosa,' said Wewers.

'There were bloodstains, Rosa's blood in the house. Some food was taken,' said Clare. 'We found the wrappings outside in the cottage. And people were smoking tik. There were some nasty pictures there too.'

'Hey, lady,' Wewers flung his arms wide, taut muscles rippling across his tattooed chest. 'Do I look like a fucking garden boy?'

Riedwaan moved the safety off. 'You can come kaalgat like that or you can put on your clothes.'

The click seemed to focus Wewers's mind and he pulled on jeans, a hoodie.

'You always do what your white madam tells you?'

Riedwaan had his hoodie twisted up and around his neck before Wewers could move. Then Riedwaan spun him around, cuffed him.

'You can tell me where she is,' said Riedwaan. 'Beautiful girl missing for three weeks, then phones from a house where we found your fingerprints.'

'That's got fuck-all to do with me.'

'Let's talk about it at the station,' said Clare.

Riedwaan had him by the neck, pushed him out the door.

'You'll fucking pay, DesRay,' he hissed.

'No, please, Chadley, I didn't say nothing.'

'You'll pay anyway, you poes.'

Riedwaan walked Wewers ahead of him, across the littered yard to the car.

The station was still fairly orderly when they arrived. The end of a long Saturday afternoon, the calm before the storm of assaults and car accidents. The desk constables listening to Rihanna, the volume so low that the music was nothing more than irritating static.

'I want my phone back,' said Wewers. 'I want a lawyer.'

The warrant officer wrinkled her nose. 'Doesn't make you look good, a lawyer,' she said, pushing the paperwork over to Clare.

'You just go with Captain Faizal and Dr Hart and talk nicely with the captain. Maybe you'll still get to church on Sunday morning.'

'I didn't eat my pizza yet,' said Wewers. 'I'm hungry.'

'No room service,' said Riedwaan. 'Sorry for that.'

Clare signed the paperwork, and the warrant officer tossed it into an overflowing tray.

'All the rooms are free,' said the officer. 'Take your pick, Captain.'

twenty-nine

Clare watched through the one-way glass of the interrogation room. Wewers didn't have any cigarettes, but he was calmer now. Waiting. He had worked out a story, made a plan. That's what the body language was telling her. It would make her job harder. She opened the door, took the chair opposite Wewers. Two coffees burning her hands. She put them on the table.

A couple in a café.

He took her offering.

Wewers snapped the lid off the takeaway cup, drank it black and unsweetened – the same way she did.

Between them, the scuffed Formica table where confessions were laid out like cards at a certain point in the conversation. Riedwaan stood by the door. Both present, and not present. It unsettled Wewers, his eyes shifting from Clare to the police captain and back.

'Chadley Wewers,' said Clare. She sat opposite him. She had seen enough Chadleys in her life to know that here, alone, separated from his feral pack, he was no threat.

'You can't fuck with me,' he said.

'I wouldn't dream of it,' said Clare. 'I ask you a few questions. You give me the right answers. Then you get to go home. You want a cigarette?' asked Clare.

He nodded.

Riedwaan tossed him the box. The flare of a match. It wasn't easy with his cuffed hands, but this was something Chadley Wewers had had occasion to do before.

'Where is she?' Clare held out the photograph of Rosalind Wagner. Gleaming skin, rapt face, the red dress.

He looked away.

'Fuck knows. If I knew, I'd take you there.'

'Taking us there,' said Clare. 'That would be a good idea. We've got your fingerprints from the house, you already know that. Also the clinic card and the Sweetie Pie wrapper you left behind there. I've seen the CCTV, Chadley. It was you buying the stuff at the KwikShop. It's your fingerprints in the cottage. You were there. So was she. Now you're here – but where's Rosa?'

'I told you,' his voice steady, foot drumming. He put a handcuffed wrist on his leg. 'I don't know.'

'Rosa Wagner phones her grandfather,' said Clare, looking hard at Wewers. 'We go to the house where she phoned from and we find a tik lolly and Rosa's blood. But no Rosa.'

'I told you mos. I wasn't in the house,' his voice a hiss.

Riedwaan scanned the fax. He handed the sheet to Clare and she checked it. 'These are your prints. Same place as Rosa Wagner was. You were up on the contour path too. Same night.'

'What the fuck,' said Wewers. 'I saw nothing at the house.'

'What did you go there for?'

'Nothing,' said Wewers. 'It's quiet. I go walking sometimes. I found that place. You can rest there.'

'He's fucking with us,' said Riedwaan.

Clare raised her palm. 'Let's hear him out.'

'I did nothing to that girl.'

'But you know her,' said Clare.

Silence.

Clare knew enough about accused men to know that they all

swore innocence. She leaned back in her chair.

'And after?'

'I didn't see anything.'

'How come?'

'I went home.'

'Take him back to the cells.' Clare stood up. 'You think about some better answers,' she said. 'Then we can talk.'

Chadley Wewers leapt at her, but not as fast as Riedwaan. His cuffed hands slowed him down.

'It's the truth, you bitch,' he snarled. 'It's the fucking truth.'

'So where is she?' Riedwaan pushed him down on a chair.

'I don't fucking know.'

'Then what were you doing there?' The muscles in Riedwaan's arms were corded – earned from a childhood carrying loads too heavy for him, and a lifetime of wariness. It was not a body you could buy in a gym. When he was filled with fury it was a body that spoke violence. That was a language that Chadley Wewers understood.

'Your prints are there,' said Riedwaan. 'She's a nice girl with an education. If she dies and you know where she is, a judge will give you life. But if you help us now, you'll have it easier.'

Wewers sat back, looked from Clare to Riedwaan, weighing up his options. It didn't take long.

'You got an entjie, Captain?'

A confession was coming. Riedwaan handed him a cigarette.

'DesRay,' he started. 'Her mom works there. That's why we can go there.'

'What are you talking about?' said Clare.

'Listen to what I'm telling you, lady,' said Wewers. 'Mrs Daniels is the maid. She cleans the house. Sometimes you go fucking mad living in a Wendy house in the wind. DesRay takes her mom's security pass. We go up there sometimes. That's all there

144

is. Now can I go?'

'Why didn't you say this before?' asked Clare.

'You think Mrs Daniels is going to keep her job after this?'

Clare and Riedwaan stood up.

'You going to let me go?'

'Not a chance,' said Riedwaan. 'You're going back to the cells until we're sure what you say isn't some tik-addict's dream.'

The warrant officers came to take him back to the cells.

'Leave your cigarettes with me, Captain.' Wewers was scratching at his neck. Riedwaan tossed him the box.

'*Jou ma se vrot poes,*' Wewers yelled after him. 'It's fucking empty.'

thirty

'Don't know how I missed that – the fact that Mrs Daniels works at the house,' said Clare. She opened the door to her office. The air smelt stale, she opened the window. 'It's on the records, the ones Sylvan Estate security gave me, and I missed it.'

'OK, so you're not Ms Perfect after all,' Riedwaan smiled. 'But what's with DesRay, the pregnant girlfriend, saying nothing?'

'She's obviously afraid,' said Clare.

'With that jerk, I don't blame her.'

'There's no evidence that Rosa had a drug problem – the only thing that might possibly link her to Chadley Wewers,' said Clare.

'Wrong place, wrong time, that's all you need with scum like Wewers.'

'If it's him, why was the TV still there?' asked Clare. 'Why was the laptop there? Why's all that shit that tik addicts steal still in the house?'

'The girl disturbed them.'

'I think someone disturbed *her*,' said Clare. 'But who? It's hard to vanish on an estate with cameras everywhere. And Sylvan Estate isn't the sort of place where people turn a blind eye to boys in hoodies.'

'The electricity was out.' He was bending over records that Ina Britz had requested from Sylvan Estate. 'Check there. It says the fence was off for an hour that night.'

Clare flipped back through the records. 'Look, seems like

146

outages were a regular occurrence. Lots of trees blown down this winter. Bad combination, edge of the forest and stormy weather.'

'Maybe,' said Riedwaan.

'Wewers insists he doesn't know her,' said Clare.

'He's lying. '

'Why is he lying?'

'He's a gangster,' said Riedwaan. 'That's what gangsters do. They lie.'

'This is different,' said Clare. 'He's afraid. Maybe he's covering for something.'

'You want to let him go?'

'Not a chance,' said Clare. 'He may not have done anything to Rosa himself, but that doesn't mean to say he wasn't there and that he doesn't know what happened to her.'

'Maybe,' said Riedwaan.

'I want to find the others,' said Clare. 'See what they were doing there.'

'And your birthday?' said Riedwaan.

'Shit,' said Clare. 'Look at the time.'

'And this is not the right time for this either.' Riedwaan had a blue velvet box in his gun hand. He was pointing it at her. Clare took the unwrapped gift. It snapped open. An oval pendant, sky-blue tanzanite.

'I saw your eyes in it.'

'That's so perfect.'

'Turn round.' Riedwaan's fingers were a whisper at the back of her neck as he fastened the chain.

'I love it.' She turned to face him again.

Clare leaned her forehead against Riedwaan's chest. She could hear his heart. The silver chain was cold against her skin.

'Riedwaan.' Now that she couldn't see his eyes, she could formulate the words she needed to say. 'I must tell you –'

'Later,' he said. 'Tell me later. I have to go see my mother.' Riedwaan's breath was warm in her hair. 'I promised I'd be there to give her supper. I'm already late.'

'She doesn't remember anything,' said Clare, drawing back. 'She won't know if it's five or six or seven o'clock.'

'But I will,' he said, disentangling himself. 'I've broken enough promises, and anyway, I've got this feeling.'

'What feeling?'

'That she's going.' Riedwaan picked up his helmet, banging the door shut behind him. Minutes later, she heard the whine of his bike as he accelerated up the hill.

'Fuck,' said Clare. Then her phone rang and she grabbed it.

Mandla Njobe's number flashing on the screen. A splinter of ice lodged itself in the base of her spine.

'You've found something, Mandla?'

'Clare,' he said. 'You must come up the Kloof. Now, right now.'

thirty-one

Clare took Valley Road, past the KwikShop, following the river up Orange Kloof. She drove past Sylvan Estate, turning up a track along the electric fence separating the estate from the mountain. Following Ina Britz's directions, she bumped past the familiar yellow-and-black warning signs strung along the razor wire at eye level. Past the place where the little girl had been found. The light was giving out, the day about to plunge into darkness.

The track petered out. She'd have to go the rest of the way on foot, as the others had, carrying their equipment with them.

She plunged her hands deep into her pockets, safe from the wind's bite. A spider's web glinted dully. Beyond, in the forest, the saw-toothed pines bit into the brooding evening sky.

An owl hooted mournfully; fear brushed the back of Clare's neck. Clenching her fists in her pockets, she gasped at the stab of pain – the forgotten quill in her pocket.

She ignored the trails of animals escaping the sprawl of the housing estates. Instead she took the path followed by Mandla Njobe and Gypsy, by Ina Britz and the Section 28 men with their digging equipment. The trees drew her in and closed ranks behind her.

Below her was the clearing. A diffused light in the surrounding pine trees, the clearing the centre of a perfect fairy circle. A depression in the ground amid the pine needles. One, two, three small rectangles of disturbed earth alongside each other. Further along, a fourth, perhaps.

The sound of spades slicing through wet earth, piles of soil heaped to one side. Ina Britz turned, lit a Lucky Strike.

Clare picked her way through the trees at the edge of the clearing. Last night's deluge had washed away any possibility of footprints or a scent trail for the leashed dog. Gypsy barked a greeting at her, and she let the dog sniff her hand. Clare greeted Ina Britz and the others, but the group was silent, transfixed by the rhythmic thud of the spade under the glare of the halogen lights.

Then it stopped. In its stead, voices low with dread, wishing away the result, no matter how often before it had happened.

At the bottom of the hole were rocks, weighting down the form beneath them wrapped in black plastic. The tracker dog sniffed the air, and then she sat back and raised her head to the sky. Her howl was long and lupine.

The men tasked with exhumation squatted at the edge of the grave, lifted the bag and laid it out. It was not man-sized; hardly woman-sized. The stench was overwhelming. Clare cut open the bag.

A young woman stared up at them.

It wasn't Rosa.

thirty-two

The dead woman's heart-shaped face had a beguiling symmetry. Her eyebrows were dark and finely shaped above her slanted eyes. They stared up at the starless sky, and it was hard to look at her without feeling accused. Her black hair was matted, and near the temples patches had been ripped from her scalp.

Piet Mouton, the pathologist, overweight and uncomplaining despite the climb, removed the plastic that was wrapped around the body. The dead woman was naked, her hipbones and ribs visible under mottled white skin. He set to work with a tenderness and precision that seemed unlikely in a man of his size.

'She's about your height, Clare. I'd say she was your age, thirty-five.'

'Thirty-six, as of today.'

'Congratulations,' said Mouton. 'Height, all that stuff I'll do in the lab, but for now I'd say she's about your height too. Five foot four, but she can't weigh more than forty kilos. Not much more than a ten-year-old.'

An old-school pathologist, he'd been looking at cadavers for decades.

He examined the corpse. The head, the neck, the chest, the arms, the legs, her bare feet. There were no visible wounds, no gashes to the throat or blows to the head that had delivered the coup de grâce.

The pathologist stretched out the arms, the palms open to the

151

sky. There were jagged scars on the inside of the wrists.

'Suicide attempt?' asked Clare.

Mouton turned her hands over. Scars there too.

'Looks to me like this is from a ligature,' he said. 'It's healed, but it must have been there for a while to scar her like this.'

'So what killed her then?'

'I have to autopsy her, but she's so thin she could've starved to death. Anorexics look like this by the time I get to see them.'

The pathologist did obligatory fingernail scrapes before tucking the woman's arms back alongside her body. It was an illusion, Clare knew that, but it made the dead woman seem slightly less defenceless.

'Any signs of sexual assault?' asked Clare.

The pathologist swabbed her. Mouth, anus, vagina.

'No visible sign that she was raped,' he said. 'But she'd had a child. And she tore badly.'

'How recently?' asked Clare.

'It's completely healed,' said Mouton. 'So a couple of years or more.'

'I need something to work with,' said Clare. 'Time of death. Give me that, at least.'

'Well, decomposition has set in,' he said.

'No need to tell me that,' said Clare. 'I can smell.'

'OK,' said the pathologist. 'At least a week. Maybe a little more. Although I'd be surprised if she's been buried that long. Too little damage, too little insect predation.'

He turned the body over. There were livid scars across her back.

'These scars come from a sjambok,' he said. 'A whip. I see them on children usually. Women too, sometimes. Usually they're from farms.'

'That's what Anwar Jacobs said about the little girl we found yesterday. She was tethered to a tree on the bridle path not even a kilometre away.'

'That child was found alive,' said Mouton. 'This woman's been dead for at least a week. There's nothing more I can tell you until I get her back to the morgue.'

The wind whined in the pine trees as the mortuary attendants carried the corpse across the rough terrain. The few crime scene officers that had been mustered were searching the area, but they weren't going to find much and they knew it. Even though the weather had lifted, it had been raining too hard and for too long for them to find tracks.

Clare walked up the wooded slope. At the lip of a hollow, the wind caught her. It seemed to come straight off the pack ice around the white continent thousands of kilometres to the south.

She pushed her cold hands into her pockets – into the quill she had picked up and forgotten. She withdrew her hand and stared at it. A bead of blood was forming on her palm, yet the pain was a relief.

thirty-three

Clare was outside the Art Deco villa where her older sister lived, in the embrace of Table Mountain. She leaned her head on the steering wheel. All she wanted to do was sleep. A motorbike. Riedwaan, nosing onto the pavement. He took off his helmet, shaking the rain off his clothes.

He opened Clare's door for her, and they walked through Julia's fragrant garden towards the house. Clare's five-year-old niece, Beatrice, flew down the verandah steps.

'My bestest aunt,' she exclaimed.

'My bestest niece.' Clare caught the little girl in her arms; she'd grown taller, sturdier; a measure of how little Clare had seen her in the past six months.

Clare's twin, Constance, came up behind the child. She flung her arms around her sister.

'Happy birthday,' they said simultaneously. Clare touched her sister's short hair. It was feathered around her face where a latticework of pale scars disappeared into the grey that she, unlike her twin, didn't try to hide.

Scars on her temple, persistent reminders of the incident in the park all those years ago, the battering she'd endured while crawling away from the hands, the hammer, the unbuckled trousers. For eighteen years the two women had been tethered to that night. Both had been altered; both had survived.

'Happy birthday, Constance.'

Her twin released Clare from her embrace and smiled at Riedwaan.

'Glad you dragged her from that work of hers she uses as an excuse not to see us,' said Constance. 'You coming in?'

Clare and Riedwaan followed her up the steps. Inside, it was all food and warmth and flickering candlelight.

The momentary silence that fell as Clare and Riedwaan stepped into the room was swept aside by Julia's offers of champagne, her taking of scarves and jackets, her reassurances that it was fine that they were late, that dinner wasn't spoiled.

'Thanks, Julia.' Clare hugged her older sister, glad of the warm sanctuary of her home. The red wine glowed; the silver cutlery glinted on the table. The aroma of Karoo lamb, minted yoghurt sauce, roast potatoes, butternut, beetroot and orange salad set aside for the latecomers, Constance serving and Julia talking, weaving them together around her table. When they had finished eating, Clare helped Constance clear the table.

As Clare put the dishes into the sink, she glanced at a photograph of herself and her twin. The two of them sitting side by side on the swing at the bottom of the garden. Before it had all happened. While there had still been parents, a garden, a family frame for the two identical girls.

'That's us at the same age as Rosa Wagner,' said Clare.

'Who's she?'

'A girl, a cellist, whose disappearance left not a ripple for three weeks.'

'Are you all right, Clare?'

'No,' said Clare. 'I'm not.'

'Then stop,' said Constance. 'Do something else. I'm no longer the fragile one. One day you'll push yourself too far and then you'll break.'

Clare ran cold water into her hands and splashed her face.

'Let me pour you a glass of this.' Constance took a bottle of Chenin Blanc from the fridge. 'At least take the edge off things. You didn't have anything to drink with dinner. There are few problems that can't be solved, at least temporarily, with a glass of wine.'

'I didn't feel like wine.'

'Pregnancy's the only thing that ever put the women in this family off drinking,' said Constance. 'Look at Julia!'

'How did she manage to do it twice?' said Clare, off-guard.

Her sister's gaze cut straight through Clare's. It had always been like that. Constance, the one person who saw her for what she was, and even loved her for it.

'You're pregnant, aren't you?'

'It wasn't planned.'

'So what,' said Constance.

'It's still not planned.'

'You can't plan everything, Clare.'

'Oh? Why not?'

'With all your cleverness you are so stupid sometimes,' said Constance. 'You're thirty-six, time passes. What does Riedwaan say, anyway?'

Clare stacked some plates.

'You haven't told him about this, have you?' said Constance.

'No.' Clare stacked some more plates.

'You must.'

Laughter and music drifted into the silence between the two sisters.

'Clare, talk to Riedwaan, tell him. Then decide what you want to do together. Just this once, don't shut out the people who love you.'

'If I tell him, I'll have to have it,' said Clare. 'And I'm telling you, I cannot do it.'

'Clare, listen to me –'

'No, you listen to me.' Clare turned and faced Constance. 'It's a mistake. It's my mistake and only mine and I will fix it.'

'You're wrong this time,' said Constance. 'Wrong.'

Constance picked up the tray with the cake, the cake forks, and the gilt-edged plates that had been their mother's and were for special occasions only. She stalked off to the dining room. Clare followed. She took her place next to Riedwaan and turned her smile back on.

The birthday cake was homemade, with a lemon zest top. Everybody sang happy birthday and Constance blew out the candles; Clare cut the cake. She couldn't eat any of it. And then it was over, and they were outside on the verandah; below, the city lights stretched away towards Table Bay.

thirty-four

Fritz was in her usual place at the top of the stairs. Clare picked her up and buried her face in the soft ruff of fur around the cat's neck. With Fritz warm and purring in her arms, Clare went through to the kitchen. She caught a glimpse of her face staring at her from the cold, black window pane. She crossed the room and pulled the curtains closed. That got rid of her gaunt reflection, but there was nothing she could do to erase her thoughts of the empty house on Sylvan Estate. Or the forest.

'There's nothing you can do now. Come to bed. If you sleep, tomorrow you'll be able to think straight.'

Riedwaan shepherded her towards the bedroom. He laid her on the bed, and pulled her dress off her shoulders. He ran his fingertips across her collarbones and down her sides, the curve of her breasts, the dip of her waist, the hipbones that angled his hands towards hidden skin warm to his touch. He used his free hand to pull her under him.

She didn't turn away from him. She made herself lie still. There was the texture of his hands on her skin to think of, the roughness of his fingertips, the smoothness of his wrist against her breast. She wanted to lose herself, to erase the kaleidoscope of images that swirled through her head. The child, the woman in the hole in the mountain, the phone dangling from the wall.

But she couldn't, and her body did not go with his, but she knew his rhythm, knew him well enough to pretend. Riedwaan's breath was warm on her face. Her own was catching in her chest.

She couldn't.

She pushed him away.

'I can't do it,' she said.

'It helps sometimes to remember that you're alive,' said Riedwaan. 'If you don't learn to shut the work out, it takes your life from you.'

'I feel like it already has.' Clare traced the scorpion on his shoulder; the ink long since become part of him.

'I thought that if I found out why people killed children, it would be like lancing a wound,' she said. 'That I'd be healing someone, something. Me.'

Riedwaan turned onto his back and looked up at the ceiling patterned by the street light outside.

'I look at these children,' said Clare. 'And I feel like I've gone mad. That little girl on Friday morning. She was one too many.'

She was silent a while. Riedwaan turned to face her.

'When I saw her, I felt nothing. Nothing. My heart didn't even beat faster. It was like I was looking at a rag or a piece of old newspaper,' said Clare. 'Like she was just another piece of rubbish.'

He pulled her towards him.

'You feel far away, you know.'

'It's these cases.'

It was too dark for him to read her eyes.

'You and Constance in the kitchen, were you talking deep stuff?'

'Sister stuff,' said Clare.

'She seemed upset,' said Riedwaan. 'The way she was watching you.'

'She's used to running people's lives.'

'She loves you, Clare.'

'Ja.'

'So do I.'

'Ja.' There was a lump in Clare's throat. 'Thanks.'

'What were you going to tell me, earlier on, I mean?' asked Riedwaan.

'Oh, it can wait.'

'It's waited all day,' said Riedwaan. 'It's been waiting since I left.'

A siren wailed in the distance, and another close by. The night's lament.

'Riedwaan,' said Clare.

He lay on his back.

'I need to gather myself,' she said. 'I think I need to be alone.'

The long low sound of the foghorn penetrated the gloom.

It was one o'clock when Riedwaan let himself out. Clare didn't hear anger in the click of the front door closing. A moment later she heard his bike start. The sound filled the night, then faded into silence as he rode up towards the Bo-Kaap.

Clare folded her hands over her belly, trying unsuccessfully to read what her body was telling her. Fritz arced up onto the bed, turning once and settling herself before falling into a triumphant slumber.

Clare, though, was unable to sleep. The little girl occupied her mind: had someone hidden her, leaving her tied up where a Good Samaritan might find her? Or had she been tethered so that she'd find neither help nor comfort – and then die?

Anwar Jacobs's words ran through her head. He'd remarked on her lack of vitamin D, said that he didn't think her legs were able to hold her weight. That's how brittle her bones were. He had said that the child may have been starving all her life.

Or that she'd never seen the sunlight.

Clare watched the moving shadows on the ceiling.

She put thoughts of the watery cave inside her own body firmly from her mind. The storm had returned with satanic vengeance, driving the waves against the sea wall. It sounded as if the ocean would burst through. There was an allure in the possibility that someday it would, and the ocean would wash away the city, and Clare with it.

She turned over, and stared at the clock by her bedside.

Sunday
June 17

thirty-five

Riedwaan freewheeled down the cobbled streets of Bo-Kaap so as not to wake his neighbours. He unlocked his front door, the smell when he opened it reminding him that he had not been there for days. A heap of post lay on the floor – bills, junk mail, a large envelope with an estate agent's garish logo. He felt the weight of it in his hands. As heavy as money. He tossed it onto the low table in front of the dusty TV.

He listened to his messages. One from the hospice, telling him his mother was fading. One from his ex-wife. The settlement had been finalised. She sounded pleased. That meant he was fucked, financially. He deleted them both.

He opened the windows, letting air into the old house. He took out the rubbish and looked at the dishes in the sink. He made himself a cup of coffee – Nescafé was as barista as it got in Signal Street. He smoked a cigarette, abandoned the coffee. He was wired enough as it was.

He stripped off his clothes, dropping them to the floor. Leather jacket, shoes, shirt, jeans, underwear. The shower water was freezing – he'd forgotten to switch the geyser on – but it felt good. The icy water needled the fog out of his head. He dried off and pulled on a tracksuit.

It was already Sunday. A day off. But it stretched as empty as a Karoo road in front of him. He had to sleep, but he stopped at his daughter's empty bedroom. It had the same look as all the children's bedrooms he'd seen in the homes of many divorced fathers. The pink bunk bed he'd finally managed to assemble. The few drawings she'd brought home to him curling off the walls. Nothing else left behind.

Riedwaan lay down on the top bunk – where Yasmin had always slept. The blank day would come, Sunday the worst now that he had no one to take to the aquarium. He had no one to take, with a ball, to the beach. He had no one to lie on the floor with to read *Beauty and the Beast*. No one, ever since his enraged ex-wife had taken Yasmin with her to Canada. So many promises to Yasmin, to both of them. But his phone would ring and he'd be off on his bike to work. Leaving his wife to explain. Again. Until she got sick of it and packed up and left.

First he'd had a woman who'd left him because he was never around. Now he had a woman he suspected might leave him because she preferred to be alone.

The curtains hung askew and a sliver of moon was visible in a rent in the clouds. Riedwaan watched it slowly slide; he must have slept, because the next thing he was aware of was the muezzin calling. Fajr, the dawn prayer signalling the fading of the night. The wolf hour passing. Riedwaan listened to the chant threading through the silence blanketing the city. He got up, but not to pray.

He flicked on the TV. He stared at the morning news while he drank his coffee – black because the milk was sour, unsweetened because the sugar was finished. The tension on the mines in the north-west had exploded into warfare overnight – thirty casualties or more. He watched a looped clip of cellphone footage showing men wearing the same uniform as he did. Firing at fleeing men. When the dust cleared, Riedwaan saw bodies and some sticks and a knobkierie littering a dry piece of veld.

The massacre had knocked the story of a child abandoned in a

Cape forest from the lead. He watched the cameras pan across a wasteland filled with smoke, dust and teargas. Government lackeys and union officials talked nervously from behind a police cordon.

'Where the fuck are you?' he shouted at fat, absent ministers asleep in their king-size beds.

The anchor didn't answer, but she did cut to a government spokesman who sweated and threatened but could not, would not provide answers or assurances.

Riedwaan fingered the last cigarette in his pack – there was nothing for breakfast. But for the grace of Edgar Phiri, North West province is where he'd be right now. Using a government-issue rifle against men who wanted enough money to feed their families.

The Cape child was up next, but there was nothing new. Just yesterday's news being rehashed. Eager e.tv journalists calling the little girl Angel. Shallow, saccharine sentimentality. Like using air freshener to mask the stench of a corpse. Then the news team's helicopter flew in close, the aerial view shifting the perspective. The clearing was close to where Rosa Wagner had made her last phone call. And Hout Bay was threaded with paths – for walkers and horse riders – that no car could traverse. The camera panned across the valley, from Izamo Yethu and its squalor to the lush paddocks along the river, across the estates and then to the castle and Hangberg beyond. The presenter's patter was a potted tale of the rich and the poor and the fault lines of violence produced by proximity.

A sugar-coated pill for the viewers: 'Mr Milan Savić is one of many concerned citizens involved in community outreach programmes.' Riedwaan sat up at the mention of his name – Savić, king of the castle in Hout Bay, had recently moved to Cape Town, his reputation preceding him. And Chadley Wewers – just this side of Milan Savić's fence? Riedwaan mulled over this as he picked up the estate agent's envelope. Before he opened it he looked up, straight into his mother's eyes boring down at him from a family portrait taken just before his father died. Now, when he paid his guilt-wracked Sunday visits, she only occasionally knew who he was.

Riedwaan slit open the envelope and looked at the offer. Someone had taken their time in typing all those zeros. He counted them. They could make quite a few problems disappear.

thirty-six

When Clare awoke, heart pounding like the waves, her nightmare was distilling into adrenalin. She had dreamed that she was Rosa. Rosa, her naked back sliding down against a white wall. Her fingers stiff and uncooperative, searching for numbers on a dial. The adrenalin cancelled the morning sickness. For the first time in weeks, Clare was up and out of bed, eager for a run. Darkness was leaching from the sky. The swell was heavy against the rocks beyond the Promenade.

A lone runner on the Promenade, whom Clare used to pace herself. Five hundred metres, and she already felt better. Her heart beat rhythmically, and she imagined that other heartbeat inside her, claiming her, imagined its skull, rudimentary limbs, infinitely helpless. This accidental being would own her more completely than Constance had ever done. She ran on, past the lighthouse, memories surfacing, she and her twin in the cool shade of a gum tree long, long ago, the tang of eucalyptus, dusty leaves rustling on a hot Namaqua afternoon. Her twin sister's face the mirror of her own, lying so close that the babies touched – knees, bellies, noses. Clare had turned away, and in that moment, for the first time in her short life, had the sense that she was herself. Just her, alone, her own separate self. The memory had spurred her on, comforted her, as much as the memory of her twin warm against her back.

Emerging from a dyad, did she now want to be lost again – in the sentimental triad of mother, father, baby?

She touched the bollard at the end of the Promenade and turned back. She ran, her feet flying across the wet concrete. The endorphins took over, and she sank into the oblivion of her easy, practised stride.

Clare showered and made herself an espresso. She took it through to her study and opened her laptop. She checked her email; nothing new on Rosa. No plausible responses to the Missing Person alerts that had gone out on the social networks. One thing was for sure, no one had seen Rosa for the last three weeks, or if they had, they weren't saying.

The results of the Dog Unit's search. Interviews of neighbours, walkers, riders. Mountain Men reports of alarm activations and vagrants, the phone numbers and locations.

Zero, zero, zero.

The innocence of everyday life made sinister because she was looking at it, reading it for something more than the jumble of human activity under whose surface a lonely girl had slipped.

Her thoughts twinning the abandoned child with missing Rosa, her mind trying to stitch fragments from yesterday into some semblance of order. She was trained to recognise a pattern, a repeat. She sought something to anchor her thoughts as her mind worked along the well-worn grooves of parental cruelty and the depravity of strangers towards a child.

Clare opened the little girl's folder. It had had been forty-eight hours ago. It felt like a lifetime.

She picked up a photograph: the waxen face, the fold of the ears, crescent lashes on waxen cheeks, wild hair, the defined widow's peak.

Clare stuck the girl's picture onto the map of Hout Bay. A lepidopterist pinning a specimen, adding a wingless butterfly to her collection of damaged and dead children.

She was wary of seeing pattern where there was nothing but coincidence. That the child was so malnourished was not unusual, she knew that all too well; that there had been no claim was not unusual either. Still, that haunted Clare. No keening mother, no angry father, no outraged uncles, brothers, promising to hunt and kill the monster who had done this. They were nowhere. There was no one.

The deathly pallor of the skin, the bones too soft to keep the wasted little body upright. Who had done this, and how had it not been seen? Or had it? Was that why the little girl had been left to die? A cry for help, perhaps, rather than an act of cruelty?

She spread out the photographs of the girl, curled and stiff, her fingernails ripped and filthy. Alongside, photographs of the muddy path, the crude shelter in the trees. The place the perpetrator had chosen was so public. She flipped through the photographs until she found the one with the leather restraint. The child had been tethered. Gently. With so many other injuries, the thong securing her had caused no hurt.

Clare ferreted in that cusp between thought and feeling, trying to identify what it was that felt familiar even as it unsettled her so. She watched the waves. They were coming into focus, the grey ocean barred with a swell that rippled almost as far as the container ships on the horizon.

She turned back to the notes Anwar Jacobs had sent her; examined again her own from the bridle path. The child. Bruises everywhere. Her face gaunt, her body frail. On her hands and feet, the nails ripped as if she had tried to dig herself out from somewhere.

Yet she had been left, tethered, where someone would find her. Whoever left the child in the forest really did seem to want her to be found. Or had the person hidden her, planning to return?

Clare scrutinised the photographs of the little girl's wounds. Her little naked body on display, its details recorded – subjected to a final assault, that of officialdom.

She set out the photographs of the abrasion on the nape of the child's neck.

Clare angled the light, peering at it closely.

Letters of the alphabet.

A tattoo.

thirty-seven

The rain had stopped, but the rush of cold air took Clare's breath away when she got out of the car. The tanzanite pendant was like an icicle on her skin.

The security guard looked up from his Sunday newspaper. There was a picture of the place on Judas Peak where the little girl had been found. Clare in the background. His eyes flicked up at Clare's face. He waved her through, and Clare took the lift to the Intensive Care ward.

Anwar Jacobs looked up when she walked in.

'How long have you been on call, Anwar? You look exhausted.'

'Ever since you found that little girl on Friday,' he said. 'Yours was my first phone call today. Looks like you're bringing me a chink of light. Come and see her.'

Clare watched her for a moment, but the child did not stir in the darkened room. Her breathing was regular, her pulse steadier, the metronymic rhythm of the drip bringing her back from the brink.

'I wanted to check something,' said Clare to Anwar. 'Something I noticed in the photographs. May I?'

The doctor nodded and left the room.

Sitting on the bed beside the girl, Clare settled herself. Felt the warmth of the little body, the swell of the breathing, the calm that descends as a child hovers on the brink of sleep.

Untangling the tresses spread across the pillow, Clare worked her fingers along the girl's scalp. Feeling a twig stuck in the hair behind her ears, her fingertips eased it out, brushing against a ridged patch of skin at the nape of her neck. The child didn't wince. If it was a wound, it had healed.

The small curled-up body inched closer to her. Clare found her flashlight. Lifting the girl's hair, she ran her finger across the skin. The child buried her face in the pillow when Clare angled the light onto her neck.

An E and an S. She could not make out the rest.

The child's hand reached upwards. Clare rested her hand on it, their fingers entwining as she did so. With the index finger of her other hand, Clare read the scar.

'Esther.' Clare said the word.

The corners of the girl's mouth lifted, a ghost smile. Clare pulled the cover up to the child's chin and tucked her in securely.

She closed the door and went to look for Anwar. She found him in a ragged armchair in the storeroom that passed as a nap room for the doctors on duty. He was asleep, the tea beside him ice cold.

'Anwar.' Clare touched his shoulder.

His chin snapped up.

'What?'

'The child,' said Clare. 'The wound on her neck. It looks like a prison tattoo.'

'Show me.' He was on his feet.

'Done with a pin and a Bic,' said Clare, as they walked back to the ward.

'She must have screamed blue murder,' said Anwar. He opened the door. 'So many nerve endings at the nape of the neck.'

'Some children learn not to cry. Judging by the state of her, she is one of them,' said Clare. 'She mustn't be left alone. I need to know if she says anything more. She is the only key to her own puzzle.'

They were standing by the little girl's bed.

'A nurse aid will stay with her. She won't be alone,' said Anwar. The child's eyes opened as he spoke.

'Anwar, look,' said Clare. 'She's responding.'

He bent over the child, but she recoiled, thrashing her arms, oozing rehydration fluid and blood where the needle had pulled out of her arm. The look on her face was one of terror. She cowered, an animal cornered, her mouth open in an endless, silent scream.

'Do something,' said Clare, turning towards Anwar – but he had already retreated to the door.

'I can't go near her. She is terrified of me,' he said to Clare as a nurse brushed past him. 'It's because I am a man. I've had children react like this before. The worst cases. The voice, the smell, it triggers panic. I think she'll be fine with you. She tolerates the nurses. You stay with her.'

The blinds were closed and the room dark, apart from the faint green glow of machines emitting electronic chirps. The girl's eyes were on Clare. The absence of expression spoke of a terror too deep for a child's simple body language of fear and reproach. She kept utterly still. Her knees were drawn up under her chin, her spine – each vertebra a misshapen pearl – showed under the scarred skin.

Clare approached the child as one might an injured bird, knowing that her size, her proximity, might again trigger panic. That the child might injure herself, rip out the drip that had taken so long to re-insert into a barely visible vein.

The child did not move; she followed Clare with her eyes until she sat down.

Despite the child's stillness, Clare felt her shrink further, as if she had retreated even deeper into some locked chamber at the core of herself.

Anwar Jacobs closed the door, pitching the room into darkness once again. Clare's eyes adjusted to the dark. The little girl's eyes

175

were gleaming.

'I won't hurt you,' said Clare. Her voice was low, the voice of a mother speaking into darkness so that a child might anchor herself to the sound. After a long silence, Clare slowly got up to open the blind. She pulled the cord and barred light fell onto the floor. The child shut her eyes instantly, her fingertips pressed tightly to the lids. She whimpered. Pain and terror in equal measure.

'The light hurts you, doesn't it?' Clare closed the blinds. She sat beside her on the bed. The child seemed lost in the cold wastes of white sheets, pillows, blanket; alone, small, bereft.

She looked up at Clare with a mute appeal.

Clare put her hand on the child's cheek, her touch slow, soft. The girl did not flinch.

'Tell me please, who are you?'

Nothing. An impossible question, she knew. But she tried again in Afrikaans. Again, silence.

'My name's Clare,' she tried.

No response.

The sound of the rain was louder, drumming da da da da da da da.

The little girl lay still. A tentative hand, reaching for Clare's. She took it in her palm, sensing the child's yearning, her loneliness. Clare lay down on the bed beside her. Face to face. She rested a hand on the girl's stiff little back. She moved closer, so that the child was curled against her chest. Thus contained, the child burrowed closer. This she was familiar with, Clare realised. A familiarity with bodily proximity. Clare's body was a sanctuary, though she herself was a stranger.

She felt the child's warm exhalation on her skin.

'Who are you, little one?' Clare whispered.

The child's breath faint on her face.

She was trying to speak, Clare realised. She had tilted her head

176

so that she might breathe words into Clare's ear. Sounds so faint that Clare was not at first sure she had spoken. Then she placed a hand against Clare's throat, and Clare covered it in hers.

The child's breath was soft as a moth-wing as she tried, and failed, to utter a word. Tears pooled in her dark eyes, spilling over. Her narrow chest shook with silent sobs.

'Where's your mother gone?' Clare whispered, but there was no answer, just her hands moving under Clare's top, finding comfort as they settled on Clare's breasts. After some time the child's breath evened, her heartbeat regular at last.

Clare lay beside her until she sank into sleep. A real sleep, this time. She pulled the blanket over Esther's shoulder. Then she moved the nurse's gift of a teddy bear into her arms. It would do for the moment.

'You look like you could do with some breakfast,' said Anwar as she closed the door behind her.

'Love to, but not right now.'

Behind the bonhomie, desolation in his eyes. Clare knew why Anwar Jacobs avoided going home. One reckless taxi driver, one red light, his son dead.

'You still with Faizal?' he asked. Between them the memory of the night when he had sought solace in Clare, who had given so willingly.

'I am.'

'He's a lucky man.'

'I'm not sure he'd agree with you this morning,' said Clare.

She zipped up her jacket.

'I need to know when she's recovered enough for me to question her.'

'That's going to be a while,' he said. 'But she'll be OK.'

'Physically,' said Clare.

'That's as good as it gets in Cape Town,' said Anwar.

He walked with Clare to her car. Watched her drive off, the traffic lights bleeding green, orange, red in the rain. She drove through the empty Sunday morning streets towards the Salt River Mortuary.

thirty-eight

The hospice was a bilious green on the outside, but inside it was comforting, calm. Cream walls, white curtains. Riedwaan walked down the corridor and put the yellow chrysanthemums on a bedside table in his mother's sparse little room. He sat down beside her and took her hand.

'Wanie, my boy,' she said with a wan though welcoming smile. *'Jy't gekom.'*

'Ek't gekom, Ma.'

She looked at him; a flare of memory gleamed on a sea of forgetting.

'I dreamed you had a son, Wanie,' said Mrs Faizal. 'The nurse said I must wait, but my time is up.'

'Not yet, Ma.' Riedwaan held her hand tighter.

'What would you know, my boy?' she said, her old tartness sparking for a moment. 'You never knew nothing. I was thinking of a name for my grandson and I thought I must tell Wanie.'

'Not going to happen, Ma,' he said, opening the Peppermint Crisp he'd brought for her. She put out her tongue so that the chocolate could melt on it.

'Ishmael.' She fixed beady black eyes on her son. Saw the grey streaks in his black hair, the longing, quickly doused, in his eyes. 'That would be the name for him. If he was born.'

Aysha Faizal, seamstress, gossip, keeper of memories he'd long let go of. Custodian of traditions he'd long since abandoned and

179

forgotten.

He felt a twinge of longing: the comfort of prostration before an all-knowing paternal wisdom. Instead, he settled his mother's pillow so that she was more comfortable.

He hadn't visited her enough, his excuse being that because she was losing her memory she wouldn't remember if he had been there or not. That was true – she didn't. What was also true, and he knew this, was that she lived for the most part in an endless present, a stretch of time alleviated only by small pleasures. A bar of chocolate, a sliced banana, his presence at her bedside.

When she awoke she'd have no idea who he was or why he was there. He sat and listened to the rain. For him too, time had no meaning here. His phone rang, wrenching him from his stupor. He stepped into the corridor. Cabbage and urine, the smell of old age.

'Faizal.' It was Edgar Phiri. 'When can you get here?'

It was a relief to walk out into the rain and to hear the swish of his wipers on the empty Sunday highway.

The security guard raised the boom and waved Riedwaan through. The building was deserted, except for him and Phiri. The colonel was pacing – not a good sign – passing back and forth in front of the slatted blinds.

'Come in,' he barked, when Riedwaan knocked. The Sunday paper lay open on Phiri's conference table.

'Colonel,' said Riedwaan.

'Dirty politics has just been replaced with filthy politics. Jakes Cwele's just been promoted,' said Phiri, jabbing at the *Sunday Times*. 'Head of Special Operations.'

Riedwaan pulled the paper towards him. Cwele smiled up at him.

'First thing he's doing is going for the specialist units,' said

180

Phiri. 'Anything that might be outside of the politicians' control.'

'That's why he got the job.' Riedwaan scanned the report: the Gang Unit was outdated for policing modern-day South Africa. Expertise needs to be redeployed.

'Redeployed. That means cutting its balls off,' said Riedwaan.

'Not quite how I would have put it, Faizal,' said Phiri, with the ghost of smile. 'But yes, that's the effect. He's got it in for Section 28s too,' said Phiri. 'Page three, look there: Clare Hart. He's singled her out. Says it creates security problems having civilians looking at crimes against children. Of course, what's needed is the preservation of law and order and the protection of national key points. He says the minister is unhappy with her approach – focusing too much on cases that make TV news. Says things must change.'

'The minister is the president's poodle,' said Riedwaan, closing the page. 'What do you know about this, apart from what's in the paper?'

'An old connection called me,' said Phiri. 'Told me off the record that the Gang Unit's already been dissolved. They're just waiting for the right moment to take the political flack. I'll be offered a toothless job with a big salary at headquarters in Pretoria. And your transfer papers are on their way.'

'Transfer to where?' asked Riedwaan.

'Economic Stability Unit.'

'What the fuck is that?' asked Riedwaan.

'The new minister's name for the Riot Squad. Apparently he thinks that's all the country needs after those mineworkers were shot.'

'You're making this up,' said Riedwaan.

Phiri handed him an envelope.

It was littered with gleaming government seals and bold signatures. Riedwaan opened it, fought his way through the verbiage.

The Economic Stability Unit, some patriotic nonsense about serving the country's best interest, an order to be on a military plane on Monday morning. Tomorrow morning. A single night away. Riedwaan thought of Clare and the conversation they hadn't finished. The conversation they had not even begun.

'Fuck them, I'm not doing it,' he said.

'You don't have a choice,' said Phiri. 'All leave has been cancelled. The cabinet says subversive elements are involved in the strikes. All police force members who are called up are obliged to report. A state of emergency has been declared on the mines.'

'How is this suddenly an emergency?' asked Riedwaan. 'It's the same shit that's been happening for months, years. Service delivery protests and now miners on strike, miners killing each other, strikers getting shot by cops who get three weeks' training in public order. What's changed?'

'The emergency is the fall in share prices.' Phiri's jaw was clenched. 'That's a genuine emergency if you're a kept politician.'

'You tell them that?'

'I haven't,' said Phiri, 'I'm not speaking in my personal capacity. Not yet, anyway. The line from above is that the stability of the country is under threat, and the Economic Stability Unit is going to sort it out. There are no exceptions, Faizal. If you want your salary, if you want to keep your pension, you get on that plane on time.'

Riedwaan took out a cigarette.

'Milan Savić,' said Riedwaan. 'You know him?'

'Heard of him,' said Phiri. 'He puts money into township soccer on the Flats.'

'He owns an estate up where that girl went missing. Got security like a private army up there.'

'What are you thinking, Faizal?' asked Phiri.

'Why does he have Stavros the Greek skipper a tourist yacht that goes out beyond territorial waters where every South American ship slips past, its hold full of coke? I'm thinking why does Stavros hire a gangster who's there the night a beautiful girl goes missing. That's what I'm thinking.'

'I don't like it when you feel, Faizal,' said Phiri. 'And I like it even less when you think.'

Riedwaan looked at his boss; Phiri looked at the rain-lashed window.

'You asked for a connection,' said Riedwaan. 'I'm getting it.'

'Just be on that plane tomorrow, Faizal,' said Phiri. His body seemed to cave inside the carapace of his pressed uniform. 'There's nothing more I can do.'

'Why not, sir?' Riedwaan faced his boss – in all the years they'd worked together, this was the first time he didn't feel his back was safe.

'I can't say,' said Phiri. 'All I can tell you is that I got this order and I was told to relay the message to you and a couple of others.'

Riedwaan stood up and turned to the window. Cape Town lay below, spread like a dirty picnic blanket under the sodden sky.

'You going to take it, Faizal?' asked Phiri.

'I had a wife, I have a daughter. Means I've got maintenance to pay. I've been a cop since '94. I don't know how to be anything else,' said Riedwaan. 'So fuck knows.'

'Can I have one?'

'I never saw you smoke, Colonel,' said Riedwaan.

'I haven't since Mandela came out of prison.'

'The end of an era,' said Riedwaan. 'You keep the box; you're going to need it.'

As Riedwaan closed the door, he heard coughing.

thirty-nine

Piet Mouton was waiting at the door to the freezers.

'Come see her. Where's Faizal?' said Mouton. 'I thought you'd bring him. Save you the trouble of explaining things to him.'

'Very thoughtful of you, Piet,' said Clare. 'He called while I was on my way here. Says Phiri's told him he's been seconded to something called the Economic Stability Unit. He's heading up to Joburg.'

'You wouldn't be the first person to have thought you'd got rid of him and been wrong,' said Piet.

Clare shrugged.

'By the way, I had an email from Cwele this morning.'

'He's up early,' said Clare. 'Did he have a sudden attack of work ethic?'

'Oh, Cwele always does his work,' said Mouton. 'It's just his aims are different to yours.'

'So, what did he want?'

'The email said that Section 28 was being terminated and that all outstanding casework was to go via Cwele and his uniformed cops. You be careful, now,' said Mouton.

'They've told me nothing yet,' said Clare, stopping outside the women's change rooms. 'And until they do, this is my case.'

'I'm not arguing with you, Clare. I'm just warning you. Be careful.'

'Tell me what you know,' said Clare.

Mouton waited as Clare put on a white coat, rubber boots, a mask.

'This is what we know. She's white, about thirty-five. She was badly nourished, that you already know. Vitamin D deficiencies, bruises old and new, and those sjambok scars on her back.'

'So what killed her?' asked Clare.

Mouton held open the swing doors to the cutting room. Clare stepped into the sepulchral space. The roof vaulted, early-morning light filtering through tall windows. Rows of empty gurneys awaited Saturday night's bloody harvest.

'Did she starve to death?' Clare's stomach turning, a sweet stench discernible beneath the whiff of bleach.

'It's what I first thought,' said Piet Mouton, 'but our lady here was asphyxiated.'

The corpse lay on a table at the centre of the room, seeming to eavesdrop from under the white sheet.

'The eyes, the tiny lesions inside her lips. My guess is someone held a pillow over her face until she stopped kicking. The state she was in,' he said, pulling back the sheet, 'it wouldn't have taken very long.'

Clare wasn't hearing him. She was looking at the woman lying on her back, her unseeing eyes fixed on the vaulted ceiling. Her hair had been swept back from her pale face in preparation for the autopsy.

'Look at her face,' said Clare. 'A vee of black hair on the high wide forehead. A widow's peak.'

'Frames her face,' said Mouton. 'Gave it beauty when she was alive.'

'No, no,' said Clare. 'The little girl, she has the same thing.' Clare's heart raced. She had something now. She recognised it: that moment when anger distils into comprehension – or the beginnings, at least.

'A not uncommon feature,' said Mouton.

'Oh, come on, Piet,' said Clare. 'The injuries are so similar. Sjambok scars. The emaciation, the paleness. I want a DNA analysis on her and a comparison with Esther. And I want it today, please.'

'Maybe you're seeing what you want to see, Clare.'

'Do the DNA,' said Clare. 'Prove me wrong.'

'It's Sunday, Clare. The labs –'

'Tell them to open,' said Clare. 'Find a graduate student, I don't care. But I want those tests done right now.' She opened her bag and took out the photographs of Esther. 'Look at this, Piet, the hair, the shape of the face, the pallor. I'm dealing with something monstrous here. Tell them to get moving. Get them busy with their Petri dishes.'

'OK, Clare, calm down. I'll do it. We'll run it through the databases. If she's in there, we'll find her. I'll let you know as soon as it's done.'

'I'm sorry, Piet,' she said. 'There's a lot happening.'

'I understand, Clare. You carry a lot on your shoulders.'

'I've got a name, the child's name.'

'Well, that changes everything. Why didn't you say?'

'A tattoo on the nape of the little girl's neck,' said Clare. 'It says Esther.'

'My wife's name,' he smiled. 'The beautiful queen who used her influence to save the Israelites from persecution.'

'She seems to know all about persecution,' said Clare, looking down at the dead woman's face. 'This possibly explains why Esther's mother wasn't looking for her.'

'But it doesn't explain who she was with during the week her mother was dead. Find that person, you'll have all your answers, said Mouton. 'Any matches to the little girl's DNA?'

'I've logged it with the Missing Person's Records,' said Clare.

'There's nothing so far on the South African database, which as you know doesn't mean much. So few records are kept.'

'Run her through the European and US databases too, if you can,' said Mouton.

'As I said, there was nothing on the little girl.'

'But if this is the mother,' said Mouton, 'maybe you'll get a hit. Anyway, you'll be interested to know that she had some expensive dental work done. When she was an adolescent, I'd say, the kind of filling you don't see much of around here. No recent dental work, just signs of an untreated abscess that must have been agony.'

'OK, but I need to know who she is before I can use dental records – if it comes to that, of course,' said Clare. 'Anything else you can tell me about her?'

'Not much till we open her up,' said Mouton. 'But there's something else with her teeth that might help you.'

He lifted the woman's upper lip. The teeth gleamed against her gums. There was a slight gap between the two front teeth.

'See this?' Mouton pointed at the right-hand tooth, which had been worn away at an angle. 'It's from playing the flute. Not as a hobby. I'd say she was a professional musician.'

Sounds of people arriving; doors opening, exchanges about a wedding someone had attended, a snatch of a popular song.

The chill Clare felt had nothing to do with the refrigerated air of the autopsy room.

'A girl called Rosa Wagner went missing three weeks ago. A cellist.

Footsteps coming down the passage, the door opening, two men in scrubs. The cutting was about to start.

'It's happened before, Clare,' said Mouton. 'People being buried alive for years.'

'In Europe, yes. I know those cases,' said Clare. 'The girl in

187

Austria, locked in a cellar by her father for twenty-four years. That's three years short of Nelson Mandela's incarceration right here in the Cape. Hidden in plain sight.'

'Go look in my office,' said Mouton. 'I went to a conference on South African Paedocide.'

'Jesus,' said Clare. 'Only here would you need that word.'

'There's a DVD of the conference proceedings in my office,' he said. 'Take it with you, it may help. There was a case years ago. Two girls, buried alive in a hole in the ground. In the Hemel-en-Aarde Valley.'

forty

Clare opened Mouton's office door. There was a picture of his plump wife on the table, his sons next to her. A half-eaten bacon sandwich on the desk. The bookshelf was meticulously arranged. Clare ran her nail along the covers until she reached P. There it was, the DVD. She slotted it into her laptop.

The social worker on the monitor was dressed in the professional woman's uniform of tailored navy skirt and crisp white blouse. In even tones she presented her findings, fact by excruciating fact. The search, the symptoms, the treatment of the buried girls in the Hemel-en-Aarde Valley.

Heaven and Earth.

A memory flickered in Clare's consciousness. She scrolled through the findings until she came to the interview she was seeking. The girl was slender, her face a blank; she wore a blue top, and her hair was braided against her head. She looked directly at the camera, at Clare, said her name, said she was now nineteen. And then she told her story, one sentence running into the other:

I grew up here on this farm. I lived with my mother and my stepfather, until the Christmas Day when I was kidnapped. I was twelve. It was early on Monday morning. We were still sleeping. We heard a knock on the door. We got up and saw the man standing in the doorway with a mask over his face.

He left with me and we walked.

He held me tightly by my arm. I had to walk with him. We walked past the house, and my stepfather came outside. He said he had to bring me back. He said to my stepfather that my stepfather must go back inside or he'll hurt me. My stepfather turned around, and we left.

When we came to the reeds he said I must lie down and take off my pants. I did what he said. When he was finished we carried on walking.

When we came to the dirt road, he turned me with my back to the road so that the cars couldn't see me. When we came to a fence, he covered my eyes. I didn't ask him why. He held my arm and we walked. All I could feel was that we climbed over a fence and over a stump.

When he took the thing off my eyes, I saw I was in a bush. I saw a white house, that's all. There was a pear orchard, and he lived just below the pear orchard. There was a little girl there. She was two years old. I asked him about the girl's mother, and he said her mother is dead. He didn't talk much about the mother. When I asked about her, he got very angry.

We couldn't talk a lot. At one time, the little girl had two dolls. He brought them for her one day. She started to play and made a bit of a noise and he broke the dolls into pieces and threw them.

And the people. We heard people talking but we didn't know who it was. They walked above us but we didn't talk or shout. We were just quiet.

When the helicopters were flying over the bush and over the rivers, he said he wouldn't walk around so much any more. He said to me and the little one that we must be glad with what we have. It was a Saturday evening that he left. He didn't come back. The child asked where her father is, and I said, He's not here yet. We waited for him the whole time, we didn't go out. Then we heard people talking but we just kept quiet.

Then I heard one calling my name. They gave me a jacket and I tied it around my body and I came out.

We were together in one orphanage. Then, when I turned fifteen they sent me to another orphanage. And her too. But we didn't live together for long. I miss her a lot. I talk about her often.

Her voice was low and urgent; it was as if a pause, even drawing breath, might make her lose the thread, burying her again in silence. When the interview stopped and the camera cut to the social worker, Clare herself could at last breathe.

Esther had shown reasonable growth in infancy. Most likely because she'd been breast-fed for an extended time. Clare thought of the symptoms to be found in a child who has never seen the sun.

A child with smooth soles, feet that had never walked or run or climbed.

It was cold outside in the courtyard. She could see the silhouettes of Mouton and his two assistants bent over the pale body of the young woman, taking out her heart. As if a muscle might tell what she had endured.

The roses outside the mortuary's utilitarian brick looked neglected, the winter pruning abandoned half-way. A pair of secateurs lay on the grimy windowsill, and Clare picked them up.

She found the growth point on a straggling branch and cut back the dead wood. She moved down the serried ranks. Red ones, then white; red ones, then white. The rhythm of her movements, find the growth point, cut the dead wood, soothed her and stilled her nausea.

Maybe this was what she should do: erect a picket fence; prune roses. Stop worrying about women who were starved and beaten, and girls she couldn't find.

Clare's phone rang. She put down the secateurs and answered the call.

'Dr Hart?' A woman's voice, unfamiliar. 'You left a message about Rosa Wagner.'

'Who is this?' asked Clare.

'Melissa Patrick. I've been away,' the woman said. 'So I didn't get your message. I am Rosa Wagner's doctor.'

forty-one

The doctor's house was pretty, a thatched roof and cream-coloured walls. Clare followed the signs to the consulting rooms at the back. The lights were on, despite the wan sunlight that was breaking through the clouds.

'Dr Patrick?' she called, as she knocked on the glass door.

'You must be Clare,' said Melissa Patrick. She was dressed in expensive yoga clothes. She looked to be a fit, attractive forty, though Clare put her closer to fifty.

'You were asking about Rosa Wagner. You said it was very urgent. How did you find me?'

'I saw from the music college records that you're her doctor.'

'You got those out of Irina Petrova?'

'Is that a problem?' asked Clare.

'It's not the main problem. As I'm sure she told you, the director's way is the Bolshoi way,' said Dr Patrick. 'She's only interested in the perfection of performance. That overrides any other considerations – if she ever had any.'

'And there are other considerations?'

'Of course,' said Dr Patrick. 'Rosa is young, she's vulnerable, she's in a big city for the first time in her life. You can imagine.'

'Rosa's missing,' said Clare. 'The college tells me she withdrew on the twenty-fifth of May. That's three weeks ago, just after she'd visited you. Since then no one has seen her. No contact at all until she left a message with her grandfather early on Friday morning.

We found the place where she called from, but since then there's been no trace of her.'

'She didn't go home?'

No,' said Clare. 'Her grandfather assumed she was at the college. And the college – if they thought of her at all – assumed she'd returned home.'

'Oh my god,' said Melissa Patrick.

'Do you have any idea what was wrong, where she might have gone?' asked Clare.

'None,' said the doctor.

'How often did you see her?'

'A few times,' she said. 'Colds, flu, the usual. It was an excuse to talk to someone, I think.'

'What did she talk about?'

'Rosa needed a sanctuary,' she said. 'I suppose coming here was an attempt to find one, even if it was just for half an hour. She didn't have the easiest childhood, but she was devoted to her oupa, as she calls him. She's a solitary creature, but here she was lonely for the first time in her life. The way she survived was to keep things to herself and play her cello.'

'What did she come to see you about the last time?'

Dr Patrick pulled Rosa's file out of a drawer.

'It was in late May,' she said. 'I was concerned about her then, I clearly remember now. She seemed agitated in her quiet way.'

'Did she tell you what was wrong?'

'There was nothing physically wrong with her,' said Dr Patrick. 'But she seemed close to breaking point. I prescribed something to help her sleep – I assumed it was just end-of-semester nerves.'

'So, no history of depression? No suicide attempts?'

'Not that I know of. Why do you ask?'

'I'm trying to form a picture of her,' said Clare, 'but it's so opaque. She seems to have organised herself, her things, and then simply walked out of her life and vanished. Until that phone call. I'm trying to work out what happened, where she might have gone, and why. Did you have any reason to think she might be taking drugs?'

'No,' Dr Patrick replied. 'At least, she never gave me any reason to think so.'

'What about the other students, do they take drugs?'

'It's not unheard of,' said the doctor. 'They're young, they're gifted, they're unmoored from their families, their homes. They're driven. I have sent a couple to rehab.'

'Have you got a name you can give me, a lead?'

'I can't –'

'Look,' said Clare. 'I understand about confidentiality, but this girl has disappeared and I need to know where to start looking. If she's alive and it's to do with money, then maybe we can find where she is and help her.'

'Lily,' said the doctor. 'She's been to see me a couple of times. I tried to get her into rehab.'

'What for?'

'Cocaine,' she replied. 'But I don't think she was the source.'

'Who, then?'

'A friend of hers, a handsome boy. Wears dreadlocks.'

'Jonny Diamond?'

'That's it,' said Melissa. 'He wasn't my patient, but I think he was part of the problem. There were rumours of tik too. A couple of the others I saw mentioned things. When I told Irina Petrova she said she'd deal with it. It seems that the boy's father is a lawyer, that he made a donation to the school, so the enquiry never happened. I do know he stopped his studies rather suddenly, but he still hangs out there now and again. I've seen him on occasion, but whatever, he was taken off my books.'

'Was Rosa part of any of this?'

'I didn't see any signs,' said the doctor. 'She kept herself apart from things.'

'Was she bullied?'

Melissa Patrick considered the question. 'She wasn't like other teenagers.'

'How do you mean?'

'It's as if she had a layer of social skin missing,' said Dr Patrick. 'But it didn't matter, her strangeness. Her music, it's such a startling gift.'

'Did you discuss Rosa with Petrova or anyone else at the school?'

'I didn't,' said the doctor. 'Perhaps I should have. But it's only with you here and her gone that the fleeting observations I made when she was sitting where you now are, seem at all significant.'

Melissa Patrick tapped the file with her fingertips. 'I was remiss, but perhaps my own life swept me away. You know how it is, mid-life and marriages. Things fall apart somewhat.'

'Did Rosa mention a boyfriend?' asked Clare.

'No,' said the doctor. 'No contraception either. She lived with her oupa, the one I mentioned. Have you spoken to him?'

'He's the one who reported her missing,' said Clare.

'Of course,' said Dr Patrick. 'You said.'

She fell silent. A thrush called from the garden, the tranquil sound strangely discordant in the doctor's room.

'What did you think when Rosa didn't come back?' asked Clare.

'I didn't think of it until I got your message.' Dr Patrick scanned her notes. 'It's not in here.'

'What isn't?'

'There was something she asked me,' she said. 'We were walking across the lawn and she asked me about cancer. She was very precise. Castrate-resistant prostate cancer.'

196

'Did she say why?' asked Clare.

Melissa Patrick shook her head. 'She asked about the tests and how long the person would live if they had it. Apparently someone she knew had a father who was sick. Rosa was worried because the person didn't like talking about illness.'

'So what was it that bothered you?' asked Clare.

'The cancer she was asking about has a poor prognosis. She asked about the treatment,' she said. 'I told her that there's a new drug. It's called Xtandi. New and very expensive. The medical aids don't cover it yet, and the State system certainly doesn't.'

'And so?' Clare prompted.

'She asked me what it cost and I told her thousands. After that she left. I didn't see her again.'

'Can you tell me a bit more about the cancer?'

'It's virulent and the prognosis is poor. Without treatment you have just a couple of months, and that's it.'

forty-two

Churchhaven, an hour's drive up the bleak West Coast, was nothing more than a scatter of weather-worn houses on a lagoon. There was no electricity, no running water, no shop. The stark white church was flanked by a crowded graveyard where two spindly palm trees – one dead, one alive – stretched into the sky.

A biting wind and the melancholy cry of seabirds greeted Clare as she walked towards Alfred Wagner's house on the lee side of the church. An old mongrel staggered down the steps, her master behind her.

'You have news?' Terror and hope in equal measure, his bent shoulders squaring for whatever burden Clare might place on them.

'No, not yet,' she replied. 'I need to ask you some more questions.'

'Come in, please.'

Clare followed the old man into the kitchen. The room was warm, the Aga nearby, a pot of moer-koffie simmering. The rich smell aroused memories of early farm mornings, just her and her father awake, an uncertain sun spilling light over the Namaqua plain.

A Welsh dresser with stencilled enamel utensils; on one shelf an empty blister pack of pills, and two unopened packs. Clare picked one up. Xtandi – expensive, unaffordable to most, the doctor had implied.

'Excuse me, but are these yours, Mr Wagner?' asked Clare.

He nodded, acknowledgement of the disease somehow shameful to him.

'Cancer?' Clare gently enquired.

'The information's all there,' he said with a flick of his fingers.

Clare picked up the serving bowl. Beneath it a stack of papers. The yellow paper used by state hospitals. A note attached, Mr Wagner's name on it. Clare, the daughter of a doctor, deciphered the scrawl: *Sorry about the news. Let me know how I can help, if you have private coverage there might be options.*

'What has my illness got to do with Rosa, Dr Hart?'

'She knew about it,' said Clare. 'She asked her doctor about it.'

He looked stricken.

'Did you discuss it with her?'

'No, no. I came to get water,' he said. 'She didn't hear me, she was listening to her iPod. She was at the table. She was reading this. I didn't know what to say.'

He took the medical records from her.

'What is there to say about an old man being told he's going to die?' He tried to smile.

'And the next day she went back to Cape Town?'

He nodded.

'I thought it best that she go, that she live her life,' he said. 'I'm an old man. I'm dying. They said so. The treatment – well, I had a little money to spare. That bought me a few months of the drug. A few more months with her.'

'And after that?'

'I did not want to burden Rosa,' he said. 'She is all I have. I didn't want to weigh her down with my old man's troubles. Not now, when she was finding her path.'

'And you are all she has,' said Clare. 'She'd do anything to save you, I suppose?'

Wagner poured the coffee, a tremor in his hand as he passed her a cup.

'There was a storm. My son drowned, Rosa was only four. She was eight when her mother overdosed. I went to fetch her from the filthy place she was in. There had been some sordid incidents, the kind that sometimes happen with stepfathers.' The unforgotten fury flashed in his eyes. 'Rosa seemed broken, but she sealed it inside herself. What could I say to her, an old man to a little girl? That is when I taught her the cello. I taught her how to make music out of what she heard from the sea, the lagoon. I taught her that her music could be a sanctuary.' He paused, took a sip of his coffee.

'She ran away when I sent her to school, she simply vanished –'

'So this isn't the first time she's disappeared?'

'Some boys at the school held her down, looked up her skirt. She freed herself, she ran. She told me it was like "the man". That's her mother's boyfriend,' he said, tired eyes glinting again. 'She slept in the veld. Someone found her and brought her back. I said she could stay at my home, be at peace here, and that I would teach her. Things I'd learned at university – Latin, Greek, and music. Useless things that muffle the world. That kept her safe. Until Irina Petrova heard Rosa play in the church for a wedding. She insisted. She gave Rosa a place, enough money to live on. Said she had to come.'

From the lagoon, a gurgle, the tide coming in.

'You didn't want her to go?'

'I had to let her go, of course. But I realise now that I had equipped her for nothing.'

'Where might Rosa seek sanctuary if she was in trouble again?'

'Why would she be in trouble?' Mr Wagner stiffened.

Clare did not say that trouble might be their best hope for finding Rosa alive.

'Did she have any friends?' asked Clare. 'Someone she might go to? A place somewhere?'

Mr Wagner shook his head.

'Could you tell me what happened that weekend?'

'Rosa was here for two nights,' he said. 'She seemed restless, though she said nothing. She played her cello most of the time.'

'Did she see anyone?'

'Nobody,' he said. 'It was just the two of us.'

'And then?'

'Then she left. I asked if she didn't want to take her dog with her.' He attempted a smile. 'She said no. I took her to the bus. It was the last time I saw her. She phoned to let me know she had arrived safely.'

'How did she sound then?'

'Not quite herself, even though she said she was fine.'

'Drugs maybe?'

'I thought of that, of course,' he said. 'Given her history. But there were no signs. I did have this feeling.'

Clare waited for him to gather his thoughts.

'But I didn't ask her and she didn't tell me. That was not our way.'

'Rosa didn't see anyone while she was staying here, you've said. But did she perhaps speak to anyone on the phone?'

He closed his eyes. The light from the window shone through the old man's hair, gleaming on his skull. 'It's the pills. I forget things. The phone. Of course. I heard her whispering, it was something about music.'

The dog came inside, wet paw prints patterning the polished floor.

'She'd just come in, brought sand inside. It was on her feet, like when she was a child. She stopped talking when she saw me, but when I went out again she said it again, I heard the word music, I heard it clearly. Her voice,' he said. 'She was pleading.'

'Who was she talking to?' asked Clare.

'I don't know,' he said. 'But the number will be on the bill. It just came. Let me fetch it.'

'Can I have a look at her room too?' asked Clare.

'Come this way,' he said. 'It's off the stoep.'

The door was painted a cerulean blue. Inside, a narrow metal bedstead, a white bedspread with a grimy rag doll propped against the pillow. A paraffin lamp and a box of matches on the bedside table. A small table and a bookshelf. Old Penguin classics; another pile of children's books – Beatrix Potter, *The Hobbit*, the Narnia books.

'You can see her books,' he said, picking up *The Wind in the Willows*. 'The characters in them were her friends, this faraway England that she could close her eyes and imagine. You can take a look, my dear,' he said replacing the volume. 'I'll go and find that bill.'

Clare looked through drawers, under the mattress, flicked through the books.

Nothing.

She opened the faded blue curtains. The lagoon, the colour of pewter, lay before the house like a bolt of unfurled silk. An interregnum of silence before the tide turned, the water flowing back towards the Atlantic. For a moment it felt as if time had stood still. Flamingos called to each other, a melancholic pleading that carried across the expanse of water. Clare closed the door on Rosa's bedroom.

The petrol gauge flashed red when Clare was half-way back to Cape Town. She pulled over at the 1-Stop. The high that comes with caffeine on an empty stomach had long since passed, and so had the early-morning nausea. It was close to lunch time, but she ordered the breakfast: bacon, eggs, tomatoes, toast, coffee.

She phoned the number that Alfred Wagner had given her. It rang until a recorded voice said: 'Katarina is probably rehearsing so please to leave a message.'

Clare stared out at plastic bags caught on a fence: they writhed in the wind. She wondered why Katarina Kraft had lied to her.

forty-three

The music college was filled with Sunday-afternoon ennui; apart from sounds of a single cello, the building was silent. Clare went up the stairs to the rehearsal room at the end of the corridor.

'May I come in, Katarina?' Clare was already closing the door behind her. Katarina Kraft was seated at the window.

'Hello. Sorry, I have to practise,' she said. But she let her bow drop.

'You don't feel comfortable if you're not busy?' said Clare. 'You thinking about Rosa?'

'I've told you all I know.'

'Why did you lie about Rosa?' There was a metronome on the piano. Clare touched it, setting off a rhythmic tap-tap-tap. 'She phoned you from her grandfather's house two days before she disappeared.'

'Really?' Katarina closed the score in front of her. 'I must've missed that. My phone, it's weird sometimes.'

'And you phoned her back.'

Katarina avoided Clare's eyes.

'She said something to you about music, I've been told.' Clare leaned forward, her gaze unwavering. 'Look, I'm curious about some of the people Rosa knew. Places where she may have been paid to play.'

Katarina shifted a little; this time she didn't look away.

'Did Rosa ever talk about money?'

'All of us talk about money,' said Katarina. 'None of us have any, that's why.'

'Did she suddenly need money?'

'Dr Hart,' Katarina was pleading, 'we played together. We practised. She's not my best friend.'

Clare put her hand over the metronome. The silence was a relief.

'It's not my fault.'

'People keep on telling me that,' said Clare. She paused and softly asked, 'What happened, Katarina?'

'I don't know. You keep on asking me questions as if I'm hiding something.'

'Why did you lie to me?' asked Clare.

'Look, Dr Hart,' said Katarina. 'People make this mistake about Rosa. They think because she's so quiet she doesn't know anything, but it's not true. Rosa is quiet because she's listening. She's figuring out what other people don't see. She knows people, she knows how to make a plan out of nothing. She knows how to fix things. Wherever she's gone, she'll make a plan.'

Katarina plucked at the sleeves of her cardigan. A man's cardigan, leather patches at the elbow.

'You'd better tell me what you know, Katarina. I will find out eventually. So, either you help me or you don't. If you know something and you've said nothing, it will be your fault,' said Clare. 'Either you live with guilt – or with fear. It's up to you to decide. I can tell you one thing, though: fear passes. But guilt will be with you for the rest of your life.'

Katarina's eyes gleamed with tears.

'Rosa phoned and said she needed money, a lot of money, and she said she'd be coming back. She asked if I'd help her.'

'And you did help her, didn't you, Katarina? But how?'

Katarina's chin sank to her chest.

'So, what did you say to her?'

'Rosa is beautiful: her face, her body,' said Katarina. 'Not like me. So she had options.'

'What options, Katarina?'

'There's someone at the school. He, ah – he'd played with Rosa. He liked her. He always said he wanted to play with her again.'

'Jonny Diamond?'

Katarina's mouth a small, silent 'oh'.

'And you,' said Clare. 'You like him?'

She shrugged.

'You played with him?'

'I did,' she said, 'but I'm nothing on Rosa.'

'But you slept with him? And afterwards he stopped talking to you?'

Katarina looked away, her silence an answer.

'And Rosa?'

'She wouldn't,' said Katarina.

'So he made her life difficult?'

'Rosa didn't seem to care,' she said. 'And anyway, she wouldn't sleep with anyone. He told me that if I could get her to play with him again, he'd –' She glanced down, her neck turning pink.

'He'd what, Katarina?'

'He said he'd be pleased with me.'

A flush crept up her neck again.

'So what happened?'

'He kept his word. He was really nice to me.'

'That's all?'

She shook her head. 'He bought me these,' she held back her hair, revealing two jet beads dangling from her earlobes. 'He bought a bottle of wine too. We drank it together.'

'And then he slept with you again?'

'He hurt me.' Katarina's eyelids flickered. 'But what could I say? Afterwards he didn't kiss me, nothing. He just went to sleep. I didn't know what to do, so I got up and went to the bathroom. Then I heard his phone beep. I don't know, something made me look. It was from Lily. She wanted to know how it was, riding rodeo on the fat cow, asking when was she going to see the pictures.'

She was silent, and Clare didn't press her.

'I started looking then,' said Katarina. 'For other messages, for photographs. That's when I saw Rosa again.'

Clare's shoulder blades tensed.

'What did you see?'

'A video clip.' Katarina stared at her fingers twisting in her lap as if they were snakes. 'Not that clear, you know how those things are. But it was definitely her.'

'Katarina, what was going on in the clip?' Clare took the girl's chin and turned her face towards her. 'Tell me.'

'Someone was fucking her,' said Katarina. 'A lot of people were fucking her.'

'Who were they?' asked Clare.

'I couldn't see their faces,' she said. 'I didn't know them. Men. Big men.'

'How many?'

'I don't know,' she sobbed. 'They stood around her, their legs were like a forest. It was horrible.'

'Where can I find him?'

Katarina looked Clare in the eye, held her gaze.

'Jonny will be at Joplin's tonight.'

forty-four

Clare crossed the empty lot to the Section 28 offices. Not much overtime happening. The security guards were huddled inside their hut; a vagrant was sliding past the fence, hunting through the bins. It was a relief to be outside, away from Katarina Kraft. Clare felt dirty. Dirty and panicked that if Rosa Wagner was alive and she played this wrong, the girl would die.

The temperature inside the converted shipping containers was several degrees colder than outside. It was late Sunday afternoon and Ina Britz's desk was clear. She'd be finishing lunch at the Italian Club in Rugby with Paula, the diminutive personal trainer who had Ina Britz wrapped around her pinkie.

Clare had a sudden pang of longing – the company, the wine, the platters of melanzane parmigiana. Instead she stopped in front of her murder map and ran her fingers across its forest of pins. The vulnerable, most of them women and their children, caught in the crosshairs of poverty and rage.

She turned and walked to the window when she heard the bike. She leaned her head against the cool pane, watched as he approached.

Riedwaan walked in with two brown paper bags, handed her one, opened the other. Chips, fried fish and a Coke for him. For her, a salad, a piece of grilled fish.

Sorry about last night, is what she should have said right off, but the moment passed and he put the food down.

'You find something?' he asked.

'I had a chat with Rosa Wagner's friend, Katarina,' said Clare. 'Now she's saying she saw what sounds like a rape tape on her boyfriend's phone. Rosa is the star performer.'

'This girlfriend know who was in it?' he asked.

'She said she didn't recognise any of the men, but there'll be more tape somewhere. We'll find it, and then we'll find them,' said Clare.

'What's the boy's name?'

'Jonny Diamond,' said Clare. 'He was a student at the college for a while but didn't finish.'

'What happened?'

'Nothing I can pin down,' said Clare. 'Some rumours of drug dealing, but whatever it was he still hangs out there. He was with a girl called Lily at the concert I went to on Friday night.'

Riedwaan opened the bag and flaked his perfectly fried fish.

Clare sprinkled some vinegar over his chips.

'Take them,' he pushed the bag towards her. 'You're going to eat them anyway.'

Clare's phone rang. Tracy Darke from Records.

'Find anything?' asked Clare.

'Diamond has a conviction for assaulting a girl,' said Tracy. 'He was sixteen at the time. The girl was thirteen.'

'What did he do to her?' asked Clare, her appetite gone.

'He took her home, gave her his father's Johnny Walker Blue and filmed her having sex with some of his friends,' said Tracy. 'The judge said he was young and gifted, so he gave him community service.'

Clare spun round on her chair, looked at the map of the valley. 'I think we should pay Jonny Diamond a visit.'

forty-five

Joplin's was small, a speakeasy wedged into an old warehouse near the Yacht Club.

'How do you want to play this?' asked Riedwaan.

'I'll go in and talk to him,' said Clare. 'You go round the back. It's the only other exit.'

Clare walked up to the entrance. Perched on a stool at the front door was a man with a crew cut, his steroid-built muscle bulking up his black suit. He opened the door for Clare. Riedwaan watched it swing shut behind her.

The lighting inside Joplin's was dim. There was a double bass, a cello, violins, a singer's mike on the small stage, but no musicians. The restaurant was half full. Dim lights, a fireplace, red wine gleaming, plates of food coming from the kitchen.

A sign on the wall: *The food is good, the music better, the girls the best!* One of them, armed with a menu, came towards Clare.

'A table for one?' A silver cross dangled between her breasts.

'I'm looking for Jonny Diamond,' said Clare. 'Where'll I find him?'

'He's on a break,' she said. 'You want to wait at the bar?'

'No,' said Clare. 'Where will I find him?'

'Out the back,' she said. 'Near the rubbish bins.'

Clare went through the swing doors at the back. Beyond some tables out of reach of the rain, yachts were restless on the choppy water. A young man with a cigarette cupped between his hands had his back to her.

'Jonny Diamond,' said Clare. 'Allow me to introduce myself properly. I'm Dr Hart, Section 28.'

He turned towards her, his beautiful eyes as blank as the water in a quarry at night, an iPhone on a table in front of him.

'You again.'

'Where's Rosa, Jonny?'

'What are you talking about?' He ground his cigarette under his boot.

'Where is she?'

'Look, we played together a couple of times. That's all I know.'

'When was the last time, Jonny?'

'Two, three weeks ago, maybe,' He rubbed his temples, working his fingers into faux dreadlocks. 'Why you asking?'

'No one's seen her since,' said Clare.

Clare allowed the silence to stretch between them until he broke it.

'Maybe she just needed some time out.'

'And why would she have needed that?' said Clare.

Nina Simone's voice drifted in, advising against smoking in bed. Jonny Diamond lit another cigarette.

'The last time I saw her,' said Jonny, 'she played, she left. If something's happened to her, it's her own fucking fault.'

'D'you always blame the woman?' Clare leaned closer.

The acrid tang of adrenalin in the air. He was less good-looking close-up. Sallow skin, dark circles under his eyes, scarlet veins in the whites of his eyes.

'Make it easier for you to sleep at night?'

'I did nothing to her,' said Jonny. 'She did what she was asked to do. Then she left.'

His band mates had returned to their instruments, a cacophony of strings being tightened or loosened.

'I've got to get back to work.'

'Not till I'm done with you, Jonny,' said Clare. 'You keep saying she played, she left,' said Clare. 'I want to know where she went.'

'How the fuck should I know?' he said. 'I'm a musician, she's a musician. She played. She was paid.'

'What did she do it for, Jonny?'

'Money.' He sat back. 'Why else does anyone do anything? Rosa, me, you. What's the difference between us?'

'Tell me, why did you get Rosa to come here?'

'It's a gig, isn't it?'

'I heard nothing about her playing music, Jonny,' said Clare. Jonny Diamond reached for his phone, but she was quicker.

'That's my fucking property, you bitch,' he said.

'Glad to hear you confirm that,' said Clare. 'It's on this, I imagine?'

'She asked for it,' he said.

'Asked for *what*?' Menace in her tone.

He was up, eyes on Clare. Behind him was the alley. A row of bins, a gate. On the other side the marina, yachts jostling in the rough waters. He backed towards the exit.

'You going somewhere, Jonny boy?' Riedwaan had his arm around Diamond's neck.

'What the fuck do you and this bitch want from me?'

'Some answers.' Riedwaan pushed him back onto the chair.

'You're fucking with me,' said Diamond. 'You don't have a warrant, you can't take my stuff.'

'Report it,' said Clare. 'I'd like to see what the judge will say. Especially when we tell her what Katarina saw on your phone.'

'That jealous little cunt,' he spat.

'Hell hath no fury like a woman scorned,' said Clare. 'And you should've paid more attention in class.'

'I'll fucking kill her.' He tried to twist out of Riedwaan's grip.

'Threats to a woman,' said Riedwaan. 'Preventative detention for domestic violence; that's in the rule book, isn't it Clare?'

'If it isn't, it should be,' said Clare.

'You can't arrest me,' said Jonny Diamond. 'I haven't done anything. She signed. There was consent.'

'You know your stuff, Jonny,' said Clare. 'I'm impressed. But I'd be far more impressed if I could ask Rosa Wagner for her version of events.'

'I don't know where the fuck the little bitch is.' Circles of sweat stained his tight white shirt. 'Whatever's happened is fuck-all to do with me.'

Clare was scanning the archived video clips.

Diamond lunged; Riedwaan tightened his grip.

But she had found what she was looking for. She opened the first clip. The screen flickered to life. Rosa, picking up her cello. Her nails were clipped short, exposing the rosy tips of her fingers. Her red dress was pulled up high as she parted her thighs and drew the instrument towards her. Her chin pressed against the instrument. Her eyes downcast, lashes fringing her cheek, the back of her neck arched. Rosa closed her eyes, surrendering to the music that flowed from her deft hands. A man stepped into the frame. A livid scar on the back of his neck. Clare froze the frame for a moment, trying to place him. Her throat was tight with apprehension.

Rosa did not look up when he said her name. The man took the cello from her, holding it as tenderly as if it were an infant, then laying it to one side. Exposed, vulnerable, Rosa raised her eyes.

Clare opened the next clip.

Men circling a petite figure spread-eagled on the floor. The nausea that gripped Clare had nothing to do with the secret she carried. It had everything to do with the man whose hands scuttled over the girl's skin. The rhythmic thrusts over the girl's inert body nauseatingly familiar from the internet: the disposable body, dulled eyes resigned to a million hits when this was over.

It was Rosa – the girl pinned under the pumping buttocks, the muscular back. Her arms were splayed, her face slack, her body jerking like a kicked doll's. With the rough concrete floor and grey prison blanket, the scene was clearly staged. The camera did not show the faces of the pack of men waiting in a circle. Predators with their prey. Rosa's eyes were open throughout, her gaze seeming to turn inwards, as if trying to unhappen what was happening to her.

Clare stopped the clip, freezing it on an image that caught her eye. Electrical cords, snaking out of the shot.

'These Lolita tapes: are they the next big thing, Jonny? Or are they just a sideline?' Clare asked.

'It's not a fucking rape video. She signed, she got fucked sideways, she got her money. That's the deal. She's a fucking musician. How else is she going to make money?' His dark eyes were slits as he hissed, 'It's not what you think.'

'Explain to me,' said Clare.

'Business,' he said. 'It was all business. She knew what she'd get out of it.'

'Tell me what she got out of this.'

'She had her price,' he said. 'Fifteen thousand fucking rand.'

'Who paid the money?' asked Clare.

'I'm not at liberty to say.'

'You won't be at liberty until you do say,' said Clare.

'You're not listening to me, lady,' said Jonny Diamond. 'She wanted to do it.'

'With all these men?'

'It was the deal. She signed.'

'Show me.'

214

Silence.

'Jonny,' said Clare, her voice low. 'Tell me where she is. We'll find her. Things will look better for you that way.'

'She took her money – and she left.'

'So where is she now?' asked Clare.

'I wish I fucking knew,' said Jonny. 'If I knew I'd tell you. She's nothing to anyone, this little bitch.'

'Murder carries a life sentence,' said Clare. 'Even if that means only twenty-five years, the chance of you making it that long isn't very high. Pretty boys who like music don't last that long in prison.'

'But I keep telling you. She counted her money, she left.'

'Prove it.'

'That's not how it works,' said Jonny Diamond. 'I'm innocent until you prove it. You've got fuck-all on me.'

'The judge isn't going to like this tape,' said Clare. 'Especially not the lady judge that we'll request, and that we'll get when your bail application comes up.'

'Someone will have seen her,' he said. 'She left with it in cash. She had her cello with her. A girl with a cello is hard to miss.'

'Who're you covering for, Jonny?' asked Clare.

'We'll charge him,' said Riedwaan, yanking Diamond's collar as he turned to Clare. 'Leave him in the cells overnight to think about his options. I'm sure Chadley Wewers will be glad to discuss terms for Jonny to pay back what he owes for the tik he took on HP.'

'Fuck this shit, I don't know what you're talking about,' said Jonny.

'I checked Wewers's phone records,' said Riedwaan. 'Looks like you two are thick with one another.'

Jonny's fists bunched, and Riedwaan cuffed him.

'Fuck you both,' he shouted, ignoring the curious patrons at

215

the door.

'Jonny, just tell us who you're working for,' said Clare. 'You don't need to take the rap.' She scrolled through the clip again, found the frame where the man's neck was in focus.

'This man works up at the castle,' said Clare. 'He drove me through yesterday. This scar, there's no mistaking it. You want to sit in jail for him?'

He held her gaze for a moment, then his eyes dropped to his lap.

'Mr Savić wanted her. I took her up there,' he said, his swagger suddenly gone.

'Savić,' said Riedwaan.

'He's the money behind the music college. Behind the scholarships. This was his pound of flesh.'

'At least you know your Shakespeare,' said Clare.

'So I can go now?' asked Jonny Diamond. 'It wasn't me.'

'There's no rush. You can relax in the cells for a bit. We've got till Monday to decide,' said Riedwaan. 'You shout for the constable if there's anything else you remember.'

'All I did was see to the lighting and the sound,' he whined. Then he growled like the dog he was: 'It was Lily who set it up. She was meant to take her home. You should ask her where your precious Rosa is.'

forty-six

It was already dark when they drove out of the police station. Clare gulped in the cold air. The paperwork was done, and Jonny Diamond was sitting with his head in his hands, alone in a cell. Riedwaan hooted as an ambulance swerved in front, its lights bleeding red as it sped through the rain.

Clare dialled Alfred Wagner's number. He answered immediately.

'Hello, anything you need, Dr Hart?' the old man asked.

'I'm tracking Rosa's movements on the Friday night,' said Clare. 'The night she was last seen. We may have a sighting.'

'You mean someone saw Rosa?' The cadence of hope. 'Who was it that saw her?'

'She did a performance,' Clare offered him the euphemism – this was not the time for the truth. 'At a house in Hout Bay. It belongs to a man called Milan Savić – a big place, looks like a castle. Do you perhaps know Mr Savić?'

'I know the name,' said Wagner. 'I believe he's one of the benefactors at the college.'

'Did any money arrive for you?'

'No. Nothing. Why are you asking this, Dr Hart? What's it got to do with Rosa?'

'I can't say right now. I'll phone you as soon as I know more.' Clare ended the call.

'No money?' asked Riedwaan.

'Nothing.'

'We've got till tomorrow morning, when the court opens,' said Riedwaan. 'If there's no charges they'll be released. And I've got to catch that plane up to the mines, first thing.'

Clare ignored the tightening in her belly.

'That's tomorrow,' she said. 'Right now, though, I want to pay Lily a call. She's up at that castle Milan Savić bought.'

'Savić,' said Riedwaan. 'I saw him on TV, talking about security issues, shit like that.'

'The latest Hout Bay philanthropist,' said Clare. 'Patron of the arts too.'

'That's not where I know the name,' said Riedwaan. 'I've heard him linked to other things.'

'Here in Cape Town?'

'No,' he said. 'Stuff up in Joburg. Savić has kept under the radar here. I've got someone who can tell me. If he doesn't know anything about him, then Savić is clean.'

'A cop?' asked Clare.

'Ex,' said Riedwaan. 'We started off in Vice, then moved to Narcotics. We owe each other favours. You've met him. Cyril Jarvis. Ex-boxer, ex-cop, currently a personal security expert. One-time Joburg club scene expert too.'

The tarmac was slippery where the mud had washed off the mountainside. Riedwaan pulled over, dialled.

His eyes crinkled at the sound of the voice at the other end.

'Jarvis. Long time.' He put the call on speaker for Clare to listen.

'Faizal, fuck you,' said Jarvis.

'I feel the love,' said Riedwaan.

'You interrupted me, you motherfucker,' said Jarvis, 'and this is one I don't even have to pay for. Hey, this isn't on video link is it?'

'You naked, Jarvis?' asked Riedwaan. 'That's ugly, even without the pictures. There's a lady present.'

The sound of a door shutting and a brief silence.

'Clare, howzit, doll,' said Jarvis.

'Hello,' said Clare. 'D'you know someone called Milan Savić, he's got a big muscle boy?'

'Ugly fucker. Scarred neck?'

'That's the one,' said Clare.

'Name's Mikey. You want my advice?' said Cyril Jarvis. Traffic in the background.

'I'm obviously going to get it,' said Riedwaan. 'Whether I want it or not.'

'Whatever you do, keep it low key,' said Jarvis. 'I heard he bought a couple of your bosses.'

'Who told you that?'

'I hear things,' said Jarvis.

'You got names?'

'Cops are so cheap, Faizal. It's like shopping at Makro. You buy one, you get one free.'

'Give me a name,' said Riedwaan.

'I heard Cwele,' said Jarvis.

'Who's the free one?'

'Don't know,' said Jarvis.

'So tell me about Savić,' said Riedwaan. 'Down here he's clean, everyone seems to love him.'

'The oke worked Joburg, but quietly. Lots of cash, no flash, but things began to get hot up here,' said Jarvis. 'So he moved down to Cape Town. Said he'd retired. Wanted the views, the culture, the feeling of living in a European city. Complained Joburg was becoming like Lagos.'

'What else?'

'He did business up here a long time. Drugs mainly. Guns, women if he had to. But nothing stuck. No convictions, not even an arrest.'

'How'd he do it?'

'Started small, quickly moved away from the man who'd get caught. Made sure he just took the money and let everyone in between pay the price.'

'He must have connections then,' said Riedwaan.

'As high as they go, he had them. His father was from Yugoslavia – the bit that became Serbia. At the end of the war he was declared a war criminal. Never got as far as The Hague, though,' said Jarvis.

'OK. And how did Savić end up here?'

'His old man knew comrades who'd come back from exile. He put some lucrative arms deals together. Consolidated the friendships. Then sent his son out here to keep an eye on business.'

'Milan did well,' said Riedwaan. 'He lives in a castle now – like something out of a Bond movie.'

'Like father, like son. Except little Milan dropped the war part and went straight for criminal. He came out here in the early 90s. Went to the most expensive boarding school in Joburg – blazers, cricket, those stupid basher hats. Kids had a lot of money, so dealing coke was easy. He finds a niche, fills it. Goes for quality, not quantity. Anyways, what's the deal?'

'We're about to pay him a call,' said Clare.

'I hope he's not expecting you,' said Jarvis. 'What you want to talk to him about?'

'A missing girl and a very nasty bit of film,' said Clare. 'Upstairs, classical music. Downstairs, extreme porn. A set-up like a gang rape by soldiers. It's pretty slick, though.'

'I heard his father had a thing for that in Bosnia – Muslim women were his favourite,' said Jarvis. 'Sure sounds like Savić. Quality, not quantity. You could say that's his motto. And drugs – you

220

Capies are so flooded with cheap shit that it left the top end of the market open. All those movie stars in Clifton, the housewives in Camps Bay. They don't want tik. Wouldn't surprise me if he's back to dealing coke again.'

'I owe you, Cyril,' said Riedwaan.

'Watch your backs,' said Jarvis. 'Savić buys whoever he needs. The rest just disappear.'

Riedwaan turned the ignition on, the wipers fighting the rain. He turned up the driveway towards the castle. The turrets vanished behind the pines, reappearing only as they turned the last bend.

'If what Jarvis says is true,' said Riedwaan, 'and Cwele finds out, we're fucked.'

forty-seven

A security guard appeared when Clare stopped at the gate. She showed him her ID and he waved her through. She watched him in the rear-view mirror, his walkie-talkie held up to his mouth. There was sure to be a reception for them. The driveway snaked upwards, the looming castle foreshortened against the sky. Some cars stood in the gravel parking lot, one of them a red Mini Cooper. The custom-made number plate said *Lily*.

'We're in luck,' said Clare as they walked up the stairs. A butler opened the door. A flicker of suspicion suggested he'd read Riedwaan for a cop.

'Evening,' said Clare. 'We're here to see Lily. She's staying with Mr Savić.' She stepped adroitly past him.

'We'd like to see Mr Savić too,' said Riedwaan, following Clare into the cavernous reception area.

'Mr Savić is unavailable,' said the butler. 'Lily is not available either, she's about to perform.'

'Police,' said Riedwaan, ID in hand.

The click of heels on the stairs; Clare looked up to see Lily looking down. A flash of recognition.

Clare stepped around the butler, taking the stairs two at a time. Along a corridor, she glimpsed the young woman slipping behind a door.

'Lily,' said Clare as she opened the dressing room.

'Dr Hart.' Blotting her lipstick, Lily left a scarlet arabesque on the tissue. Her cool green eyes rested on Clare.

'Tell me how it works, Lily.' said Clare. 'Does Milan Savić fund the college?'

'Yes, he does. The galas for our donors, the private parties, the cruises. It works very well. The director asks no questions. What we do after, we've played is our own business.' She appraised herself in the mirror. 'We're performing again soon. Please excuse me so that I can prepare.'

'Where's Rosa?' asked Clare.

'I told you already. I don't know. She's not here, certainly.'

'But she's been here in the past, hasn't she?'

'Milan Savić said Rosa was beautiful, that she was just right,' said Lily.

Riedwaan appeared in the doorway and Lily glanced at him in the mirror. She raised an eyebrow, stood up and slipped off her costume. Her body was magnificent.

'This your boyfriend, Dr Hart?' she asked, sitting down again and rifling through a tray of makeup. Clare looked at Lily's fine, unfeeling face in the mirror. She was painting on a sweep of black eyeliner.

'Jonny Diamond is in custody,' said Clare. 'He filmed what was done to Rosa on his phone.'

Lily swung round.

'Nothing happened to Rosa. What she did was business. It's legal in this country, Dr Hart. The film industry is big business and this is art, if you like,' said Lily. 'She was well paid. What Rosa did, what all of us do, it's only difficult the first one, two, maybe three times. Then it's nothing. The same as playing music. Only more money. I don't see why you're hassled about it. Money is hard to make, in my experience. Rosa got her cash. What's the problem?'

Lily turned back to her face, her mouth a hard line.

223

'I saw the film,' said Clare. 'What happened to Rosa would unhinge most people.'

'I talked to her afterwards,' said Lily. 'I took her to the bath-room. She wouldn't speak. She wasn't bleeding or anything. She was fine. She had fifteen thousand rand in cash in her bag. How much finer can you get for an hour's work?'

'So you tried to speak to her?' asked Clare.

'I tried, yes,' said Lily. 'I said I'd give her a lift. Take her where she wanted to go. She just said no.'

'And after that?'

'Nothing, really,' said Lily, her face impassive. 'She just said I must open the side entrance and let her out. So I did. I watched her. She spoke to a man.'

'Who?' asked Clare.

'I don't know. This place is crawling with men.' She grimaced. 'He was one of the security guys.'

'Did she know him?'

'How must I know?' she said. 'It was too far away. He stopped her, they spoke, I think he pointed down the hill. Then he went back inside with one of the other guards and she walked down the road then turned the corner. She was gone.'

'Well, nobody has seen her since,' said Clare.

Lily half-shut her eyes and applied gold eye-shadow to her lids.

'There's nothing much for me at home either, Dr Hart,' said Lily. 'Maybe Rosa's the same.'

She took a short green dress off its hanger and stepped into it.

'I've got nothing to hide,' said Lily. 'Jonny's in shit because he shouldn't have been filming on that stupid phone of his,' said Lily. 'But here's the man to ask,' she said, looking at the figure reflected in the mirror. 'He's the one who wanted her to perform for him.'

'And you're the one who offered her up, Lily darling,' said Milan Savić. He smiled at Clare as he enveloped her hand in his smooth palms. Noticing Riedwaan, his eyes betrayed a flicker of curiosity.

'To what do I owe the honour of this visit?'

Lily stepped up to Savić, turning so that he could zip up her dress. 'She's here because that pretty little cellist you wanted so much to play with is gone, Milan.'

'Mr Savić,' said Clare. 'I've seen the film.'

'Jonny filmed the shoot,' Lily explained. 'Dr Hart's seen it.'

Savić's face was impassive.

'Pirate copies. It's going to kill art,' he said. 'Isn't Rosa perfection?'

'She's missing, Mr Savić,' said Clare. 'She's disappeared.'

'That has nothing to do with us,' said Savić. 'This is a dangerous country for women, we all know that.'

'Where is she, Mr Savić?' asked Clare.

'I have no idea,' said Savić. 'She was here, we made a film. I have not seen her in the flesh since. It was all perfectly above board. A business arrangement. You'd like to see, yes? Come to my office, Dr Hart, Captain. We can clear this up immediately.' Savić cupped Clare's elbow and shepherded her down the passage.

Riedwaan held back, watched them walk away.

'You're not following your girlfriend?' Lily said to Riedwaan, leaning against the window frame.

'You don't trust him?' asked Riedwaan.

'No woman should ever trust a rich man. A poor man – like you – he's going to be grateful: feed him a bit, fuck him a bit, and he's happy. He knows he's lucky. A rich man? Never. You don't make him happy? He buys a new one. You don't fuck him how he wants? He does it anyway. Because he's got money, and you have nothing.'

Her eyes glittered – tears or spite, it was hard to tell.

'You want to leave like Rosa did?' Riedwaan said. 'Just turn your back and leave everything behind and feel proud of yourself again?'

'Here I have everything I want – except pride. And what's that worth, anyway? Can you eat it? No. Can you smoke it? No. Sleep in it? Of course you can't.'

'But what about Rosa?'

Lily shrugged. 'What about her? Pretty girl, talented. She let them all fuck her, and she took the money. She didn't come back. Can you blame her? No.'

'Do you blame yourself for that?'

'I just arrange things, that's all.' Her voice trailed off. 'I warned him. I could see that with her things would go wrong. It broke her to do that stuff, but she did it anyway.'

'Why did she do it, then?'

'For one more year of an old man's life.'

Lily brushed past Riedwaan and walked down the corridor, her hair metallic in the light.

forty-eight

Milan Savić led Clare downstairs. Music suspended in the chill air – Bach, Clare guessed – voices, glasses clinking.

Savić ushered Clare in, the guard called Mikey closed the door. 'My study,' said Savić.

He poured a whiskey and soda for Clare. She left it untouched.

'There's a studio downstairs, but everything's locked now – Sunday, you know – and anyway that's not what you are here to see, I'm certain. You are looking for that lovely cellist.'

'Take a seat, Captain Faizal.' Savić looked up when the door opened. 'You're just in time. Help yourself. Water, cigarettes. Everything's there.'

Savić pointed the remote at the television screen. An image of Rosa Wagner appeared, her hair loose, her dress diaphanous, revealing the contours of her body. She was playing a solo. She seemed to escape the camera's hunger for her skin as she played. Her body, the bow, the exquisite instrument, were transformed into a single living entity. The music filled the room with a rich, compelling, yet infinitely melancholy sound.

'Beautiful, isn't it?'

Clare looked at Savić. He smiled at her.

'She is truly gifted,' he said. 'She is also beautiful and delicate, but this you have surely noticed,' said Savić, turning the music off. 'It's most unfortunate, these young men and their phone cameras.'

The ice in his eyes tempted Clare to release Jonny Diamond into his custody. 'Who is this for?' asked Clare.

'I trade in pleasure,' he said. Clare Hart and Milan Savić sat opposite each other. Riedwaan leaned against the wall, watching. The light etched shadows under Savić's eyes, his nose, his fleshy mouth.

'Whatever form it takes. Music. Art, food, wine, women. I provide it all,' he spread his hands, 'if it is legal, of course. Rosa was paid very well for this particular performance. If she chose to do extras, she would not be the first to do so. Nor would it be my responsibility – as an employer, you understand.'

Savić touched a wooden panel and it slid open. On a shelf, a stack of files precisely arranged. He ran his fingers along their spines and pulled one out.

'Here's her contract,' he said, turning to Clare so that she could read it. Rosalind Wagner's ID number, a bland description of her role. A date, a signature. 'There it is – signed and witnessed in triplicate.'

Clare skimmed through the legalese. 'Okay, but where's Rosa?' she said, putting it back on the table.

'Rosalind apparently decided to leave us, Dr Hart.' His eyes were glacial. 'I have told you this. Lily has told you this. She was even offered a lift – my personal driver. She refused –'

'Do you mean Mikey?' Clare cut in.

He leaned back in his chair, face composed, hands steady, though a tightening of the sensuous lips betrayed him.

'Remember this, Dr Hart: Rosa approached us. Of course, she knew I wanted to use her, and at first she refused. But then she needed money. She did what was required.'

'I've seen what was required,' said Clare.

'The world has Catholic tastes, Dr Hart,' his tone unctuous. 'Not always pleasing to everyone. Many of the girls who work for me – musicians, dancers – are beautiful. These are girls who know what they are trading; they give what they have in order to get where they want. Our mutual friend, Irina Petrova, she had many contacts in the orchestras and ballet schools of the old Soviet Union. She organised for them to come here, to the music college. Sometimes they perform here. It works well. Everybody wins.' He smiled, shrugged.

'But Rosa did not want to work in that way,' said Clare.

'That is precisely what made her so appealing, Dr Hart. And in the end, the real pleasure is in capitulation. The girl you want, coming to you, begging you for the thing she finds so repugnant. What one must find and tap into is the need – that is the true pleasure. Ah, it is a pleasure for the connoisseur.'

'You know that her grandfather is dying?' said Clare. 'That's the reason she did it.'

'What does it matter why?' A dismissive sweep of his hand. 'In the end she came to me and she gave herself over. The rest is unimportant.'

'She was here,' said Riedwaan stepping up to Savić. 'We've seen what you did with her, that's not so important – you have your contract, you've dealt with your conscience, such as it is. What is important, though, is the fact that no one has seen Rosa Wagner since she was here. How do you feel about explaining that to a magistrate?'

The guard cracked his knuckles, moved towards Riedwaan. He had a few centimetres and fifty kilograms on Riedwaan. He also had a gun in his hand.

'Mikey, Mikey, relax,' said Savić. 'The captain means no harm. This can all be resolved. We'll sit around a table and talk. This indiscretion will be resolved.'

There was a discreet knock on the door. The butler, and a man with sloping shoulders carrying a lawyer's briefcase in his hand.

'Ah, Henry,' said Savić. 'Let me introduce you: Dr Hart, Captain Faizal. We were just getting to know each other, weren't we?' Leaning over, he laid his hand on Clare's arm. 'I was just explaining the nature of our project.'

'Dr Hart, Captain Faizal,' said the lawyer. 'Do you have a warrant?'

'Come, come,' said Savić. 'There is no need for that. This was all a misunderstanding. Everything's in order, unless there's something wrong with the contracts you drew up, Henry?'

The lawyer's sagging shoulders shifted.

'Those contracts are watertight, Mr Savić. You know that.'

'Of course they are,' said Savić. 'It's resolved now, is it not, Clare?'

The use of her first name was an uninvited intimacy.

'Nothing is cleared up,' said Clare. 'I want to know where this girl is, and you have given me no answers at all.'

'Are you suggesting she's on my property? Where would I keep her?' Savić stretched his hands out. 'Please, look around. Be my guest. There are no secrets here.'

'Mr Savić, sir,' said the lawyer. 'There is no girl, there is no warrant, there is no need to speak further to this woman or her colleague. You'll be hearing from us, Dr Hart, Captain Faizal – and so will your superiors.'

'Lawyers,' said Savić with a wink. 'Never invite them to a party. They can't leave their work at home. But now I must return to my guests below. Mikey will show you around the castle – you can check for Rapunzels in the tower and Bluebeard's wives in the basement. And then we'll continue this conversation another time?'

Taking a sip of water from a gold-rimmed glass, Savić stood up.

'It's late. Mikey, the lady is tired. Will you show them around and then show them out?' He ushered the lawyer out, and followed him.

The three people left in the room eyed each other and went downstairs to the cellar. Clare and Riedwaan stood aside as Mikey unlocked a metal grille at the end of the steps. It was cold, the smell of damp not quite masked by the opulent arrangement of lilies on the reception desk. Beyond that, another door. A room full of consoles, couches with plush cushions, bottles of mineral water.

'The studio,' said Mikey. 'You can look, but there's nothing to see.' In one half of the room, stacks of lights, cables, tracks for cameras. On the other side, a set, props stacked neatly on a stripped bed. Bed sheets, all different colours – black, red and white – lay in a pile with laundry tags.

'No pretty cellists here, you can see. No bodies neither,' said Mikey. 'You'll have to find another tree to bark up.'

'They didn't shoot us,' said Clare, navigating the precipitous driveway.

'You don't need to if you own the police,' said Riedwaan. 'You can just pay to make inconvenient evidence go away.'

'Chadley Wewers, Jonny Diamond, Milan Savić, his lawyer. They all told us the same thing.' Clare pulled over, turned to Riedwaan. 'Maybe they aren't lying.'

Clare got out and looked down at the valley twinkling below.

'Rosa Wagner left the castle and walked this way, I'm sure.' The road ahead disappeared round a bend. 'She was terrified, she was humiliated. She first washed herself, trying to erase the pain and the shame. She was trying to keep her mind on the money – the time it would buy for her grandfather, for the two of them.'

Riedwaan came to stand beside her.

'She didn't go back to Handel House,' said Clare. She raised her eyes: through gashes in the cloud, the sky swarmed with stars. 'So where did she go?'

Riedwaan's lighter flared briefly, he inhaled deeply. He knew she needed time to think.

'What if I've followed the wrong lead? I'll have lost Rosa another thirty-six hours of her life,' Clare said.

'You've looked where the evidence led you,' said Riedwaan.

'I've failed her,' said Clare. 'Now what do I do?'

'We go home, we sleep, we look at it tomorrow.'

'There is no "we" tomorrow,' said Clare. 'You're leaving in the morning.'

He had no answer to that.

'I'll take you back to your bike,' said Clare. 'And we need to talk.'

Riedwaan killed his cigarette and flicked it down the slope.

forty-nine

Clare took the ocean road, the wind pummelling her car. She opened her window, welcoming the clean, cold air. She parked, went upstairs, and filled the cat's bowl. She turned the shower on as hot as she could bear it and scrubbed herself. It was only when she was done and when she looked at herself in the mirror that she realised she'd been crying.

'Stupid woman,' she said to her reflection. 'Tell him. Get it over with.'

She'd left telling him for so long now, there seemed no way of bringing it up casually, in a way that was natural. Simply to say: I'm pregnant and I'm going to have a termination – all in one easy sentence. As she'd practised so often, the words circling in her thoughts but fading to silence when it came to speaking them.

Tell him.

That's what she wanted, surely? The only option. Or not.

Riedwaan let himself into the flat. There was no sign of Clare, just Fritz outside the bathroom door, her tail flicking.

'Clare?' he knocked.

'No, please.' Her voice, muffled.

He opened the door. Fritz shot inside, rubbing her head against Clare's thighs. Crouched between the shower and the toilet, Clare sat, her arms wrapped around her legs. Riedwaan dropped down beside her.

'Are you sick?'

'I've made a mistake.'

'Tomorrow. Review everything again,' said Riedwaan. 'There'll be something. You'll find it.'

'It's not that.' She dropped her head onto her knees. 'I'm fucking pregnant.'

'Pregnant.' Riedwaan squatted beside her. 'Why didn't you tell me?'

'It's a total fuck-up.'

'It might be a fuck-up,' Riedwaan put his hand on her shoulder. 'But it's not a mistake. When did you find out?'

'I did the test yesterday,' she said.

'But you've known for longer.'

'Yes,' she said. 'I suppose I've known.'

'And you didn't trust me enough to tell me?' Anger, pleasure in his tone.

'It wasn't you I didn't trust.'

Fritz was butting her face against Clare's, demanding attention. She pushed the cat away.

'I can't do it. I can't have a baby, be a mother, clean up mashed food, all that shit.' Her face was streaked with tears. 'The amount of care – just for a cat; it feels like too much sometimes.'

'Clare,' said Riedwaan, smoothing her hair as she dry-heaved. 'It's a baby, not the end of the world.'

'For the first time in my life I don't know what to do,' said Clare. 'And it feels wrong. I feel wrong. I'm not a mother.'

Riedwaan put his hand on her back.

'What do you want?' he asked.

'For this not to be happening,' she said. 'It's not like I wanted it. It's just that my pill didn't work. Like I say, it's a mistake.'

'You can't control everything, Clare,' said Riedwaan, standing up, pulling her up too.

'That's what I'm afraid of,' said Clare.

'You just need time to get used to it,' said Riedwaan. 'We'll get used to it.'

'I don't want to get used to it,' said Clare, not looking at him. 'I want to fix it and I can't think about it. Not now. I've got to find Rosa Wagner. I've got to find out who did that to little Esther. There's no one else looking out for either of them.'

'Clare, that child is alive. She's recovering.' Riedwaan took her by the shoulders. 'Talk to me. You can't run from this.'

'I'm sorry, Riedwaan.' She disentangled herself, as she always did.

'You got a whiskey?' he asked. 'We both need one.'

'Jack Daniels, it's in the fridge.' Riedwaan put his hand on the small of her back, guided her into the kitchen.

'That's all there is in here,' said Riedwaan, opening the door. 'Whiskey and mayonnaise.'

'It's been worse,' said Clare.

'Riedwaan poured a splash for her, a stiffer measure for himself.

'Drink it,' he said. 'It's medicinal.'

The fire in her belly felt good as she took a sip.

She turned to Riedwaan and said, 'Look at us, neither of us can hold a relationship together.'

'I'm here,' he said. 'I'm not going anywhere.'

'Apart from Joburg in the morning.'

'I'll be back.'

'You need to think first,' she said.

'For me there's nothing to think,' he said. 'It's you who's the thinker.'

'Not now. I have to sleep.' Fatigue had plagued her almost as long as the morning sickness. 'Will you hold me?'

He pulled Clare close, led her to the bed, drew the duvet over them both. For a moment, fragmented images of Rosa and then little Esther flitted through her consciousness; they merged, whirling past her mind's eye as her breathing evened.

Riedwaan lay and listened as the wind dropped. Apart from the sound of the sea, the city was silent.

His phone vibrated, Phiri's name on the screen. Riedwaan eased himself out of bed and closed the door behind him. Clare shifted in her sleep, her body taking possession of the bed.

'Colonel,' said Riedwaan, stepping onto the balcony.

'Cwele's like a heat-seeking missile,' said Phiri. 'And you're the target.'

'I thought there'd be trouble.'

'This is more than trouble, Faizal. Let me hear your version of events.'

'Clare Hart and I were up at Milan Savić's castle this evening,' said Riedwaan. 'It's where Rosa Wagner, the girl Clare's looking for, was last seen.'

'Did you find her?' asked Phiri.

'No,' said Riedwaan.

'OK, so tell me what you did find.'

'Places downstairs for making porn,' said Riedwaan. 'Places upstairs for gentlemen's entertainment.'

'I take it you had a warrant?'

'No, sir,' said Riedwaan. 'No warrant.'

Silence.

Riedwaan felt for his cigarettes, but he'd left them in the kitchen.

'I spoke to Cyril Jarvis, my Joburg connection,' said Riedwaan. 'He says Savić moved out of Joburg, went off the radar, but there's no reason to believe he's stopped business.'

'You have evidence, I presume?'

'Nearly,' said Riedwaan.

236

'What is Savić meant to be up to, exactly?'

'Dealing,' said Riedwaan. 'Drugs, women, extreme porn, that's my theory.'

'What's the rest of your theory?'

'Jakes Cwele's in Milan Savić's pocket,' said Riedwaan. 'Cwele gets moved to Cape Town and promoted. He gets oversight of the Gang Unit and Section 28. This goes higher up than just another cop taking some small change.'

'How high up?'

'I'd say right to the top,' said Riedwaan. 'Wouldn't be the first time, we both know that.'

'You got proof of that, Faizal?'

'I just know it,' said Riedwaan.

Phiri was silent for so long that Riedwaan thought the connection had dropped.

'You get on that plane tomorrow morning. Got to get you out of town.'

'Sir,' said Riedwaan. 'How often have I been wrong?'

Phiri ignored him and said, 'I'll look into it.'

'And Clare?' asked Riedwaan.

'Clare, I'm afraid, will have to take care of herself,' said Phiri. 'Cwele's cancelling her contract.'

'Section 28 is her baby,' said Riedwaan. 'She's not going to let her cases go, she's not going to let Cwele bury the truth.'

'She doesn't have a choice,' said Phiri.

'With all due respect, sir, I don't think you know Clare like I do.'

Through the window Riedwaan could see Clare sleeping; she looked so young, her blonde hair spread out on the pillow. She turned onto her side, curling herself around her stomach. The duvet gaped, revealing softer contours than her clothes suggested.

Monday
June 18

fifty

A streak of light dirtied the sky as the first calls of the sea birds drifted up and Clare's phone rang.

'Leave it, Clare,' said Riedwaan. 'Finish talking to me.'

Disentangling herself from his embrace, she answered it.

'Piet,' she said, sitting up. 'What?'

'Sorry to phone so early, Doc,' said the pathologist.

'I'm awake,' said Clare.

'The woman we exhumed yesterday matches the DNA of Esther, that little girl you found on Saturday.'

'What sort of a match?'

'Mother,' said Mouton. 'Daughter.'

'But the woman died at least a week ago.' Clare was already up and opening her cupboard, pulling out clothes.

'That solves why Esther's mother wasn't looking for her,' said Mouton. 'So, the question is, who was Esther with? Find that person, you have all your answers, Doc.'

Clare ended the call, pushed the duvet aside and sat next to Riedwaan.

'The woman in the woods is Esther's mother.'

'Clare,' Riedwaan took her by the shoulders. 'That woman's dead. For ever. The child is alive, she's recovering. It's happened, it's past.' He put a hand on her belly. 'Talk to me about what's between us, about what's going to happen. You can't run from this.' The flicker of new life so close, consoled by his warm palm.

All Clare desired in that moment was to lean in and relinquish herself, but she pulled back.

'I'm not running,' she said. 'I just have something to finish. When it's over I'll be able to think.'

'Clare, you've just told me you're going to have a baby. Our baby,' said Riedwaan. 'This is our lives, our future.'

'We'll talk,' she said. 'I said we would. Just not now.'

'What will we talk about?'

'I'll tell you what I've decided.'

'I've got to catch a plane to Joburg now –'

She was out of his grasp, at the front door, keys and bag in hand.

'Clare, this – a child – it's something we decide together.'

'I know,' she said, her head down, pulling on her boots. 'Just not now. Anyway, it's not a child, not yet. It's just a mistake – a few cells growing, blame my faulty pill.'

'You're not going to end it while I'm away?'

She stopped, her back stiff.

'Clare, answer me,' he said. 'This isn't only about you.'

'For now it is, Riedwaan,' she said. 'You'll let yourself out, then?'

The door shut, and she was gone, striding towards her car. Then she turned at the lights and disappeared into the reluctant morning.

fifty-one

There were few cars about, and in Salt River a rag-and-bone man had stopped his cart at the entrance to the morgue. He was negotiating with two bergies trying to sell him a shopping trolley of scavenged street signs. *Botha Avenue*, one of them, *Rhodes Drive* another. Clare leaned on her hooter.

'Sorry, my lady.' The scrap merchant raised his whip. The donkey jerked forward as the sjambok came down. The animal trotted past, nothing but forgiveness in his eyes.

Piet Mouton was in his office. The smell of the bacon sandwich on his desk was overwhelming.

'Doc,' he said, when she walked in. 'You're as white as a sheet. You not feeling so good?'

'I've felt better,' said Clare, taking the visitor's seat. 'It's just the bacon.'

'First it's bodies, now it's bacon,' said Mouton, 'We're never going to make a mortician out of you.'

He handed Clare the report on the DNA match.

'We ran it through the databases. There's a name there. Read that. I'll get someone to bring you a cup of tea. I've got to get started. Looks like it was a busy weekend.'

'Thanks, Piet,' said Clare. 'And if you've got some tea, that'd be great.'

Clare opened the report on the DNA match. The coding was clear. Mother and daughter. The algorithms of the corpse's genetic makeup had churned through Clare's database, producing a name and a nationality: Esther Previn, German.

Born and bred in Berlin, the dead woman had been reported missing a decade earlier. The last time she was seen alive was at Daddy Cool, a youth hostel wedged between a row of clubs on Long Street. In an interview, the hostel manager had said she was on her way to India. That was it – apart from the name of a lawyer, Jens Bekker, and a Berlin phone number.

'From the professor.' A mortuary attendant in white overalls and white rubber boots handed Clare a mug of tea.

'You're a saint,' she said. 'Thanks.'

'Prof says to just close the door when you done.'

'Sure,' said Clare, picking up her phone.

A woman's voice answered. Clare gave her name and asked to speak to Bekker.

'In connection with what matter is this?' the secretary asked after a brief delay. 'He is busy.'

'Tell him it's about Esther Previn,' said Clare. 'She went missing in South Africa ten years ago. We have found her body. Tell him this and he'll want to talk to me.'

A man's voice, incredulous.

'Dr Hart? This is Bekker. You are telephoning on behalf of Fraulein Previn?'

'No,' said Clare. 'We've found a body, and we've matched it to the Interpol missing persons' data bank.'

'This is not possible,' he said. 'It must be someone else.'

'There's something I need to know – did Esther Previn play the flute?'

'Yes, yes,' said the lawyer. 'She was with the Berlin Philarmonic, how do you know this?'

'A DNA test. There is no doubt it's her. Please tell me what you know about Esther Previn.'

244

'The fraulein had a breakdown and went travelling. She left Germany, went to South Africa. She played in the Cape Philharmonic. That is all the family knew. People thought she might be in India. She had written once to say she was going, but they weren't sure.'

'So, no one looked for her?'

'She was not a child, remember that,' said the lawyer. 'She was a woman of twenty-five at the time.'

'Why was she declared dead?' asked Clare.

'Her things were found by the sea – her flute, everything. They think she went into the sea and drowned.'

'Where was this?'

'On a beach near a forest – I think it was a forest, along a coastal route. You know the place?'

'Sounds like Nature's Valley,' said Clare.

'*Jawohl*. That is the place,' he said. 'No body was ever found, but I understand there are sharks there.'

'Did the parents not follow up on this?'

'Both of them had passed away,' said the lawyer. 'There was a sister, but she and Esther were estranged. The parents left a large estate. The details had to be resolved. But she was declared dead many years ago – I suppose you have found the skeleton?'

'What we found was a body.'

The lawyer was silent.

'Well, as long as she remains deceased,' said the lawyer. 'It would make for a lot of legal difficulties if she were alive.'

'She's only been dead a week,' said Clare. 'And nobody has looked for her.'

'But the important fact is, Esther Previn is dead,' said the lawyer.

'Yes, she's dead,' said Clare. 'She also suffered a great deal before she died, that's for sure. But there's also a child, a little girl of three or four – we aren't sure yet, as she can't tell us. We've established that she is Esther Previn's daughter. The little girl is very much alive.'

There was a long silence.

'Now that does complicate matters,' said lawyer. 'Where has the child been all this time?'

'In a place where neither of them seems to have seen the light of day for many years – the child perhaps never,' said Clare. 'But we have no idea yet where they were held, or by whom. All I can tell you is that the child – whose name is Esther – will need a great deal of care. So I would ask you to find someone who will claim her.'

'Of course. This is most unfortunate.'

Clare's phone vibrated on the desk.

'I have another call coming in. Please excuse me. I hope to hear from you soon.'

'Is that Dr Clare Hart?' A voice all mink and manure. 'This is Cassie's dressage teacher. She gave me your private number.' A claw in the voice. 'The hotline is hopeless. It's like phoning an Indian call centre. It probably is an Indian call centre.'

'Cassie?'

'It's been terrible for her, I can tell you. Her poor horse, he pulled a tendon when he bolted and it's touch and go whether they'll be ready for the national trials in July.'

'Has Cassie told you something?'

'No, no,' said the woman. 'Cassie's fine, but I've been so distracted with her that I didn't pay attention to the other poor girl. This cellist.'

'What about her?'

'I saw her picture in the paper,' said the woman. 'And I said to Cassie, I've seen her. I'm sure it was her. So she said that I had to phone you at once, it was your case too.'

Clare closed the folder on Esther Previn and her daughter.

246

'Where did you see her? When?' she asked.

'At that garage with the KwikShop. It was the Friday. Must've been the twenty-fifth of May.'

'You're sure of the date?'

'Absolutely,' said the woman. 'One of my horses had colic. I was up all night leading him. They die if you don't, you know, the intestines twist and they keel over. Too ghastly.'

'Do you know what time you saw her?'

'It was late,' said the woman, 'One, maybe two in the morning.'

'And it was definitely Rosa Wagner? Long black hair, slim, brown skin.'

'Oh, absolutely,' said the woman. 'She was wearing a red velvet dress and carrying a cello case. It got stuck in the door. I helped her get it out.'

'Did you speak to her?'

'She just said thank you and went round the back to where the loos are.'

'And you didn't see her again?'

'No,' she said. 'Which is funny, because I walked my horse up and down that road all bloody night. It was my daughter's wedding the next day and, as you can imagine, I looked a wreck. Jemima was furious.'

'Did you see any cars that night?' Clare asked. 'Round the time you saw Rosa?'

'Not a thing,' said the woman, 'until that absurdly expensive vet of mine arrived and did sweet blow all and charged me anyway. So sorry that I don't have more to tell you, Clare.'

'That's plenty,' said Clare. 'Thanks. Send my love to Cassie. She's a fine girl.'

Clare closed the file on the two Esthers. The mother was dead, and the daughter was alive and safe with Anwar Jacobs. She felt a surge of hope that Rosa was alive and that she was going to find her.

fifty-two

Clare swiped her security card and the door to the Section 28 offices opened. She put her coffee and croissant on the desk and opened Mouton's report on the DNA match. Mother and daughter. The coding was clear. Esther Previn and the little girl slowly coming back to life in Anwar Jacobs's orderly hospital ward. Clare made her notes, put the file away, and opened the folder with Rosa Wagner's name on it.

She took it over to the map on the wall, marked a place in red. The same place Chadley Wewers had been on Friday night, where he had bought cheap party food en route to the dismal cottage in Sylvan Estate. She stepped back from the map, her finger on her cheek. She dialled and waited for the officer on duty to pick up.

'SAPS.' Exhaustion in the woman's voice.

'Chadley Wewers,' said Clare. 'I want to ask him a couple more questions. Don't let him go yet.'

'He's long gone, Doc,' said the officer. 'Him and Jonny Diamond, that other low-life you brought in. Both of them released last night. I thought the order came from you.'

'Not mine,' said Clare. She turned round and glanced at the Hout Bay Police station on the other side of the muddy lot. 'And not Captain Faizal's either.'

'We were told to let them go,' said the officer. 'They've both lodged a complaint against you.'

'What for?'

'Wrongful arrest. I'm sorry, Doc, but we were just following orders.'

The vehicle turning into the parking lot caught Clare's attention. Her heart gave an annoyingly anxious jump. A shiny black Pajero, not Ina Britz's old Jeep that she'd been looking out for.

'Jakes Cwele,' she said to the officer at the other end of the phone.

'I think so.' The officer's voice muffled, as if she didn't want to be heard. 'There's even more rumours than usual. Someone said Major Britz is going to be arrested.'

'Dr Hart.'

Clare turned to see Cwele filling the doorway.

'Can I come in?'

Without waiting for her response, Cwele sauntered into her office. She stepped sideways, putting the desk between them.

'You released two suspects,' said Clare. 'Why did you do this?'

'Police business is no concern of yours, Dr Hart,' he said, leaning his torso across the desk. 'And Captain Faizal is on his way to join the Economic Stability Unit. There are enough stray bullets up there to keep his attention.'

'With all due respect, sir,' said Clare. 'Do you have a reason to be in my office?'

'You are suspended, Dr Hart.' His voice was thick with menace. 'The 28s are finished. You are going back where you belong. And Ina Britz, once she's answered corruption charges, will write the report she's instructed to write.'

'No chance of that,' said Clare.

'Major Britz does not have the luxury of your privileged position.' He stepped around the desk, ran a finger along Clare's wrist. 'She will write what she's told in the end. Because otherwise she'll have nothing. That you can be sure of.'

'What are these corruption charges?' demanded Clare.

'I ordered an audit of the 28's expenditure,' said Cwele. 'Several unverified invoices were found. For petrol, for coffee, for flowers. This is where it starts. This is where it must be rooted out.'

'You're telling me this, having just released two suspects in a possible abduction case?'

'There was no proof,' said Cwele, 'plus you entered the home of a well-respected member of the public.'

'Milan Savić,' said Clare. 'Yes. You may be interested to know that Rosa Wagner – this girl you are happy to see disappear – was last seen at the home of Mr Savić. We had every reason to go there.'

'You went without a warrant,' said Cwele. 'A powerful man with lawyers and connections, and you decide to drag the good name of the South African Police Service through the mud?'

Cwele took a letter out of his pocket and put it on her desk. Clare did not even glance at it.

'Your suspension order, Dr Hart.' He smiled a slow, triumphant smile. 'And the terms of the investigation into your activities.'

Clare grabbed her keys and headed for the doorway. Cwele moved fast for such a big man. He pinned her to the door. Hard hands. One on her left wrist, one on the right. There were no cameras to catch what he was doing. He knew that. And she knew that.

'I'm not finished with you, Dr Hart.'

'But I'm finished with you.'

Clare raised her right knee fast and hard. He bellowed as she ran down the steps and yanked her car door open. She had wrenched the car into reverse before the front door flew open.

Cwele filled the doorway. He made the perfect target, framed there – if she'd had a gun in her bag. Clare watched him in her rear-view mirror, imagining herself turning, firing, the doorway empty again, the sunlight streaming back inside. But the guard was already opening the boom for her and she was turning into the road filled with Monday-morning taxis, and the moment was lost.

fifty-three

Clare wished that her heart would slow down. Her hands were shaking on the wheel. Part rage, part fear, part revulsion. The traffic lights up ahead were red. She stopped, opened the door and threw up, and felt better.

'Ag, shame, my lady.' The beggar was watching her through fake Ray-Bans, holding up his sign. He moved in front of Clare's car; he'd had the sign laminated. *No fingers, small change, pleese help.* He wasn't moving out of her way.

'You promised me something next time.'

It was true, but all she had was a fifty. She gave it to him and he got out of her way.

'God bless you, my lady,' he said, as Clare turned into the garage. 'God bless.'

The parking in front of the KwikShop was blocked by a Land Rover with a horsebox, so Clare drove around to the delivery area at the back of the building and went into the KwikShop. The television was muted, actors silently shouting at each other on the screen. The single cashier was slumped over a magazine. *Mercy* said the sagging nametag on her green-and-yellow uniform.

'Hello, Mercy,' said Clare.

The cashier glanced up.

'Have you seen this girl?' Clare pushed a photograph of Rosa over to her.

Mercy did not look at it.

'No.'

'She was seen in here, in your shop, three weeks ago. Her picture's been everywhere. In the papers.' She picked up a copy of *The Voice*, pointed to a photograph on page three.

'I read, I saw,' said Mercy, popping a piece of gum into her mouth.

'You didn't think of phoning the Section 28 hotline?' Clare struggled to conceal her impatience. 'It was in all the papers, on TV, with her picture.'

Mercy eyed Clare. 'I left home, came here. I never told anyone till one of my cousins saw me in Cape Town. It was four years after I left. I never wanted them to know. I never wanted to go home again.' With a long red nail she tapped the picture of Rosa. 'Maybe this girl's like me.'

'Her grandfather –'

'I also had a grandfather.' Mercy folded her arms. 'He's why I left.'

'I'm sorry, Mercy. But imagine that you had a grandfather you loved,' said Clare. 'This girl was going home to him – he was sick – she'd earned money to save his life, but she never made it back home. Three weeks later she phoned him, asking for help. When I arrived to help her there was no one, just blood on the wall.'

'You should write for *Isidingo*.' Mercy took the photograph from Clare, studied it a long time.

'She bought some Grandpa headache powder, and some pads. She asked for the toilet key,' said Mercy. 'I gave it to her. She was gone for a long time, then she brought it back. She gave me the key.' She turned the photograph over. 'She had a big guitar case with her. It got stuck in the door. The lady with the horsebox, she came in, helped her, and then she was gone.'

Mercy pushed the photograph back to Clare, shifted on her stool.

253

'That's the last you saw of her?' asked Clare.

'She walked that way, into the dark.'

Mercy pointed down the tree-shadowed road that wound its way up the valley. Big houses, paddocks, a streetlight or two, cameras that had seen nothing, and the soaring sweep of Judas Peak.

'Did a car come by?' asked Clare. 'Did she get a lift?'

'No, she was just gone.'

Mercy blew a big pink bubble. Popped it.

'Can I have the key to the bathrooms?' asked Clare.

Mercy unhooked a key, already reaching for her magazine.

Clare walked around to the women's toilet and unlocked it. She looked inside, nothing but chipped white tiles and the smell of bleach.

She pictured Rosa, remembered her grandfather's story about her schoolgirl panic, her running away from playground harassment. Boys pulling up her skirt. Looking, laughing.

Clare washed her hands in the stained basin Rosa had used, returned the key. On the garage forecourt, she stepped over water puddles iridescent with oil. She studied the tree-lined avenue. Mountain Men Neighbourhood Watch signs everywhere. Nothing moved, but there was a tall steel pole where the oaks reached the vanishing point.

Clare dialled Ina Britz, but she didn't pick up. A text came through instead.

Shit + Fan here. Cwele's checking all the 28 accounts & is looking 4 U. sez U assaulted him!? Stay away. Will call later. VOK!!

Fuck, indeed. Clare paused a minute, dialled Mandla Njobe.

'Mandla,' said Clare. 'I need a favour. Pictures from the Neighbourhood Watch cameras. Can you go into the office?

'I'm here, Doc,' said Mandla. 'What do you need?'

'Friday, twenty-fifth of May, two people saw Rosa Wagner at

254

the KwikShop. The same place Chadley Wewers did his late-night shopping on Friday. It's on the way to Sylvan Estate.'

'What's Captain Faizal say?' asked Mandla, respect in his voice.

'Right now, he's on a plane out of Cape Town,' said Clare. 'Official orders.'

'Why? The Cape is what he knows, we need him here.'

'Economic Stability Unit,' said Clare.

'Doing the dirty work for dirty politicians,' said Mandla. 'And Wewers – did you ask that piece of rubbish if he was at the shop three weeks ago?'

'I would if I could,' said Clare. 'Jakes Cwele released him, so you have to help me. I'm relying on the Neighbourhood Watch cameras, the ones you Mountain Men monitor.'

'Eish,' said Mandla. 'What time was this girl there?'

'It was late, one or two in the morning. Then she walked up the road. There are some facial recognition cameras half-way up, I want to know if she passed that way.'

'We already checked those,' said Mandla. 'They don't show anything.'

'Please check again,' said Clare. 'From one till three, on the twenty-fifth of May.'

'OK, I'll call you back.'

Clare thought of Riedwaan, about to head north to sprawling Joburg with its Highveld dust and veld-fire smoke. It took her a long time to compose the text she wanted to send him. She put her hand on her belly. *Jirre, vok, jy's in die kak, meisie*, is what Ina Britz might say.

Then her phone rang and it was Mandla and she could stop thinking and start doing again.

'You find anything, Mandla?'

'There's a picture of a girl with a funny suitcase at 2.03.'

'That's her. Tell me what you can see.'

'Not much,' said Mandla. 'She goes into the shop, comes out, goes round the back, goes back into the shop, then she's out and she just walks into the dark.'

'And that's it?'

'She takes her case and walks down the road,' said Mandla. 'No vehicles, nothing. She's there – and then she's not.'

'And further down the road?'

'There's a camera there,' said Mandla. 'But it didn't pick her up.'

'OK,' said Clare. 'I'll check it out.'

She ended the call, shoving her phone into her jacket pocket. An articulated truck with engine trouble pulled up behind the garage, blocking the exit. She was about to ask the driver to move when she saw the black Pajero pull into the filling station. Cwele and a couple of uniforms went into the KwikShop.

Clare slipped around the side of the building. A path led down to the road, the one that Rosa had walked that dark night not too long ago. She looked up at the mountains, gilded by the low solstice sun. Wednesday would be the tipping point, the sun at its lowest point in the sky. In two days' time light and warmth would slowly begin to return to the Cape. Right now, though, with Cwele hunting for her, it was not hard to imagine herself in Rosa's position.

fifty-four

The plane was on the tarmac, the doors still open, flurries of icy air laden with fumes. Riedwaan looked around him. The cabin was filled with cops. You could smell them, Axe deodorant, shaving cream, braais they had had with their families, the sweat that comes with an old plane in a storm at the start of a runway.

The ground crew was scurrying under the fuselage; it was clear that they'd still be sitting for a while.

Clare wasn't calling him back.

He looked out of the window. Storm clouds swirled around Table Mountain and the granite spine that led all the way to Hout Bay and the tip of the peninsula.

He thought about the baby. About the shutdown in Clare's heart. He knew the reason: a reluctant twin, she'd fought all her life to be separate. For Clare, this would mean the end of that.

Riedwaan closed his eyes. Shut out the hard-eyed, sunburnt men and their familiar complaints, their stories about the 'old days', a time when the Economic Stability Unit was still called the Riot Squad and the Constitution hadn't fucked up law and order and the cops' right to sort shit out. Their silent, gaping audience was a group of raw recruits from the Flats – Mandela's Children, the generation born into post-94 democracy.

A *Cape Times* lay on the floor, the front page aflame with reports of riots, falling share prices. That's why he was on this fucking plane, sitting between men whose trigger fingers were itchy. His phone flashed. He opened Clare's message – terse yet tender.

He put the phone back in his pocket, thinking about how to reply – when it rang, a muffled buzz against his heart. He answered without checking who was calling.

'Faizal,' turning away from the man sitting next to him.

'I'm so sorry, Captain.'

It was the sweet-faced hospice nurse. Khadija. That was her name. He could picture the brisk little badge on her left breast. But he knew what was coming; her tone was too gentle.

'It's your mother. If you can come now, Captain.'

'Tell her,' said Riedwaan, the burn in his chest making him want to hit someone, 'tell her I'm coming.'

He was unbuckling his seat belt, standing up, and grabbing his hold-all.

'Sit the fuck down, Faizal,' ordered the Economic Stability Unit's commanding officer; thin, blond, with Klipdrift-bloodshot eyes, he was coming at him down the narrow passage.

'This plane's taking off, man,' he shouted.

'Without me,' said Riedwaan.

The officer pushed him back towards his seat; Riedwaan dropped his bag but kept his balance. Then he had him by the front of his officer's uniform. The engines were revving. The officer saw the look in Riedwaan's eye. He hadn't survived this long in the police by fighting for principle. But here was a situation where he could hand his boss a wanted man's head on a platter.

'I'm not going to stop you.' The officer smiled a Judas smile. 'But you step off this plane, you're disobeying orders, and I'm taking that as you handing in your resignation, Faizal.'

'Take it any way you want.' Riedwaan let him go, wiped his hand on his trousers. He shouldered the bag and pushed past the officer. There was a widening gap between the stairs and the plane, but Riedwaan jumped, ran down the steps and crossed the wet tarmac.

The officer stalked back to his seat, saw Riedwaan's cellphone flashing on the floor where it had fallen. He stamped on it, crushing the phone underfoot.

fifty-five

Rosa. Clare could imagine how she had felt. Money small compensation for the shame. Her skin burning. The loathing, the nausea setting in. Hiding herself in the shadows under the avenue of trees.

The pavement was broad and leafy, the path alongside marked with regular piles of horse dung. Apart from the distant thrum of a lawnmower, all was quiet. This road, Clare knew, meandered up towards Orange Kloof. Further along, there was a short-cut across the Disa River, which led to the music college and Handel House.

At the end of the road was Sylvan Estate and the house where Rosa had made her last phone call. There were few exits along the road skirting the mountain to her left, other than turn-offs to secured estates. The road curved towards the river, and Clare could no longer see the garage where the Pajero had parked. She breathed easier for it.

She kept going, a kilometre or two, imagining Rosa seeking shelter. She arrived at the vanishing point, a steel pole with its facial recognition camera – the latest anti-crime deterrent in Hout Bay. Clare looked up at it, imagined its electronic eye scanning her face, transmitting her image to the Mountain Men computers.

Clare called Mandla Njobe again. 'You're picking me up on your monitors?'

'I see you, Doc,' he said. 'Sharp and clear.'

'And if it was night?' asked Clare.

'We'd still see you,' said Mandla. 'It wouldn't be as clear, but if she was as close as you are, there'd be enough street light for a shot.'

'So you're saying Rosa didn't make it as far as this?'

'That's right,' said Mandla.

'How far can the camera's eye see?' asked Clare.

'In the daytime, couple of hundred metres, easy,' said Mandla. 'The one nearer the garage the same. Less at night, though. But Doc –'

'What is it?'

'You be careful. The mountain's not safe that side.'

'I'm walking down a road in broad daylight, Mandla. If there's something there, I'll call you. If there's nothing, I'm going home,' said Clare. 'I'll be fine.'

'Captain Faizal asked me to watch out for you for a while.'

'That's sweet of him,' said Clare, unable to contain her irritation. 'But I can look after myself, thank you.'

Clare looked back at the way she had walked, the bend in the road that hid the garage from view. If the distance between the surveillance cameras was greater than a kilometre or so, there had to be a blind spot. If Rosa never got this far, where did she go?

Clare turned, walked back slowly, concentrating on places where she may have hidden her unwieldy cello case. A couple of copses of trees, the undergrowth dense. But there was no sign of disturbance. Clare retraced her steps. Further down, a footpath leading towards a house set back in the trees, but it was blocked off by coils of razor wire. A bit further on a disused driveway, the gate and the wall topped with electric fencing.

Again, no sign of disturbance. Certainly no sign of the cello case.

She was another hundred metres down the road when she noticed the sign, partially obscured by a tree. The faded face of the tear-stained bokkie, warning hikers not to start mountain fires. Clare stopped. The sign marked the end of the contour path. A notice pasted onto the sign: *Private: No access for horses.*

Below it was a new gate, securely padlocked, but there was a narrow pedestrian entrance. Clare looked up the winding path. She opened the map; the path was marked. It led up to the Back Table, a vast swathe of land between Hout Bay and the Table Mountain that tourists knew, with its flat top and expressionless stone face. It was probably not the dark Rosa feared so much as people. Clare imagined the silence of the mountain, broken only by the distant sound of running water, beckoning. If Rosa had taken this route it would explain why she never appeared on the next camera.

Clare walked up the path. It was overgrown, but not unused. It wouldn't be easy to carry a cello case up here, but not impossible. She walked on, looking for a place where Rosa may have stopped, may perhaps have hidden the instrument.

But there was nothing. The path took Clare to the place, skirting Savić's electric fence, where Mandla had found Wewers's nocturnal picnic site. Sylvan Estate was below, and the house where Rosa's blood streaked the wall.

Clare tried to call Ina Britz, but all she got was voicemail. She tried Mandla Njobe, but the reception had dropped. She sent a message instead – and, after a moment's consideration, she sent one to Riedwaan too, saying that she was tracking Rosa's last known movements. There would be a bar or two at some point, and she trusted that the messages would be sent.

Clare pushed on along the path. It took her up the steep pitch of the mountain. The path forked above Sylvan Estate.

She checked her map again. The fork was not marked. Had

Rosa walked this way, her cello strapped to her back? Tough going – a desperate measure, perhaps, on a dark road late at night. Clare looked back. She could see the road to the KwikShop below, glimpsed the black Pajero cruising along the treed avenue. The car stopped, just shy of the spot where she had turned off the road.

Cwele, his window down, hunting.

For her.

Clare wiped her face. She was sweating, despite the chill air.

But she couldn't go back. Not yet. Not with Cwele getting out of his vehicle, walking towards the KwikShop.

Clare looked up the overgrown, unmapped path that led up the mountain. Rosa could as easily have stumbled across Wewers, or someone like him, someone worse. She checked her phone; still no reception. The vast silence of the cloud-wreathed peaks behind her seemed to urge her to turn and walk back, get help. Mandla Njobe, that's who she needed. She considered getting back-up, but another vehicle was pulling in behind the Pajero. Uniformed officers. If she went back now they'd see her, and her chance to retrace Rosa's footsteps would be lost.

She pressed on up the mountain.

The trees soon swallowed her. The valley, the estate, the fishing village, the traffic – it was all behind her. The fallen needles on the wet earth absorbed the sound of her footsteps. Apart from the drip of water from the trees, there was no sound or movement. Her only sensation was the tang of her own sweat as she licked her lip. She stopped. Above her, Judas Peak and the cold, dark sweep of the pine forests. The roar of the waterfall was audible even here, the water cascading down smooth rocks and whirling white and dangerous downhill to swell the already bursting Disa River.

She looked down. Mist shrouded the trees. Fingers of light

touched the old farmhouse at the bottom of the valley. A child following behind a woman bending down to the earth.

Paradys.

The place where Rosa had sought peace, sanctuary.

Clare's unease was strengthening, but the boy had stopped to look up at her. His mother followed his gaze. She put her hand over her eyes and looked up at Clare. The child waved at her, his arm jerky. Clare hesitated a moment, then she followed the path down to Paradys.

fifty-six

Riedwaan pushed open the dingy doors of the hospice. His mother's room was quiet; the young nurse was at her bedside, the matron too. They both stepped back. Riedwaan walked over to his mother's bedside. His mother looked up at him, unblinking – as she had when he'd stayed out too long as a boy.

He put his hand over her face and closed her eyes and his mother was gone for ever.

'I'm so sorry for your loss, Captain Faizal,' said the nurse, pulling the clean white sheet up over the body. Riedwaan turned towards a window streaked with rain that seemed to dissolve the modest houses beyond the fence.

'Sometimes death is a release.' The nurse rested a hand on his arm, a cheap engagement ring on her second finger.

'When we went in to give her breakfast she had passed. She looked very peaceful.'

'All dead people look peaceful,' said Riedwaan. 'That's the way the dead are.'

'For the funeral arrangement.' She gave him the undertaker's card: *Muslim Burial Society*. Riedwaan turned it over and read the inscription on the back. *'Every soul will taste Death.'*

Wanie. His mother's nickname for him echoed through his thoughts. After that, the silence between him and his mother was complete. He leaned his head against the window, grateful for the coolness of the glass.

Riedwaan looked at the jumble of numbers on the undertaker's card. They'd make sense once he'd punched them into his phone, which he was reaching for in his breast pocket. Nothing there. Not in his jeans pocket either. Must be thirty thousand feet above sea level, on its way to Johannesburg. Fuck. He hit his forehead against the window frame. Fuck.

He opened the drawer beside his mother's bed. Tissues, a dog-eared photograph of Riedwaan's father, old copies of *YOU* magazine and the Qur'an. The cellphone he had bought her lay there, tucked under the Arabic verses she'd tried so hard to read ever since going on Hajj with his father.

The phone was dead, but he plugged in the charger and the little Nokia flickered to life. Riedwaan wanted Clare to say goodbye to his mother. He wanted her there with him. But she wasn't picking up. Not at work, not at home, not her mobile.

'Wanie, boy.' Riedwaan took a while to realise that someone was calling him. It was his uncle, older than him by thirty years, but turning to him to make the decisions. The time, the mosque for the funeral prayer, the graveyard.

'Wanie, tell us what you want. The family is gathering at your home in preparation for your mother's *Janazah*.'

The funeral rite. The decisions to be made within an hour of the passing, the body to be buried before the end of the day. Riedwaan, the oldest and only son, must see to the arrangements, the comforting, numbing rituals a path trodden by many down the centuries. There was a body to be washed, there were prayers to be said, so that an old woman could be bedded down under the earth before sunset.

Riedwaan dialled the Imam's number and the day's inevitable events were set in motion.

fifty-seven

The skies were lowering and it was starting to rain when Clare reached the woman and boy in the vegetable garden. Nancy Stern, watchful, drew the child towards her as Clare approached.

'Hello, I'm still trying to find Rosa Wagner,' said Clare. 'She was seen at the KwikShop three weeks ago, and I think she may have been headed back here.'

'Nobody comes this way unless they have a purpose,' said Nancy Stern. 'You've already asked us, anyway. We haven't seen her again.'

The boy twisted a little, looked up at Clare. His mother settled a firm hand on his shoulder.

'Maybe you saw her, Isaac?'

The child glanced from his mother to Clare, shook his head wordlessly.

'We already told you all we know,' said Nancy Stern. 'We're quite alone up here, as you can see. And you must know that it's not safe to walk alone on this part of the mountain.'

'I still think she may have tried to come this way,' said Clare. 'She was up at the castle. Something happened to her there, it distressed her terribly.'

'Milan Savić.' There was ice in Nancy Stern's voice. 'We lived here in peace until he came. He has brought the evil of the world to our valley.'

'What evil do you mean?'

'His men walk through our land,' said Nancy Stern. 'We see them going up towards the mountain. They're from Hangberg. Tattoos on their bodies, nothing in their eyes, nothing in their souls. We used to have peace here. Till they came, carrying those loads on their backs. We've seen them.'

The drizzle was turning into cold, hard rain.

'Let's go inside, Dr Hart. Tell me what you know, and I will try to help you.'

She led the way up the steps and opened the kitchen door.

'We leave our shoes out here,' she said, slipping off her boots and putting them on a shelf on the back stoep. Clare did the same. Her socks were wet, so she took them off too. The flag-stones were cold, but the wooden floor of the kitchen was better and the Aga emitted a welcome heat.

There were three plates on the kitchen table, with a half-slice of buttered bread on one, though the house was utterly silent.

'Your husband's out?'

'You'd have seen him if you'd driven up. He went down for supplies,' said Nancy Stern, busying herself with the kettle. 'We were running short of a few things, it's been hard to get down the road.'

She set out a teapot, two pretty floral cups. She put out a mug for the boy. His beanie was pulled low over his ears. He watched as his mother poured tea and handed Clare a cup, accepting his own in silence.

'Three weeks ago, Rosa was at the castle. She did a performance –'

'If you can call it that,' interjected Nancy.

'Any idea what they do up there?'

'Of course I know, how can I not know? It's an abomination.'

'Did Rosa tell you?'

Nancy shook her head, sipped her tea.

'Who, then?'

'You hear things, you know.'

Clare put her cup down.

'Rosa was last seen at the KwikShop down the valley, then she walked out into the night and simply vanished,' said Clare. 'I think she might have tried to come here.'

'Seeking sanctuary,' said Nancy Stern.

'She never arrived?'

A door slammed somewhere inside the house and the little boy jumped.

'It's the wind,' said his mother, instructing him, 'go close the windows in your father's study.'

The child slid off his chair and disappeared into the house.

'This is not a safe country for girls, Dr Hart,' said Nancy. 'You of all people should know this. There are few places that welcome women with open arms. Just look at that mountain.'

The mist was pushing against the window, Judas Peak just visible above.

'There are endless places there to lose a girl. Or her body. All those crevasses, the tunnel.'

'But the tunnel runs the other way,' said Clare. 'From Hell's Gate down to Camps Bay. It takes drinking water down from the dams.'

'There's an older one too. The Woodhead Tunnel. It was bricked up because it was dry. Dangerous.' Nancy Stern pursed her lips. 'My husband followed those men up there one day. They carry the stuff down into Camps Bay. Drugs, you know. Stuff that delivers people to the devil.'

Dealers avoiding roadblocks on routes leading out of Hout Bay. Clare's stomach lurched at the thought of Rosa encountering one of them on the mountain.

Nancy Stern threw Clare a quizzical glance. 'Did you not arrest one of those men?'

'Excuse me. Can I use your bathroom?' asked Clare, the tea rising in the back of her throat.

'It's down there,' said Nancy, pointing to where the boy had disappeared.

Across the hall was Stern's office. On impulse, Clare stepped inside. It was the same as when she'd glimpsed it on Friday afternoon. She glanced at the heavy old bookshelf, which held few books apart from an old Bible. She thought she heard a vehicle, but when she listened for it there was nothing but silence.

On the desk were folders, paperwork, accounts and delivery logs. Stern's diary was open. She flicked through it. A farmer's neat listings of orders, sales, modest procurements for the farm, notices of meetings about the land dispute with Savić.

'Dr Hart.'

Clare turned, guilty and startled. Nancy Stern was standing in the doorway.

'The bathroom is that way.'

'I grew up on a farm,' said Clare. 'This study, the smell, the journals. Just like my father's.'

Nancy looked at her, expressionless.

'Sorry. It caught my attention.'

'The past does that sometimes,' said Nancy, turning on her heel and going back to the kitchen.

Clare walked down the corridor. The doors along it were shut, a child's shoe abandoned outside the last one.

'Isaac,' said Clare, softly.

There was no answer.

She went into the bathroom, turned on the tap and splashed the icy water onto her face. The nausea was gone but she felt lightheaded; her face in the mirror ashen.

The door opened and she swivelled round.

The boy had his beanie in his hand and his face was turned up

270

towards her. Clare stared at his dark hair, the widow's peak. What she was seeing was impossible.

'Isaac.' Clare knelt down so that they were at eye level. 'Esther?'

His extended arm was taut as a rod. He was pushing a book into her hands. A rain-damaged, dog-eared old Penguin. Clare opened it and a photograph fell out. She picked it up. A girl sitting on a white beach; a cerulean lagoon behind her.

Rosa.

Clare looked up, but the boy was gone. The door at the end of the passage was ajar. She ran towards it and pushed it open. Pines pressed close to the back of the house, their comradely branches beckoning. The little boy was zig-zagging between the trees.

The back of Clare's neck prickled, but it was too late to run. The blow to her head pitched her forward into darkness.

fifty-eight

Riedwaan's house in Signal Street was filled to bursting. Aunts and cousins were arriving, solemn as they climbed the stairs to the open door. Riedwaan stepped outside with his uncles to meet the hearse bumping along the cobblestones. He helped the men carry his mother's body back into the house where she'd been born. They laid her down and left the women to do the ritual washing before they shrouded her body in the snow-white cotton of the *kafan*. A cousin recited prayers and verses from the Qur'an, the familiar intonation holding the mourners together, comforting them until the *Janazah*.

When they were done, Riedwaan went back into the room. It smelt faintly of camphor. His mother lay swaddled for her final rest. The last of the women closed the door behind her and he was alone with her. He sat down in the chair that had been set there for him and bent his head, seeking the long-forgotten solace of prayer. The words themselves, though, were imprinted in his mind. He had heard them being intoned since before he could speak, and later as a boy in the madrassa. But Riedwaan's mind was not on God, and his thoughts drifted instead to his father and his mother – this woman with her shrill love, her swift hand always ready to punish real and imagined transgressions, who had fiercely guarded her fragrant biryani recipe, and whose deft fingers had folded samoosas he would never eat again.

He put his hand on her worn-out body, thanking her for the

first and last time for her dignity. She had taught him how to fight and how to love. She had created a world for him that had shielded him from the insults and exclusions borne by boys like him in Bo-Kaap.

Riedwaan's chest burned, but his eyes were dry. In the end he had failed her. He had divorced the wife she had chosen for him, and Yasmin, her only grandchild, had left with her mother to live in Canada. His obsession with a job that he had just abandoned in five, inflammatory minutes, had cost him his family. He swore on his mother's body that he would not let that happen again. Riedwaan lifted her body and laid her on the bier. She was light as a bird.

There were even more people in the house when Riedwaan left his mother's side: the extended family, neighbours, as well as Khadija – the nurse who had been with her at the end. The Imam arrived and prayers were said and then it was time to go to the mosque.

Riedwaan left the women in the house as, together with his mother's brothers and his cousins, he carried her body out of the front door for the last time. The sun had slid down in the sky when the funeral party spilled out onto the steep cobbled street, and they carried his mother at shoulder height to the mosque.

She was laid down, and the community of men who had known and loved her gathered around. The Imam took his position in front of her. Facing away from Riedwaan and the other mourners, he performed the *Salatul Janazah*, and then the funeral prayers were over and his mother was carried to the waiting hearse.

Riedwaan stepped aside for a moment as a brief argument broke out concerning which brothers should go in which car. He fiddled for a moment with his mother's phone and sent a text to Clare. He waited for a reply, but nothing came. An uncle took his arm, guided him to the vehicle that would lead his mother's final journey. The old Mercedes coughed to life, and the hearse and the small procession of male mourners moved down the steep streets of the Bo-Kaap to the Muslim burial ground in Observatory. Riedwaan felt himself being swept along once more in rituals that had buoyed him ever since he was old enough to go to mosque with the men.

fifty-nine

No. Clare had meant to say it.

Such a small word, one might as well not bother.

She tried to get up, but her ankle gave way and she fell again. Clare, her mind a blur, crawled through the mud towards the trees where the boy had fled. She hit her hand on something hard. A stone. She picked it up but Nancy was on her again, as strong as a nightmare, her fury a match for Clare's desperation. She hit Clare again, a glancing blow, and when the darkness cleared again, Clare was on her back and Nancy was on top of her, her face as close as a lover's.

'Rosa came here. She came to you,' said Clare. 'She came for help.'

Nancy spat in Clare's face.

Clare did not flinch.

'If she's alive, tell me where she is,' said Clare. 'You must tell me where he keeps her. Let me go – and save yourself.'

'Rosa is the one who must be saved.'

'From what, and why?' Clare demanded.

'She was wilful,' said Nancy. 'He chose her and she defied him.'

'Your husband?' said Clare. 'What has he done with her?'

Loyalty and desperation. The battle evident in Nancy's face.

'People will look for me,' said Clare. 'And they'll find me.'

'Not here,' said Nancy. 'Not ever.'

'Mistakes happen, Nancy – you can make it right,' said Clare.

'You understand nothing.'

'Nancy, you can do it. Let me go,' said Clare. 'Otherwise there'll be police, prison, a trial, an asylum. If you help me, you can make things end differently.'

A glimmer in the woman's blue eyes. Hope, or hatred – Clare was not sure. Perhaps both. But right then Nancy had a stone in her hand. She raised it again and brought it down hard on Clare's head.

Clare came round, overwhelmed by a dank, rotting smell. It permeated everything. Her hair, her skin, the marrow inside her bones.

It was silent, no light at all to hold the darkness at bay. Blackness all around, and especially above her. Clare felt the earth pushing down on her. Above that, the weight of the night. Or the indifference of the day, perhaps. Clare had no idea where she was, but sensed that she was underground. She screamed, but the walls blocked the sound. There was no one to hear – that her mind told her; it was her body that would not accept this.

She was lying on a narrow bed, covered with a blanket. Metal bit into her throat. She tried to move, but further than a metre, she gasped for air. Floating spores seemed to fill her lungs.

She put her hands out – feeling into the darkness. The wall was damp, she felt the sliminess of mould on plastered walls. This prison had been custom built.

Beyond, the thrum of water.

She felt below the mattress, Braille-read the ridges with her fingertips.

She pulled against her restraint, leaning as far as the chain allowed her. The marks, enigmatic as runes, signifying perhaps the passing of days, weeks, years.

Clare collapsed back, gasping. She lay still and stared into the darkness; regulated her breathing.

She heard it then.

A whimpering.

She opened her eyes; it was her own voice.

She concentrated on the pulse of cells in her belly: defiantly alive.

sixty

The Muslim graveyard was right next to Groote Schuur Hospital. The road to the place where the world's first heart transplant had been performed was clogged with cars and hustling taxis. In the bustle of Observatory, the burial ground was an oasis of quiet, the graves packed as close to each other as the houses of the living in this windy corner of working Cape Town.

Riedwaan's father had been buried there three decades before. The thought of his father's peace in Paradise being shattered by the arrival of his mother brought the glimmer of a smile to Riedwaan's heart, if not to his lips. His parents' arranged marriage had been an endless wrestle of wills, and his father's murder had deprived Riedwaan's mother of a perfectly matched combatant.

He was seven when his father died – required to be the man of the house, the only son then, as he was now. Thirty-five years lay between himself and that boy, but walking now, with his mother's body on the bier on his shoulder, that interim was erased.

He stopped with the other pallbearers – his mother's body almost weightless – at the edge of the grave and lowered her in. His mother he laid gently on her side, facing Mecca. He tucked her white shroud around her. The final prayers were said, and then there was a hand on his back and he relinquished her to the earth, stepping back so that a board could be placed over her to protect her from the sodden earth flung from the spades of the diggers. Her grave filled, and at last she was gone, back in the embrace of the earth.

It was too cold, too dark, too wet to linger at the graveside.

Riedwaan moved through the mourners. Touching his shoulders – the rough hands of working men, the smooth palms of men who sat behind tills or desks – all giving quiet comfort to him.

Numbness took the place of guilt, and Riedwaan pulled his collar against the rain. He lit a cigarette. He wanted Clare, he phoned her again.

'When I need you, Clare,' he said to the silent phone, 'where the fuck are you?'

Riedwaan's anger had already turned into a tight, hard knot of dread.

sixty-one

Breath, touch, memory. In the darkness, that's all there was. That, and a single note – the dripping of water. Clare counted the drops, each hanging for one maddening second onto the next. Time lost all meaning; seconds, hours, days merged in the absolute darkness. The chain around her neck made it hard to breathe. The leather restraints around her wrists and ankles made it impossible to move.

An electric light, a sudden blinding Cyclops eye in the low ceiling, was switched on. It pinioned Clare, illuminating her surroundings, but bringing neither comfort nor recognition. She blinked away the blindness. She was on a single bed. There was a blue table, two mismatched chairs, shelves on one wall. Two plastic cups, two spoons, two plates, a notebook and a yellow Bic. Steps – seventeen of them – and a trapdoor in the roof. Four uneven walls, the blooming damp a mad yellow wallpaper covered with pencil marks: music unfurling, ordered pennants of notes on wavy lines with treble and bass clefs.

The door opened. A woman's feet, her ankles, a long skirt.

Nancy. She took a bottle of water out of her basket and held it to Clare's lips. Her throat burned with thirst. There was no fight in her, not over this. Instead, she gulped the water that was poured into her mouth, telling herself what all prisoners tell themselves: just stay alive. Later, the capitulation could be undone.

'Where's Rosa?' Clare demanded. 'She was in here. What have

you done with her?'

'If you struggle I will tighten this.' Nancy yanked the chain around Clare's neck. 'You will keep still?'

Clare's heart hammered, a trusting heart beating in unison deep within her body.

She complied, and Nancy released her.

'I knew you would come,' said Nancy.

'What do you think you are doing with me?' asked Clare. Her helplessness made her want to lash out and it was all she could do to keep still.

'I'm fixing things,' smiled Nancy. 'And right now, I'm going to wash you.'

'I can wash myself,' said Clare.

Nancy didn't reply. She was setting things out. A cloth, a bowl, a flask of warm water.

'Where's Isaac?' asked Clare.

'He has been found,' said Nancy, her voice sharp. 'Brought back.'

'Isaac's not your son, you may as well admit this.'

Nancy stared at Clare, her blue eyes blank. There was a swelling on her cheek, not yet discoloured.

'He's Esther's child, isn't he?'

'Isaac is mine,' said Nancy. 'He knows it.'

'No,' said Clare. 'He knows the truth. He's terrified of you. He's terrified of Stern too. I saw that the first time I was here, and I ignored it.' The weight of all the things she had not paid attention to was a stone pressing on Clare's chest.

'His father has punished him for what he did,' said Nancy, but she wasn't looking at Clare. She was looking at her work-hardened hands. 'He will never do it again.'

'And your face, what happened?'

Nancy flushed.

'Noah hurts you too, doesn't he?'

'He knows the Lord's way,' said Nancy. She took a facecloth, wiped Clare's face, and then lifted her hair.

'He hurt the others,' said Clare. 'Esther, her mother. I saw the scars from the sjambok on their backs.'

'Chastisement is necessary.'

'Esther Previn,' said Clare. 'Was she the first one?'

Nancy brushed Clare's hair hard, making no accommodation for the bruises on her neck.

The pain brought tears to Clare's eyes.

'She was different,' said Nancy, a tremor in her hands.

'What made her different?' said Clare. 'Was she your friend?'

'Esther joined our household. She came to us, believed with us. Together we healed her.'

'Then what happened?' Clare's voice a whisper. 'Noah liked her? Started sleeping with her?'

'He told me Esther was my sister-wife.' Nancy reached in the basket and brought out a towel. 'He said if I was a good wife I would accept her. I tried, I really tried.'

'It must have hurt, though,' said Clare.

'It was meant to be good,' she said. 'It *was* good – until Isaac was born. Her ways were not Noah's ways, and she defied him. He had to do what he did.'

'What did he do, Nancy?' coaxed Clare. 'Tell me. It makes it easier sometimes. Just saying what happened.'

Nancy looked at her warily.

'He beat her, but it was for her own good, she didn't want to listen,' said Nancy.

'That's not all, though,' said Clare. 'What did he make you do?'

Nancy turned away, it was as if Clare had slapped her.

'Esther tried to leave, didn't she?' said Clare.

Nancy scrubbed Clare's legs and then her belly. Clare braced

282

herself, tightening her muscles against the woman's rough hands.

'She was going to take our children.'

'Her children,' corrected Clare. 'I've seen them. Esther, Isaac. Their hair, the widow's peak, just like their mother.'

'We could not let that happen – no, no, Dr Hart.' Nancy knotted her fingers. 'They were born here in Paradys, they were chosen. And they were mine.'

A distant drip-drip punctuated the silence.

'Is it that you can't have children?' Clare's hand rested on her arm. 'That's why you've done this, isn't it? That's his hold over you.'

Nancy took the stopper off a small bottle and the sweet smell of orange blossom filled the air. Clare's stomach turned.

'It is my fault,' said Nancy. 'I couldn't be a proper wife. I had to find another way.'

'Nancy,' said Clare. 'Stop. Look at me.'

She raised her eyes to meet Clare's.

'Show me your back, Nancy.'

Nancy hesitated for a moment, then she undid her buttons. She turned around, letting her blouse fall. A network of white ridges criss-crossed her bent back.

'Your husband should be in prison for that,' said Clare. 'What he's done, what he's made you do for him, is monstrous. You can stop it all, Nancy. Walk out of here. Walk down that mountain and get help. For yourself, for Isaac. Put a stop to your suffering.'

'No.' The venom in her voice made Clare recoil. 'I couldn't give him children. Always, there's something wrong with me. It's a mark of my sin and it was his duty to make me understand.'

'How old were you when you married him?'

'Sixteen. See this.' Nancy pulled at the silver chain around her neck, held out the silver disc that dangled from it. Nancy's name entwined with her husband's. 'Noah gave this to me on our wedding day. That's the day we became one.'

She tipped oil into her hands and rubbed them together. Bending over Clare, she worked the oil into her skin.

'Are you preparing me for him?'

Nancy poured more oil onto her palm.

'You did the same with Rosa, didn't you?' said Clare. 'She needed a mother, she needed a friend, and you took advantage.'

'Rosa came to us,' said Nancy.

'For sanctuary,' said Clare. 'Not for this.'

She dabbed oil onto Clare's hair.

'These marks,' said Clare, turning to the wall. 'It's Rosa, her music, her trying to stay alive.'

'She was fed, she had water, she had air,' said Nancy. 'There was no reason for what she did.'

'You'd promised her a haven and she came, believing you would help her.'

'Rosa had been at the castle,' said Nancy.

'So your husband saw Rosa up there? Noah participated in it all?'

'No, no,' said Nancy. 'He was there because of the land dispute. Savić wouldn't speak to him.'

'But he saw Rosa there?'

'She wanted to cleanse herself, and my Noah offered her a place that would shield her from the world. A place where she could bury her sin.'

'This hole, you mean?'

'People don't always know what's good for them,' said Nancy. 'Noah told her to take the path. He said she must be sure that she was not seen, and that I would be waiting for her. That is what she did. That is what I did. I carried her cello up for her and brought her home. Like Esther, she was chosen.'

'How can you expect anyone to live here, hidden from the

sun?'

'It is a sacrifice,' said Nancy. 'You will get used to it.'

'Please, Nancy,' begged Clare 'Let me go. Don't condemn another child to this living hell.'

Nancy gave Clare a quizzical look. Then she put the oil and the towel back into her basket.

'I'm pregnant,' said Clare. 'It's not only my child, there's a father too. He will look for me.'

'No matter,' said Nancy. Her eyes were cold. 'The child will be born. If it's a boy it will see the light of day and I will be its mother.'

'And if it's a girl?'

'She stays down here, with you,' said Nancy. 'And when she bleeds for the first time, Noah will bless her with children too.'

Nancy picked up her basket and went up the stairs without another word.

Clare had played her last card, and she had lost.

sixty-two

Riedwaan's family had his house in order by the time he got back from the graveyard. His aunts and cousins had cooked a meal for which he had no appetite but which he was obligated to share. The warren of rooms was redolent with the smell of cooking and furniture polish. The house had been cleaned almost to his mother's standards. If she had walked in that minute and run a finger over the surfaces, it would have come away clean and she'd have had to walk on and look for other faults.

He ducked out of the back to find that all his shirts had been laundered and were drying on hangers in the garage. Riedwaan tried Clare's cellphone again, but there was nothing. Out of range or the phone off or the battery dead.

He tried her sisters, Constance first, then Julia, but neither of them had spoken to her, neither knew where she was. Nothing strange about that, Clare wasn't one for telling people where she'd be and when.

And yet he didn't believe it. He was about to try again but voices were calling and he joined his family at the table, with him at its head. The photograph of his parents forever frozen on their wedding day hung on the wall opposite. The two of them facing a future they'd had no part in planning.

He ate what he could, smiling at shared stories about his mother, then slipped into silence as the conversation shifted to other things – weddings, new babies, a scandal involving a neighbour. It took Riedwaan some doing to persuade his most tenacious aunts that he'd be fine alone, that he needed to be alone. It was almost midnight when he saw off the last of them, saw them out the door and into their cars.

His last resort was Ina Britz.

She picked up, groggy and clearly pissed off.

'Where's Clare?' said Riedwaan. 'She's hasn't answered her phone all day. Nobody's seen her.'

Wide awake, Ina shushed her wife.

'She was in this morning early – and ever since then half the cops in the Cape have been looking for her.'

'Which half?' asked Riedwaan.

'Cwele's half,' said Ina. 'Something happened between Clare and Cwele this morning. His version is that he informed her that her contract had been cancelled, and that she responded by assaulting him.'

'And her version?'

'I never got it. There was chaos – Cwele and his people crawling over everything, looking in everything.' She gave a hollow laugh. 'Can you believe it – I'm under investigation for misuse of state funds.'

'What the fuck?'

'There were two tanks of petrol for 28 vehicles and two missing slips,' said Ina. 'But it's got bugger-all to do with that, of course.'

'You don't need to tell me that, Ina. Did she say where she was going?'

'Only thing I know is she's not with Cwele,' said Ina. 'He's got a warrant out for her arrest. And if he had her, everyone would know about it. Her only value to him is as a scapegoat. But if anyone knows how to find her, Faizal, it's you.'

Riedwaan took off his white funeral robe, pulled on his jeans and leather jacket. He found his gun and his keys and his helmet, pushed his motorbike out of the garage.

Rain needled his face as he headed at double the speed limit for Beach Road. The streets were empty, the restaurants closed, the bars closing. He pulled up outside Clare's flat. Fritz sat in the window, motionless except for a warning flick of the tail when she heard the bike stop. A light was on. She was home, she was ignoring him. That was fine. If she was alive he could be angry with her. If he was angry he could make up afterwards.

Riedwaan rang the doorbell.

No response.

He dialled her number. He could hear her landline ringing inside, then her voice on the answering machine, telling him to leave a message and she'd get back to him.

He stepped back from the doorway and looked up. Just Fritz staring down at him. He unlocked the door with the key she had never really given to him. She simply hadn't asked for it back – the closest Clare had come to making a commitment, he suspected.

He knew as he stepped inside that she wasn't there, but he called her name anyway as he went upstairs.

The only greeting silence.

The kitchen was untouched: her tea cup, his half-finished mug of coffee on the table. Fritz's food and water bowls empty. Riedwaan filled them, and the cat appeared. She only did that when she was really hungry.

He picked up his helmet again and ran down the stairs. Her scarf – a deep blue, the colour of her eyes – lay at the door. He picked it up, breathing in the smell of perfume layered over the musky scent of her skin.

He stuffed the scarf into his pocket. He didn't like the thoughts that prompted him to do so, and headed back into the night to look for her.

sixty-three

Darkness, thirst and cold; Clare was suspended in an unbearable present.

'You're pleased to see me.' Noah Stern's voice compelling her attention.

He smiled at the refusal he could see in her eyes and slipped the chain from the horizontal pole above the bed. Clare lunged at him, but he pulled the chain tight. It bit into her throat.

'Please,' she gasped.

He loosened it; the relief overwhelmed her.

'Thank you.'

Stern smiled; there was little he did not know about capitulation.

He was very close, his breath on her face, his hands hard and cold on her breasts. He squeezed, saw the pain in her eyes. He kneaded, feeling the fullness. He was reading her body, simple as the alphabet, her quick tears revealing her hidden tenderness.

His other hand, quick and cold as a snake, was low on her belly. Knowing, kneading, owning. He let her go. Satisfied.

'Accept, endure, and we will be content together, you and I. If you don't, you will fight until you break. In the end, it is all the same.'

'I will fight. You will never own me,' said Clare.

'Fight as you wish. You won't be the first. But by delivering up this child to me you will have made up for what has been taken from me.'

289

'What have you done with Rosa?'

'Rosa came to us, never forget that,' he said, suspending the chain from the pole again.

He put two fingers over her mouth and trailed them down the soft skin under her chin. Then he turned around, switched off the light, and left her there.

Clare slowed her breath. Counted each inhalation, each exhalation.

Tuesday
June 19

sixty-four

Riedwaan stood in the emptiness of Clare's Section 28 office. The coffee on her desk ice-cold. The croissant next to it untouched.

He checked the files she had made for little Esther, the notes about the woman found in the forest. He tried to make sense of it all, went over each detail again and again. Piet Mouton's number on a pad next to the files. The pathologist was a man who divided the world into two categories: idiots and non-idiots. Riedwaan Faizal he'd classified on their first meeting as a non-idiot, and they had become friends – if that's what you call a person you meet across a corpse rather than a restaurant table.

Riedwaan phoned Mouton. He was awake. Just. He'd soon be heading off in the dark for a couple of hours of peace in his office before the cutting started.

'Piet, did you see Clare, hear anything from her?'

'I saw her yesterday. She didn't tell you?'

'I haven't spoken to her. I'm looking for her, don't know where she is.'

'That dead woman she found,' said Mouton. 'She made me do a check. DNA matched the kid's, the one under Anwar Jacobs's care. It's the girl's mother.'

'When did she die?'

'A week ago,' said Mouton. 'She was suffocated. Obvious from the veins in the eyes, lesions on the inside of the mouth. Brain and lungs telling me lack of oxygen. Somebody murdered the woman before that child was left there.'

'Did Clare say anything else?'

'Just that she was searching for the killer,' said Mouton.

'She mention Rosa Wagner?'

'No, nothing about her,' said Mouton. 'You'd better find Clare quickly.'

'That's my plan,' said Riedwaan.

'Faizal,' said Mouton. 'Watch out for Cwele.'

Riedwaan froze. 'Tell me?'

'He's got it in for her,' said Mouton. 'He's looking for her. He's got a call out for her, asked our security to alert him if she comes back to the morgue. Told me I have to let him know if she makes contact.'

Riedwaan fumbled for a cigarette.

'Same goes for you,' said Mouton. 'I'd steer clear of any official building, if I were you.'

'No reason to go near one,' said Riedwaan. 'I'm not a cop any more. You won't be mentioning this call, Piet?'

'I'm not a cop either,' said Mouton. 'Now go find her.'

Riedwaan found a match, inhaled, the nicotine focusing his fury on Clare's notes. They were posted alongside photographs, call logs, CCTV images and interviews. He walked over to the map of the valley. Three starred places. Mandla Njobe's name at the first one, where the little girl had been found. Next, the empty house with Rosa's blood, and the last one where the dead woman's corpse was dug up.

A lethal triangle.

It wasn't getting lighter, but the darkness was pierced by the lights of the day's first vehicles on the road. Riedwaan took his mother's Nokia out of his pocket. None of his contacts in it – but he was now an ex-cop, so they were useless anyway. Only one person he could rely on, who'd keep Cwele off his trail.

He dialled Mandla Njobe, got him as he was about to leave for his pre-dawn run.

'It's Faizal,' said Riedwaan. 'I can't find Clare.'

'Ina Britz told me yesterday that Cwele's also looking for her,' said Njobe. 'I spoke to Clare. She was up near the KwikShop.'

'Doing what?'

'Tracking Rosa Wagner,' said Njobe. 'It's the last place she was seen.'

'She find anything?'

'She said she'd call me if she did. If not, she'd go home,' said Njobe. 'I didn't hear from her, so I didn't think about it again.'

'She's not at home,' said Riedwaan. 'She's not at work. No one's seen her.'

'There's a patrol up there,' said Njobe. 'I'll get them to check it out. Meet me at McDonald's.'

Mandla Njobe was sitting at a table when Riedwaan arrived. The place smelt of stale chip oil and cheap coffee.

'She's not up there?' asked Riedwaan.

'They checked,' said Njobe.

'So where the fuck is she, Mandla?'

Njobe held out a breakfast roll.

'No, thanks,' said Riedwaan. 'Just the coffee.'

'Eat it,' ordered Njobe. 'They gave me your bacon, and you got my egg.'

'It's not that,' said Riedwaan.

'You don't eat, you're no good to her,' Njobe insisted. He spread out a map of Hout Bay. 'We need the police, Faizal,' he said. 'We can't do this alone.'

'We have to,' said Riedwaan. He ate his breakfast. It tasted of nothing, but Njobe was right. He'd been running on empty.

'Cwele's after you too?' asked Njobe.

'Me – and he's nailed Ina Britz,' said Riedwaan. 'He wants Clare too. She did something to him that he's not going to forgive.'

'She's a good girl,' said Njobe, dialling. 'My boys like her. They don't like your new boss. But they'll help.'

'I appreciate that,' said Riedwaan.

Njobe was holding up his hand and speaking rapidly in Xhosa. When he hung up he said, 'The other Mountain guys will do the suburbs. We take the dunes. She goes running up there sometimes. I've told her before it's not safe, but she says she needs to be alone to think.'

Riedwaan looked outside at the windswept sand washed a pale orange by the early-morning sun. He'd once before found human remains there, a woman taught a lesson she was too dead to remember by the time it was finished.

His gut twisted as they set out.

sixty-five

A trapdoor opened; blinding light. Clare's eyes adjusted, focusing on the dark shape coming down the stairs.

'Clare Hart.' He lingered over the name: the clipped C, the sensuous drawn-out vowel, the unsounded R seeming to leave an opening, suggesting vulnerability. 'It is a beautiful name, but one you will learn to forget.'

His hand hovered near her face. Clare recoiled, her horror bringing a smile to his lips, but Noah Stern did not touch her.

'The name carries with it your history, your memory – your past and your future. None of which exist for you any more. For those who love you, who might search for you for a while, the name will be a burden. We will change it, lessen the heaviness within you. I saw this with the first one.'

He slipped his fingers under the chain and caressed her throat.

'Esther tattooed her name on her daughter's neck with a Bic. She inked it there, just like prisoners do,' said Clare, her voice hoarse. 'Esther lives on. You failed to erase her.'

Stern's eyes blazed, but he continued as if she had not spoken.

'You will relinquish the ties that bind you to family. You will forget the story you have been told about yourself. It may take years, but in the end you will give yourself up.' He cupped her face in his hands. 'An obedient wife, willing, finally, to trust her husband with the life he chooses for her.'

'I want to know where Rosa is.'

'You would know, I imagine, how hostile the world is to wilful young women.'

'It's the wilful ones who make it,' said Clare.

'In my experience, they end up here.' He smiled at Clare. 'You wished to see her – and now you will.'

Stern moved the shelves aside, revealing a low steel-covered door. He tapped in a code and it swung open.

'Get up,' he ordered, slipping the chain off the pole suspended above the bed.

Clare stumbled towards the opening that led deeper into the mountain.

The muffled sound of water.

She stepped into the dimness, Noah Stern's hand on her back.

He stopped, turned sideways.

'Rosa,' he said.

There was a bundle on the floor. Wrapped in black plastic, it looked like a body bag.

'I've brought you a friend,' said Stern.

Clare dropped to her knees.

'Rosa?' she whispered.

The bundle moved. A pale girl tried to push herself up, but her arms collapsed. She stared up at Clare. Her blank eyes reflected Clare back to herself. Two tiny pinprick selves in the girl's pupils.

'Bring her here,' ordered Stern.

'Take the chain off me, then,' said Clare. 'Otherwise I cannot help her.'

He removed the chain, and Clare gathered Rosa into her arms.

'Water,' whispered Rosa. 'Please.'

'There's some through there,' said Clare. She helped her through and laid her on the bed.

Clare held a bottle to her lips and drip-fed the girl as if she were a wounded bird.

'It's been three days. Thirst flays the mind,' said Stern, watching Rosa's throat convulse. 'Little else is needed to tame the body.'

Clare lifted the plastic. The girl was naked.

'She will die, Stern,' said Clare, turning from Rosa's battered body. 'Get her out of here; get her to a hospital, save yourself.'

'I'm not the one who needs saving,' he said to Clare. 'Dr Hart, unless you wish to live here alone, unless you want to give birth alone, you will have to find a way to keep her alive.'

'Leave me unshackled then,' said Clare, stepping away as he approached her with the chain. 'Otherwise I can do nothing.'

'There is little you can do in the darkness,' he said, weighing up her words. 'But just remember: down here, if you do what I say, you are free.'

Stern turned on his heel and went up the stairs. The door closed, plunging the hole into darkness once again.

Clare lay next to the naked girl, covering her with the blanket, with her own body.

'You survived.' She felt the girl's breath on her cheek.

Clare's thoughts spiralled in the silence. The distant throb of the river was a sensation rather than a sound. Time passed. There was nothing else for it to do. Time passed. Surely, it passed. There was no way to tell, apart from the regular rhythm of Rosa's breath that brushed Clare's ear.

Rosa's voice brought her back into the ink-black present.

'He made me help her,' she said. 'Just like he made you help me. Esther, the little girl –'

'She's alive,' said Clare. 'She's going to be fine.'

Rosa was silent for so long that Clare put her hand up to her face to see if she was still awake. Rosa's eyes were wide open, staring into the darkness.

'My life, it's as if I'm in a movie. And that night, the trees, the light, something wasn't right; I knew that. I looked down that

299

avenue into the darkness. The oaks leaned into each other and whispered to me. Those trees – now that I live buried among their roots, I know – they were warning me. They were telling me to run. I heard them, but I didn't listen. That was my mistake. I know that now. I'm sure you know what your mistake was too.'

'I know,' said Clare.

'You know what happened at the castle.' She lay still, her mind back in the moment that had unhinged her life. Both their lives.

'I saw,' said Clare.

'That's why you're here.'

'Yes.'

'You know why I did it?'

'I know.'

'So you know I didn't walk back towards the light,' said Rosa. 'But I felt so dirty – and my mind, it was in pieces. I wasn't strong enough. I put my cello and my bag on my back and walked into the night. I walked up the road, climbed the path. I was hurting. I came here. Nancy was here. It was as if she'd been waiting for me. He took my cello and leaned it against the wall.'

'Noah Stern?'

Rosa ignored Clare's question.

'I try to run the movie in reverse, another version. Me, walking back to the shop, back into the light, back inside. I pick up the phone. I phone my oupa, I tell him. He fetches me. I give him the money for his cancer pills, enough to buy him and me a few more days.'

Rosa was quiet again, her exhalations marking the moments.

'But it never happened. That's how life is,' she said. 'Nothing gets undone. It was like I had a fire under my skin. I left that place. I walked faster, faster down the hill, trying to get away. There was the garage. I went in. I had to find some water again. I got the key, but nothing helped – their hands on me, inside me,

300

burning, burning me. I wet my hair and I walked to the trees. I knew the path was there – I'd walked there before. I knew it went to Paradys. Nancy is his wife. I knew her, she had combed my hair in the sun and told me that I would find sanctuary there.'

Rosa shifted, leaned on her elbow and faced Clare.

'A woman makes you feel safe,' said Rosa.

She sank back onto the bed.

'I was wrong.'

'Me too,' said Clare.

'I've thought so often about what Nancy knows.'

'Everything,' said Clare. 'She's his handmaiden.'

Clare put her arms around Rosa.

'When you first visited them, what did Noah say to you then?'

'It was Nancy who did the talking. He just watched and smiled and went about his business. I didn't really pay much attention to him.'

'And after you arrived here at Paradys?'

'The next morning he asked me if I'd spoken to anyone. I told him no, I'd come straight from the castle. I told him I didn't want to see anyone. Not after what I had done, not yet. He made me coffee. There was bread, a jar of honey. We sat at the table and he watched me eat. Then he asked me if I would help him in the shed.'

'Bastard. So that's where the entrance to this hole is.'

Rosa's breath quickened. 'Yes. He was standing at the door and said to me, "After you" – like a real gentleman. There were three boxes on the floor. He gave me the smallest one. He pointed to a door, some steps. It was, a cellar, I thought. He came after me. There were seventeen steps. I counted, I don't know why. And then there was another door. It opens with some kind of code. He leaned forward while I held the box and he opened the door and then it was too late and the chain was round my neck.'

'Is that where you found the little girl?'

'Yes, she was curled up on a mat on the floor. Her eyes were open. He turned her onto her side, to face the wall. Then he took my dress, he took my panties, he bent me over the table, his hand on the back of my neck, his voice was in my ear telling me I was unclean –'

Clare shook her head in the dark, stroked Rosa's forehead.

After a long pause, she asked, 'Where was her mother?'

'That's exactly what I asked her,' said Rosa. 'Poor little thing, she looked like she wanted to cry when I said mother. But that was all, and then he put the light out and it was as dark as it is now.'

sixty-six

Riedwaan's search had taken him and Njobe along remote tracks that led up the slopes of the Sentinel. Higher up they had found a dead dog, a strand of wire twisted around its scrawny neck, but no trace of Clare. That left Riedwaan with no comfort at all.

The cold sun was already sinking behind Judas Peak, the trees cast spectral shadows across the parking lot behind the garage and the KwikShop. Mandla Njobe, Riedwaan Faizal and two Mountain Men security guards were standing next to Clare's abandoned 4x4.

'It's nearly four o'clock already,' said Njobe. 'We've been searching for Dr Hart all day. Why the fuck did you only find her car now?'

'We looked everywhere for the doctor,' said the younger guard.

'Cwele was looking for her too,' chimed in the other. 'And for you, Captain.'

'You spoke to him?' asked Riedwaan.

'Didn't get a chance,' said the younger. 'Cwele's so busy telling you what a grootkop he is, you don't need to say anything.'

'Don't give me any shit about Cwele.' Njobe's voice was lethally quiet. 'I want to know why you only found the car now?'

'We did one last patrol,' said the older one. 'We drove this way. Came in for coffee. Those guys had fixed their truck and moved out so we saw the car.' He pointed to the eighteen-wheeler chugging up Victoria that had blocked Clare's vehicle from casual view.

'I sent you here this morning.' Njobe's fists bunched. 'This is Dr Hart's life we're talking about.'

'We looked, sir, both of us. The truck –'

'Useless fuckers is what you are,' said Mandla Njobe. He turned on his heel.

'It's my fault, Faizal,' he said. 'I should have come myself.'

'It should have been me.' Riedwaan walked away from the men. 'Leave them. We know this is where she was last. We start here. Now.'

Riedwaan peered into Clare's car. Everything seemed to be in order. Everything – except for the fact that her car had been parked here for twenty-four hours and that its owner had vanished.

'The KwikShop security cameras,' said Njobe, 'what do they show?'

'Nothing much,' said the older guard. 'Just going in to the shop, then leaving.'

'She buy anything?' asked Riedwaan.

'Nothing,' the guard replied. 'She went in, she talked to the cashier, she went out, walked out of shot, then she's gone.'

'Here's Mercy,' said Njobe. 'The girl who was on duty yesterday. She's back on shift.'

Riedwaan turned around when the cashier appeared.

'You spoke to Dr Hart,' he said to her.

'Yes.' Her hands inside the pockets of her uniform. 'She was looking for that girl who went missing. Rosie whatever.'

'Rosa Wagner,' said Riedwaan. 'What did you tell her?'

'That she was here,' said Mercy. 'It was a few weeks ago. Late at night.'

'What else?'

'I told her she used the bathroom and then she walked out and she vanished.'

'That's it?'

'That's it.' Mercy chewed her gum, blew a pink bubble.

'Then Dr Hart left?'

'Yes,' said Mercy. 'She walked out. Round the corner. I didn't see her again either.'

'What about her car?'

'I didn't think about it. I didn't see it, that big delivery truck was parked here, it just left.'

'We radioed everyone, Captain,' said the second Mountain Men guard. 'Nobody's seen her. She's just gone.'

'You not the first cop who was looking for her,' said Mercy.

'What do you mean?' asked Riedwaan. This wasn't the time to explain that, as of yesterday, he wasn't a cop.

'He was here,' she said. 'Got a fat stomach like a politician, drove a Pajero.'

'What did you tell him?'

'Nothing. I don't like him.' Mercy eyed Riedwaan. 'I don't think he liked your doctor lady. Not like you.'

'Did he see the car?'

'He didn't park this side, so I don't think so,' said Mercy. 'He took two Cokes and he didn't pay for them and then he left.'

'Cwele.' Njobe turned to Riedwaan. 'Clare must've seen him.'

A bell tolled in the valley. Riedwaan counted four, one for each hour of the afternoon so far and already the light dimming, fading towards evening. He swept his field glasses along the neglected firebreak that ran below Savić's fence. The castle rose above the trees, silhouetted by the last rays of sunshine.

Riedwaan dropped his glasses. The overgrown track cut across the mountain to where Wewers had sat eating Sweetie Pies while a girl was running through the trees.

'Keep looking for her here, Mandla,' said Riedwaan. 'Right now, there's someone I have to see.'

305

sixty-seven

The light flickered on, illuminated the contours of Rosa's face. Clare flinched, her eyes hurting. She braced herself, but there was no sound, no one approaching.

'This happens sometimes,' said Rosa. 'There's light, there's food, and then it's gone again.'

'Does it mean someone is coming?' asked Clare.

'Eventually, yes, *he* comes,' said Rosa. 'The first time, he came back three days later. Three days of darkness. No clothes, just me and the little girl and a bottle of water and some biscuits. We broke them into little pieces to make them last. Then he came down and he told me to bend over the table again. When it was over, I ate the orange he peeled for me.'

Clare brushed the tears from Rosa's face.

'Listen to that.' Rosa inclined her head.

Clare heard nothing, just the sound of water.

'You know, I arrange the sounds of the water. It's my own "Water Music". It's what kept me sane for a while, but I can't hold on much longer.' She buried her head in Clare's arms. 'Clare, please help me, help me die. I can't do it alone.'

'There's a way out of here,' said Clare, aware of the pulse of the life deep within her – her nameless comrade, her own reason to live. 'We'll find it, Rosa.'

'You don't think I've thought of everything, tried everything?'

'This time there's two of us,' said Clare.

'There were two of us the last time,' said Rosa. 'It didn't help.'

'Did Esther tell you how long she was here?'

'She didn't know, she thought maybe ten years,' said Rosa. 'She used the babies to count off the years.'

'And did she know about Isaac?'

'Yes, she knew,' said Rosa. 'She told me she was his mother up there in the sunshine until he was two. It's what kept her obedient all the years she was buried here with her shadow children – that's what she called them.'

'Little Esther, you mean?'

'Yes, her, the one who lived – but also the others, the girls that died.'

'How many were there?'

'Three,' said Rosa. 'He didn't come when she gave birth. It was only little Esther who lived.'

'Her mother was suffocated. I saw the autopsy report,' said Clare. 'But why, after all this time, did Stern kill Esther?'

'It wasn't him.'

Rosa's face was close to Clare's in the dark.

'Esther was very sick. She'd been sick before, but this time she knew she was dying. She'd already tattooed her name onto her daughter's skin,' Rosa's voice caught in her throat. 'She told me that the only time he let her out was to bury the babies that died, the ones that were stillborn. That's where we got the idea.'

Rosa stopped, her fists clenching.

'What idea?' Clare prompted.

Rosa's voice broke, but she pushed through. 'He said it was her fault they died, that she must clean up her own mess.'

Clare stroked her hair, untangling the curls.

'We talked about all that, here in the darkness. And then we decided. She wasn't strong enough, so it had to be me that held my hands over her face until she stopped moving. Stopped breathing.'

Rosa stopped speaking; her words faded into the silence.

Clare took Rosa's hands, felt the bones, the strength that came from making music.

'That took real courage,' said Clare.

'She endured so much, for so long,' said Rosa.

'I meant you,' said Clare.

Rosa withdrew her hands.

'Stern found Esther here, dead. He was so angry. He didn't say anything. Just went upstairs to fetch a hammer. He brought it back and he spread out my fingers, here, on the table. I thought he was going to break all of them, but all he did was break the little finger of my left hand.'

She held it up – crooked and swollen.

'This is the hand that holds the strings so that my other hand can draw the music from the cello.

'After he broke it, he told me that I would have to bury her. But first I had to bandage my finger so that I could dig her grave. He fetched a spade. The little girl clung to me, wouldn't let me go, and when he came back, he didn't care either way, and I was so frightened that my only chance would slip through my fingers that I tied her onto my back, even though I knew it would make the digging and the running harder.'

Rosa was crying now, raw animal sounds. Clare held her tightly against her own body until she could find a way to speak again.

'The grave had to be deep, he said. I dug and dug, then I put Esther's body inside and dropped the stones on her chest like he said I must so that she didn't swell up and betray us, and I filled in the grave again. The wet soil hit her face looking up at me –'

'I saw her face too, when we found her,' said Clare.

'She must have been so beautiful once,' said Rosa. 'But the horror of what happened to her was marked on her for ever.'

As it will be on us unless we get out of here, Clare thought.

'What happened then?' she said instead.

'Then the wind dropped, and there were men's voices, and he turned to listen, and that's when I ran. I ran until I fell. The child was too heavy, so I slid her off and tied her to a fallen branch. I told her I'd come back. Her eyes were closed, I think the starlight hurt her when the clouds parted. She'd never been outside, never seen stars. I covered her – an old piece of plastic lying nearby – and I ran, and ran. There was a fence. A hole under it, it looked like it was burrowed by some animals, maybe porcupines. I tried to slide through it in the mud, it scratched my skin, all along my back. At the house I broke a window, it threw my face back at me. The alarm didn't go off. I wanted it to scream – my throat was so tight – but it didn't, I saw the phone and dialled – the only number I've ever known.'

'Rosa, I heard you,' Clare said. 'Your oupa brought your message to me.'

'That's why you're here. *My* message. *My* fault.' Rosa's voice seemed to stumble, fall. 'But he found me there, in that nice house, and it was him who hit me on the head and dragged me back into the forest, my feet were bleeding. When I woke up I was here again, in this hole.'

The light flickered and went out, plunging them into an abyss of darkness.

sixty-eight

Riedwaan walked down the side of the harbour where rusty fishing boats listed at anchor. The last boat pitched and rolled as the swell muscled its way into the sheltered area. Chadley Wewers squatted over a tangle of nets, iPod earbuds disappearing into his hoodie. He worked at the net, fingers familiar with the knots since he was a boy. Riedwaan stepped over the gangplank and Wewers looked up at him.

'Entjie?'

Riedwaan offered him his packet. Threw him a lighter.

'You lost, Captain?' Wewers stood up before lighting his cigarette.

'Tell me about it,' said Riedwaan, his back to the open sea. He had a clear view of the harbour, the marina, the parking lot, the Sentinel grim behind Hangberg.

'That girl who went missing,' said Riedwaan. 'Rosa Wagner. The one who was in that house other side of the valley. Where'd she go?'

'You still scheme I know something about her? You fucken mad?'

'You tell me,' said Riedwaan.

'Me and DesRay, we've got a laaitie coming,' said Wewers. 'I got a second chance. I'm fucken taking it with two hands.'

'Changes things, a woman and a child,' said Riedwaan.

'You got kids?'

'I fucked up,' said Riedwaan. 'Don't make that mistake.'

'That's what I'm trying not to do,' said Wewers. 'I keep telling you the same fucken stuff and you don't hear me. My life, I'm turning it around. Why do you think I'm working here?'

'This girl,' said Riedwaan. He held out the photograph of Rosa Wagner: gleaming skin, red dress, cello. 'You saw her.'

Wewers studied the photograph.

'Fuck you.' He lit the cigarette.

'You nervous?'

Wewers was silent.

'If you tell me, I can help you. You and DesRay. The baby too,' said Riedwaan. 'You tell me what's happening. Where this girl is. You're safe.'

'I've got work to do,' said Wewers.

'You know what's been going on up at the castle?' asked Riedwaan.

'Why would I know anything about people in castles?' said Wewers. 'Do I look like a fucking fairytale?'

'Rosa played music there,' said Riedwaan. 'Maybe you saw her.'

'I like Tupac, not Beethoven.'

'Just wondering why you were walking up there,' said Riedwaan. 'You see anything?'

'Trees, rain, owls, mud,' said Wewers, his face shutting down. 'That's it.'

'What's with the walks?'

'Part of rehab. Fresh air, community, exercise.'

'You think about it,' said Riedwaan. 'A new start. You and the baby.'

'Why you trying to help me?'

'I was like you once,' said Riedwaan. 'Someone helped me.'

'Cheap shoes, Mr Price jeans, old leather jacket, that's what it did for you. What did it do for him?'

'He's dead,' said Riedwaan. 'Gangster like you shot him.'

'Where's the gangster?'

'He's dead too.' Riedwaan flicked his cigarette overboard.

'What you trading?' said Wewers.

'The docket,' said Riedwaan. 'The assault charge you're paroled for now.'

'That's fuck-all.' Chadley Wewers stood up. 'It cost me fifty bucks the day I was paroled. A little fish told me that the only witness is feeding the crayfish. It's gone long time, that case.'

Wewers pushed past, but Riedwaan grabbed him, twisting him into an iron embrace.

'Don't fuck with me,' said Riedwaan, his lips almost touching the metal piercing of the boy's ear, his pistol against his head.

'OK, chill, man. I heard some weird sounds. A girl's voice, maybe others.'

'What others?'

'Maybe a man.'

'That's it?' Riedwaan dug the barrel of his pistol into his temple. Defeat in Wewers's eyes, the look of a dying man.

'The girl.'

'Rosa?'

'I dunno. She was naked. Running.'

'Where?'

'Downhill.'

'To the estate?'

'I'm telling you,' he said. 'I don't know where, who the fuck she is.'

Riedwaan twisted the barrel, the metal drew blood.

'OK, OK,' he said, angling his head away from the gun. 'She was running for her life. Like an animal. She made sounds like an animal makes.'

'She ran out of the estate?'

'No, man. She was running towards it. She went in. She ran down the hill. That's why we saw her. Like a ghost with her shiny skin. I'd been smoking a lolly, I thought I was seeing things.'

'What are you not telling me?' said Riedwaan. He moved the trigger back, a loud click.

'A man was after her,' he said.

'Who, you motherfucker?'

'I don't know, Captain, I don't fucking know, man. He was sommer there, like he'd come out of the ground.'

'Where did he go?' asked Riedwaan.

'Into the estate, after her.'

'Who was it? Savić? Mikey? Jonny Diamond?'

'I don't fucking know,' Wewers whined.

The barrel bored into his temple, and it bled.

'I'm going to put in a complaint,' he gasped. 'I've got rights. Colonel Cwele, I'll tell him.'

'Tell him what you fucking like.' Riedwaan had his face on the ground. 'I've finished as a cop – and I'll kill you if you don't give me more. Tell me who he is, otherwise I take you with me. Easy place to escape, up there. Easy place to take a bullet in your back when you run away.'

'They were just fucking gone, man. Like ghosts, like the mountain swallowed them.'

'You know him, Wewers,' said Riedwaan. 'And he saw you there, didn't he?'

A wet stain spread across Wewers's crotch.

'Give me a name.'

'The farm up there. He shoots anyone who comes near his land,' said Wewers. 'I don't know his fucking name. But he saw me. He knows where to find me. And he knows where to find DesRay.'

Riedwaan eased the trigger back.

'Why do you go up there?'

'Your roadblocks fucked up business,' said Wewers. 'So now we just walk the shit through. We use the tunnel, the old dry one to Camps Bay. It was that fucking simple till this girl shit happened.'

Riedwaan let him go, holstered his gun. Wewers knew better than to move fast, but Riedwaan didn't turn his back on him until he was out of range.

He phoned Mandla Njobe as he ran to his bike.

'Meet me up on the mountain,' said Riedwaan, ready to accelerate. 'Paradys.'

sixty-nine

The trapdoor opened.

Noah Stern stood there, his eyes slits.

Clare's heart leapt when she saw her jacket. The familiarity of it, its warmth as she put it on over her naked body was an unbearable comfort. For Rosa he had brought a cloak.

There was a red smear on his white shirt.

'What have you done to Nancy?' asked Clare.

He glanced down, his hand flew up.

'Where is she?'

Stern had Clare by the throat.

'You corrupted her. You turned her. She paid the price.' Each sentence punctuated by a blow to her face.

'Leave her, please,' begged Rosa. 'Clare didn't know anything. How could she?'

'Your words were the poison.' Stern pulled Clare closer. 'I caught her when she was leaving.'

'Where was she going?' Clare asked through the red fog of pain in her head.

'She was wearing your boots, walking down the mountain. Walking away. From me, from my family, from what I've built here. She was about to destroy it all. The vision we had. I would never let that happen.'

'Where's the boy?' whispered Rosa.

'He is nothing,' said Stern, turning on her in fury. 'Now move.'

315

He moved the shelves again, and a door was revealed.

A cold exhalation as the door swung open onto to the coffin-shaped room where Rosa had lain in the dark.

'Inside,' he ordered.

Clare could not do it.

Stern took Rosa's damaged hand and squeezed. The scream compelled Clare, and Rosa stumbled in after her.

He pulled their restraints tighter. Torchlight flickered on the far wall.

'Remove that rubble,' he ordered, thrusting a spade at Clare.

The sound of the water was louder here.

'Where are you taking us, Stern?' Clare turned on him. The claustrophobic space, the smell, her rage closing up her throat.

'You try anything with that,' he warned, the hammer swinging lightly in his grip. He pulled Rosa against his body. 'This little hand is finished,' he smiled, splaying out her fingers.

Clare had no choice. Not yet. She looked at the loose bricks near a wooden doorframe, gripped the spade and began to dig at the rubble. At last some loosely packed bricks tumbled to the floor.

The breath of the tunnel was foetid.

The darkness inside was absolute.

'Clear the way,' ordered Stern.

Clare dug, chipped away at the wall.

When the opening was big enough he yoked them together again: Rosa in front, Clare behind, shackled like slaves with a looped chain around their necks. Hands tied behind them, the two women lurched into the thick black air of the tunnel.

Stern closed the door behind them and prodded them into the darkness. Unable to feel their way, the women stumbled along the rock-strewn floor and up a steep incline. Up ahead – in the distance – the roar of water. A sound at once ominous and

316

welcome, drawing them on.

He walked them fast, their feet bare and bleeding.

Stern's foul breath was hot on Clare's skin.

She tripped and the chain tightened, a hurtful saviour.

He had them. Clare matched her rhythm with his, and she was able to walk without falling.

Rosa kept stumbling – trying to shield her swollen hand.

She fell hard. Did not get up.

Stern kicked her, but she lay there, inert.

'She cannot go any further.' Clare's voice a whip in the darkness.

'Then she can die here.'

'No,' whimpered Rosa. 'Take me to the water, please, to its music.'

Stern was moving from one foot to another, agitated, lost in his own scheme.

'Let me help her, Stern.' His name hard as a stone on her tongue, it seemed to draw him back. 'Noah.' She tried that. Conciliation in her voice. 'Please, we can't just leave her here. I'll help her, stay with her.'

Still he hesitated.

'Noah.' Clare's voice submissive. 'Tell me where you want to take her.'

'I have to clean up,' he said.

'So no one will find us?' said Clare.

'No one will find you,' he said.

'Then let me help her up there. Unchain her. Unchain me. There's nothing that we can do. Not here, at the centre of the earth. Not with you.'

He gave a half-smile, removed the chain from Rosa. From Clare.

She dropped beside the girl.

'Rosa,' Clare's voice was strong; she had her arm around Rosa's shoulders. 'Stand up. Get up. Walk.'

'I can't.'

'You must, Rosa.' Clare pulled her upright. Rosa's head flopped against her shoulder. 'I'm with you. We'll walk to the end, out of this place. There's water up ahead. Listen to its music. It's calling you.'

'There's no hope, Clare. It's over.' But she was getting to her feet.

Clare half-carried, half-led Rosa onwards.

Stern behind them; an executioner's footsteps.

Hearing him walk was like seeing the end of the world. But hearing him meant that it was not yet over, the long trudge of this forced march. With the steepness, Stern's breath was coming faster now.

They slowed, the tunnel angling towards the right, towards the water that thundered off the cliffs. The sound seemed to make Rosa straighten, pulling her along ahead of them.

Clare put her hand in her jacket pocket. She curled her fist around the porcupine quill. Sharp, stubby, lethal. She tested its point against the pad of her thumb. The pain a lifeline.

She focused her thoughts, kept walking in the darkness.

seventy

The night sky was awash with stars, and there was ice in the wind. Riedwaan heard the water before he saw it, the rush of the river as it plunged towards the bay. He and Mandla Njobe, with Gypsy trotting at their heels, zig-zagged between the trees that screened the farmhouse.

Paradys.

There was a watchfulness to the house, although the surrounds were cheerful enough. Rows of turned earth. A vegetable garden waiting for the weather to warm up. Sheets heavy with rain dragged on the washing lines – no one had bothered to bring them in. A plastic scooter lay abandoned on the lawn. A few shrubs stood to attention around the wide verandah. There was no one about.

Riedwaan knocked, waited. He pushed open the front door. The wind gusted into the silence, rustling the clothes of the woman sprawled on the floor. Black boots – neat, small, like Clare's. He dropped to his knees, his hand against her neck. No pulse. No chance, not with the way her skull had been split.

A bloodied silver pendant rested on the woman's high-necked blouse. Riedwaan picked it up, angling the silver disc to read the inscription. *Forever one.* He turned it over. *Nancy & Noah.*

'Mrs Stern,' he said. 'Where the fuck is your husband?'

The woman stared up at him, mute.

'Faizal,' called Njobe, squatting at a desk. 'Here's a boy, look here.'

There was a gash in the wood, splinters around it. Riedwaan sank to his haunches. The boy lay under the desk, his arm at an unnatural angle. A contusion on his temple.

'Looks like the desk broke the blow,' said Njobe.

Riedwaan put his finger on his pulse. Faint but steady.

'Get the helicopter,' he said. 'Anwar Jacobs. Get him here now.'

Riedwaan yanked down one of the curtains and covered the child.

'You go look for Clare, Faizal.' Njobe was on the phone already.

There was no one else alive in the house, of that Riedwaan felt certain. He checked anyway, going from one room to the other. In the kitchen, evidence of an interrupted meal. Three plates. The woman, the boy – and the man. Nobody else. Nothing else.

The pantry door was ajar, the shelves packed with bottled preserves. It was hardly big enough for a child to fit into, and other than a couple of cases of beer, the pantry was empty.

Riedwaan went out to the back stoep. The curtain of night lay thick and heavy on the mountain.

A dark shape, indistinct at first, as his eyes adjusted to the dark. A solid shape under a tarpaulin.

A vehicle.

Where was Clare? Where the fuck was she?

He pulled Clare's scarf out of his pocket. The smell of her caught the back of his throat.

Footsteps thudding, nearer.

Riedwaan's gun at the ready.

'Jesus, Njobe, you'll get yourself fucking shot like that,' his finger easing the trigger back. 'The kid OK?'

'Helicopter's on its way,' said Njobe. 'I told them where to find him. Nothing more I can do there except sit. No Clare?'

'Nothing here,' said Riedwaan, stuffing Clare's scarf back into his pocket.

'That hers, by any chance?' asked Njobe.

'You mean this?' Riedwaan pulled it out.

'Now Gypsy will find her,' Njobe smiled.

Riedwaan whistled; the dog appeared, one paw up, ears alert. He held the scarf out, and she whined.

The dog nosed this way and that, her concentration absolute. She picked up the scent next to the shed. Riedwaan tried the closed door. He drew out his service pistol and fired at the lock. The door swung open. He shone his torch inside, found a light switch. A single bulb glowed weakly.

Gypsy was whining at a door hidden by clutter surrounding it. Riedwaan pushed it open. A row of electrical switches. He tried one, but apart from a fan's distant hum the room remained dark. He felt along the wall. Another switch: this one worked. Everything was illuminated in the windowless room: a desk, a work table, stacked shelves neatly packed.

The Alsatian made straight for the table, cocking her head and whining urgently. Riedwaan pushed the table. It was heavy – oak maybe, or ironwood. A scuttling spider – large and hairy – drew Riedwaan's attention to the floor. The creature disappeared into a groove that ran along the floorboards. Riedwaan put his finger into it, felt cold metal, and lifted the trapdoor.

A flight of stairs dissolved into the darkness below.

Riedwaan went down. Inside the small room, there were two thick shelves that held some tiles, packets of grouting, tools. Gypsy rushed at the bottom shelf, her short, sharp bark a declaration of triumph.

Riedwaan tipped the shelf, the tiles smashing to the floor. Behind it a metal contraption, a sliding mechanism for moving the shelves.

He tipped the contents of the top shelf too, and a heavy steel door appeared. He put his shoulder to it, pushed it open. The stench made him gag.

He felt for a light switch, flipped it.

A bed, a table, chairs, a pile of notebooks on a shelf, three Bic pens, a pared apple, and a child's drawing of a woman with a cascade of hair. A flash of silver on the floor. Riedwaan picked it up. The oval tanzanite shone in his hand.

A hole in the ground with mouldy walls. Riedwaan's flashlight revealed pencil marks, a neat musical score on plastered walls that were patterned with damp. A dungeon. Custom built. Empty.

Gypsy was scratching at the far wall. Another door here. Locked.

Riedwaan had his pistol out, took aim.

'Faizal,' said Njobe. 'Stop.'

The Mountain Man held his hand up. He had his flashlight out, trained on the lock. A tiny piece of wire protruded from the lock.

'Back,' said Njobe.

Gypsy yipped.

'This whole thing's booby-trapped.' Njobe's voice was barely audible. 'We open that, it'll blow and take us all with it.'

Njobe had his palm against Riedwaan's chest. He was pushing him back up the steps.

'I can't leave her in there,' said Riedwaan.

'You touch that, you kill her.' Njobe had him half-way up the steps.

Clare's scarf lay on the floor.

Gypsy whined. She wasn't moving.

'This is what Wewers was talking about.' Riedwaan tried to twist out of Njobe's grip, but Njobe had six inches and fifty pounds on him. 'The tunnel. This is what he was talking about.

We have to get to her, she's in there.'

'Faizal, stop – you need to think, man,' said Njobe. 'If they're alive, they're way ahead of us. Go up to the top, cut them off at Hell's Gate.'

seventy-one

This was the end: the tunnel, so steep for so long, had flattened out. An opening ahead, an O into the darkness outside. As Stern pushed them through, Clare lost her footing; she fell, her hand curling around the rock that had tripped her. She stood up, held onto the rock.

Stern had Rosa now. He was pushing her ahead of him, onto a metal platform servicing the Apostle Tunnel alongside. The channelled water tumbled and swirled into the catchment pool below. At the maw of the weir, the water circled, a predator looking for its prey before it plunged down the Apostle Tunnel that led through the mountain to Camps Bay.

Rosa's sudden scream was a soprano above the relentless bass of the water.

Stern was smiling. He loomed over her, a knife in his hand. Her hair in his left hand was a gleaming black snake. He yanked hard, snapping her head back, exposing the slender curve of her throat. The knife was pressed against her skin, silencing her. She had braced herself – her bare legs cold against the metal.

A knife clattered against the granite cliff.

Clare's aim was not true to its mark.

The rock had glanced off Stern's shoulder, making him lurch backwards. Then he was up, and he was moving. He came at Clare, a howl distorting his face, his lips pulled back. He grabbed at her. She ducked under his arms but he caught at her hair, throwing her to the ground. He kicked her hard – again and again and again – in the belly, in the back, aiming low – killer blows.

Clare could do nothing but curl around herself, around the life inside her.

Riedwaan stopped to catch his breath. The path he had followed was punishingly steep, Paradys invisible in the mist below. He scanned the mountainside. The wind – both ally and enemy – had dropped. There was enough starlight to navigate by – he would see his quarry ahead of him if he broke cover. But he too would be visible – as well as audible.

He climbed higher, higher, to where the path entered the ravine. Hell's Gate. It was narrow; the earth muddy, treacherous. He slowed, felt his way up the crevasse.

He slipped, caught at a branch; a stone skittered from the path, dancing towards the river below. The torrent drowned all sound.

He steadied himself. Kept on. Past an orchard of peach trees, the remains of old houses where, a century before, stonemasons who'd built the tunnels and dams had lived.

He climbed the next hundred metres; the slope was vertiginous. Riedwaan kept his back to the granite. It was slick with moss. The drop below was sheer, the waterfall churning below. Spirals of spray whirled upwards, vengeful furies that grabbed at his soaked legs before falling back, thwarted.

It was impossible to climb higher – the valley had tapered to a point. Riedwaan stopped, cast his eyes about him. The waterfall had burst forth from its channel in the cliff. Up ahead, the mouth of a tunnel gaped, a silent scream in the darkness.

He reached for a handhold. It held. So did the next one. He stepped into the water. The sound was overwhelming; its force sucked the air inwards, pulling him towards the vortex below.

Rosa scrambled on all fours. Ignoring the agony of her hand, she clambered away, struggling to get out, away from him.

She pulled herself up the stairs leading up from the platform. She was out, and the air was clear and clean.

Roosting crows rasped their outrage at being disturbed. Oblivious to Rosa's ordeal, they settled and were soon silent.

She looked up: the clouds were torn open, the stars bright beacons in the night sky.

Rosa squatted, listening to the cascading water. Apart from that and the pulse of her heart, all was quiet.

She clung to the cliff, tried to focus: what now? How to get down?

Behind her, the mountain. A great stone mother, she thought, and as she did so, she sank into oblivion.

A man's voice.

'Rosa, Rosa.'

A hand on her forehead, a jacket around her shoulders, covering her.

'Clare,' she heard herself saying.

'Where the fuck is she?' said the man's voice.

seventy-two

Clare's head snapped back, her hair coiled around Stern's fist. Winded, she lay in a foetal position on the platform.

'Run, Rosa,' she gasped. But Rosa had disappeared.

He pulled her up, into a bloody embrace.

Forcing her body to lie flaccid in his arms, Clare's hand brushed her jacket. The quill protruding from her pocket pricked her fingertip, and she recoiled. The movement triggered Stern, and he bit her arm, sinking his teeth deep into her flesh.

She winced, lifting her arm in a sudden parabola and stabbing at his face. The quill plunged into his right eye, piercing the eyeball as it lodged in the socket.

Stern howled, one hand on his wounded face, the other gripping Clare's arm.

He toppled, pulling her with him. In a deadly embrace, they plunged into the weir where the water churned before being channelled through the darkness of Judas Peak on its journey to Camps Bay.

Clare fell, sank deeper and deeper into the wild water, her killer clinging to her like a succubus.

She stuck two fingers into his gushing eye socket, and with a thrashing movement he released her. She was free, fighting back towards the surface, the turmoil of the water unbearable. Grasping at the metal stairs that led up to the platform, Clare clung to them as the water pulled at her, snapping her body this way and that. Then something fleshy, heavy hit her sideways, hit her hard. Noah Stern's drowned face touched her lips before being dragged into the vortex.

She would die too if she went down. Her arms flailing, her legs kicking against the water, Clare fixed her eyes again on the metal stairs. Two quick strokes, and she'd be across the maelstrom, she'd be there.

She struck off, but she was no match for the water. It took her in its grip and tossed her like a leaf along with the rest of the debris. She whirled towards a precipice where the water rushed over the edge of a pool before tumbling into the Apostle Tunnel.

The breath filled her lungs, held her ribs against the unbearable pressure of the water. She was sucked downwards, the turbulence tossing her about. She curled herself into a ball. Fragments of her life drifted in front of her as she was whirled down – her mother, sitting in the deep shade of a blue gum, her mother who had drifted quietly through her life, never swum against the current. Clare held this image, felt herself succumbing to its allure. She curled herself up around the burn in her lungs, which crescendoed as the din of the water receded.

She opened her eyes to the blackness around her.

At last, silence.

Her hair glistened, her eyes were closed. Her torso and legs were submerged in the water that swirled around her, determined to pull her down, ever downwards. But Stern's body held her up. He had caught against a metal strut and stuck fast.

The current held Clare's head against Stern's neck. His eyes were fixed on hers.

Riedwaan bent over her, yanking her limp body up into his arms, releasing her from the dead man's embrace. She was out of the water, on a ledge next to the stairs. Pressure on her chest,

Riedwaan's face inches above hers. Her lungs heaving, spewing water. More pressure, more gently this time. She inhaled deeply, spluttering as she did so; exhaled. Breathed.

He had his phone out.

'Don't you leave me, Clare,' his face hovering over hers. 'Don't you fucking leave me.'

Riedwaan's pleas, the chatter of the chopper working its way up the valley, were remote. Just the ripping pain low down in her pelvis.

coda

Summer sparkled. Black oystercatchers called to each other on the rocks. Flocks of terns, white streamers against the blue sky. A gentle swell ran up the beach, gulls strutted along lace edges left by the waves.

The slap of the water against the sides of the yacht was soporific. The sunshine was as warm as a mother's hand on the back of Clare's neck. The pain that had been her companion for six months, reminding her that she was alive after all, no longer there. The fractured ribs had knitted and the gashes had closed.

'Lucky,' is what the doctor had said. 'You won't scar.'

'Not where you can see,' Clare had replied.

'Therapy,' the doctor had advised.

'No one can erase what's in my head,' Clare's reply.

Rosa Wagner stepped out of the cabin and onto the bright white deck. Behind her were the musicians, their instruments gleaming. She stood erect as the murmurs of the audience died away. A brief shadow of wariness in her wide-set eyes.

Clare leaned against Riedwaan's shoulder. He drew her into the circle of his arm, said nothing as two trucks pulled out from behind the Yacht Club and drove up towards the castle. Their purpose, their cargo someone else's business now.

Rosa called Esther over, looked down at her and smiled. It was hard to tell, even now after bald facts had been laid out, which one had kept the other alive. Rosa pulled the little girl close. There was a steadfastness to her chin and a set to the tiny shoulders.

An old man and a boy stood at the edge of the deck. Mr Wagner was wearing his best black suit. The child at his side, neat in navy-blue trousers and a white shirt, wore his hair longer now, yet it barely concealed the scar on his temple. Rosa and Esther carried the urn over to them, and Alfred Wagner helped them open it. The breeze took the ashes, lifting them through the air. The children, wary strangers who were learning to be siblings, watched as their mother's ashes drifted towards the waves.

Rosa turned to Clare.

'We're alive today – me and Esther – because you came looking for us.' Rosa sat down and took her cello between her knees. 'And I'm human today because of my music, and the music of the water in that dark place.'

She placed her left hand on the frets, while her right hand brought the bow up into position. She drew her bow across the strings. A plangent note lingered and drifted back into silence. Then she drew from the cello a complex ordering of sound that drifted over the water.

Esther's wordless song rose up over the music, drifting along with it. When the music came to an end, a smile teased at the corner of her mouth.

As Rosa swept the child up, her smile broke free, and she laughed. The sound seemed to startle her, and she buried her face in Rosa's neck.

Her laughter, the music, hung in the air.

Rosa bowed, and the small audience clapped.

The sudden noise startled the infant in Clare's arms.

Ishmael Hart, three weeks old, looked up at his mother's face. Clare saw herself reflected in her son's serious brown eyes. He appeared to be taking the measure of her.

The infant yawned, closed his eyes, and fell asleep.

'Are you going to marry me?' Riedwaan said quietly to Clare.

'It's nice of you to ask,' she said, holding their child against her body. 'But no, thank you. It's strange enough with a baby. Being one, becoming two.'

Clare looked at Riedwaan.

'Marriage. Being two, becoming one. That's a step too far.'

acknowledgement

The testimony on pages 186–188 is a that of a young victim of abductor and serial rapist Johannes Mowers, who is currently serving a life sentence. The testimony is a transcription of a recorded interview by Kathryn Smith, from her installation *Psychogeographies: Walking Back the Cat* (11th Havana Biennale, 2012).